POINTMAN

A Novel of Love, War, and Drugs

By

Robert L. Owens

POINTMAN

Delizon Publishers

ISBN: 978-2-36523-036-0

Delizon books and other media products are available at special quantity discounts, for use as premiums and sales promotion, or in corporate training programs. For more information, please send your email to the Director of Sales, sales@delizonpublishers.com, contact your local bookstore or write to our Europe Office:

Delizon Publications,
19 rue des Alliés,
64000 Pau, France

Cover design by
Delizon International Book Publishers
www.delizonpublishers.com

This novel is dedicated to my family and to those men who have shared the bond of battle.

Based on actual events

"Loud unexpected noises still rattle my soul
and carry me back. And I remember…."
-Robert L. Owens

Part I

Chapter 1

South Vietnam--Thursday, February 12, 1970---8:15 p.m.

Warren Steele predicted his own death would be both swift and violent and that vision haunted him as he stalked forward, leading the column of soldiers across the rice paddies and toward the dim lights of a solitary Vietnamese hooch. Steele's eyes were wide and reflected the fear, but his expression was not unusual. For months, he had endured the same feelings, the same terror, and now it was no different. The night air was dead still and humid and his stomach tightened and churned. Sweat rolled down his face and stained his hat and shirt, and yet his dry mouth made it difficult to swallow.

He crept forward, his rifle leveled at his waist, and each step prepared him to instantly dive to the ground. His pace was slow, purposely slow, bent, and quiet and this approach coupled with his down-curved nose, slumped shoulders, and shifting head and eyes made him look like a vulture. Except for his breathing and the footsteps of the soldiers trailing him, no sounds were heard. Only silence existed. In another place, this could have been a pleasant evening for a moon-light walk. But not here. Pausing, Steele wiped his face with his shirt sleeve, sniffed, and wished that he could snort a vial of heroin to relax.

During the daylight, he was convinced no one could beat him as pointman. He was calmer and could sense if the enemy were near. The Viet Cong might smell the Americans' shaving cream scents or their sweaty uniforms and hear their radios squawk, but he could smell their fish sauce and oily hair and there was just a feeling…an eerie feeling during the day that alerted him.

In the light of day, he could stalk and kill with ease and he didn't crave the heroin. But at night, it was different. Steele's mood darkened with the sunset and his body and mind called out for the drug. The heroin watered his eyes and made his nose drip, but he needed it to bolster his nerve and to face the hand of death that always seemed to strike the pointman first.

With the full moon staring at him like a cyclopic yellow eye, Steele felt alone and exposed as he knelt in the open paddy and watched the woodline looming beyond the hooch. The hard-mud dike fifteen feet ahead offered the only protection, but he had no desire to advance. Every step was closer to the woods, a possible ambush, and he continued to stare and wait. He wished that he could see into the darkened woodline that faced him, but he could not. The mangrove and nipa palm trees did not allow the moon's rays to penetrate and the swamp appeared to be the entrance of a massive, horizontal cave and he had no idea what lay ahead. If only he could see into the woods, to know if the Viet Cong were hiding in the maze, watching from the shadows, lining him up in their sights, and simply waiting to kill him.

Inhaling deeply, Steele stood before his imaginary cave and expected to confront this beast of battle once again. The confrontation, the actual fighting was nothing new and nothing to be feared---it was the wait and the terminal aspect that generated fear---and yet the absurdity of the situation was that the clash had a strange and powerful allure. Like the heroin, the thought of battle coaxed him onward. He both hated and loved the roars of enemy fire, the flashes of igniting weapons and explosions. All shook his body and soul with exhilaration and mainlined a high that surpassed any drug.

Every twenty feet, Steele dropped to one knee and raised his starlight scope. The moon's rays made the green field of vision too bright and he squinted until his pupils contracted to black dots capable of admitting the magnified light. He scanned in a half-circle and then focused on the hut. Candlelight squeezed through the bamboo sidewalls and filtered through the trees surrounding the dwelling, but nothing moved. Nothing made a sound. Instinctively, his focus shifted back to the trees, less than seventy-five meters beyond the hooch. If any Viet Cong or North Vietnamese Army soldiers had infiltrated the area, they'd be hiding in either the homes of political supporters or in the marshy woodline.

Steele lowered the lens and glanced back at three soldiers, who mimicked his every step and now waited for him to advance. Their hats shaded their eyes from the moonlight, but the closest soldier's face was beaded with sweat, his jaw was exposed, and he clenched his teeth in anticipation. Sixteen other soldiers crouched in single file, staying widely-spaced, but they blended into the night and resembled the harvested mounds of rice stalks that dotted the paddies.

Steele raised the infrared scope and the mounds transformed into men. He recognized two immediately: Sergeant Brooks and Lieutenant Gomez.

Sergeant Mike Brooks carried the other scope allotted to the platoon and, as he watched the flanks, Steele bet that he was silently cursing Gomez for selecting a position so close to the woods. At the same time, Lieutenant Roberto Gomez, the only man who wore his helmet on night missions, squatted next to his radioman and whispered into the receiver-transmitter.

As pointman, Steele stood and was imitated in turn by the column of soldiers, who lifted with their legs, grunting and struggling under the weight of their packs. When he crept forward, the column followed. When he stopped, they stopped. He was like the head of a green centipede with legs weaving out of unison, meandering across the fields and into the unknown.

Nearing the hooch, Steele's path was blocked by three interlinking canals which formed a square "U" around the dwelling and he noticed the smell of ducks and dead fish rising from the water. Banana trees grew near the canal and circled the building, separating it like a tropical island from the flat sea of rice fields. Steele knelt in the shadows, hidden for the first time from the moon's glow, and listened. Conversation in Vietnamese could now be heard, emanating through the walls of the hut, but the tones were not of panic or alarm. The men had been silent and their presence had not alerted any animals, human or otherwise, and they advanced.

The pointman paralleled the canal, leading the soldiers to the access, and stopped near the dwelling. Bending under a tree, a branch hooked Steele's hat and exposed the thin face of a nineteen-year-old man, whose nose stretched his face forward and tugged on a scar below his eye. His face had been molded by a tough life in a tough town and Vietnam had only served to refine the sculpture. He swore silently at the distraction and then smelled the air for any clues of danger. None existed, only the septic scent of the canal, and he focused on his approach.

He pulled his hat lower, stepped past a wooden plow, and peered through the cracks of the door and into the room. Once he had peeked in on a couple making love and he had eagerly watched before entering. Only one candle flickered and he stood to the side of the bed, listening, watching, and smelling the scents of their passion. With eyes closed, they rocked, grunting and kissing, unaware of his presence. He stood still, a voyeur of the night, absorbing the pleasures of the dark.

He had been attracted as a boy to the same sounds, interpreting the moans long ago as pain while witnessing his mother and her lover intertwined, an open door experience that his mother thought he would neither notice nor care. She was wrong on both assumptions. He observed and enjoyed, just like his pointman experience. The rhythmic sounds and the months without a woman pushed and pulled on his emotions. He coveted her and longed to stroke her breasts, touch her skin, and penetrate her. His mind spun, whirling in seconds, and he imagined separating the lovers and bringing the act to a different conclusion with the woman's legs wrapped around him.

His body tensed and he held his breath as they moved faster and faster approaching the climax. He tapped his foot ever so slightly to the beat, disappointed that the column waited outside and rushed him for time. He wanted more, wanted to watch, wanted to take part, but he could no longer wait.

Steele stepped forward and slid the rifle barrel between the couple. The cold shaft immediately stopped the man's thrusts and changed the woman's moans to a high-pitched scream at the presence of a stranger. Steele said nothing. Like the little boy experience, he only smiled and stared with curiosity and eagerness. Watching the show was a sensual experience, but controlling the scene was more of an aphrodisiac and a wild rush of emotions surged through him.

He could have lingered longer on that night. He longed for the same entertainment, a display of love, affection, and carnal pleasure, but tonight he observed only a family of three eating as he peeked through the cracks of the door. A woman poured more tea, while her son picked at the flesh of a fish caught from the canal and her husband held a bowl under his chin, shoveling rice into his mouth with chopsticks.

Switching the selector on his M-16 rifle from "safe" to "semi" to "full" automatic, Steele inhaled deeply. He was ready. If they reached for any weapons, he would kill all of them. It was ironic. They had seconds to either live or die and none of them even realized that they were about to make that choice.

Gripping the wooden door latch, Steele slowly raised it until wings flapped and cackling erupted from the chicken coop and set off a noisy chain reaction from the ducks and a penned-up water buffalo. Steele froze and held the latch steady. He couldn't risk having them see or hear the bar being lowered.

The Vietnamese man, short, thin, and in his mid-thirties, set his bowl on the table and listened, cocking his head. He wiped his lips with the back of his hand, rose from his chair and walked toward the door, wondering what had caused the commotion and the animals' reaction. He had no idea what waited for him beyond the door.

Steele had to move. He could have waited, surprising the farmer with a weapon pointed at his face when the door swung open, but he preferred to act. He shoved the door inward, leveled the rifle at the man's gut, and ordered, "Get back!"

The family's reaction was immediate. It was doubtful that the three Vietnamese understood Steele's words, but the armed soldier instantly changed a sense of calm to one of terror. None of them reached for weapons. None existed to be grabbed. They instinctively huddled together and their voices pled in Vietnamese, high-pitched and rapid, appealing for their safety…none of which Steele could understand.

The father stood near his wife while she squatted and held the youngster in her arms. Their eyes had widened with shock and fear, unable to comprehend why they were suddenly being confronted, while their hands shivered, their heads bowed, and they retreated to the back wall of the hut.

Steele swallowed heavily. With his M-16 still leveled at the family, they didn't dare move as he looked around the room. Everywhere in the Mekong Delta, he saw the same things: the one-room bamboo hut with no windows, the hard-packed mud floor, the thatched roof, and a small family bunker, constructed above the floor and resembling a large mud casket.

Kneeling, Steele stuck his head into the opening of the bunker/casket. His action was quick, a fast glance into possible danger. The motion exposed his head, but Steele looked into the dark bunker and was relieved to see it was clear. The enemy had nowhere else to hide in the hooch and he felt safe and in control. Lowering his rifle, he leaned against bags of rice stacked in one corner, glanced at the flames and glowing red charcoal of a cooking fire built on the floor, and smelled the odors of *nuoc-mam* fish sauce fermenting. Candles flickered and waved with any movement of air, offered the only light, and created ghostly shadows dancing on the bamboo walls. A makeshift mantel hung on the wall, holding two candlesticks, and smoke rose from burning incense, paying homage to Buddha and his teachings of peace.

Since the Vietnamese offered no resistance, Specialist Four Warren Steele motioned them to lower their hands and they complied, slowly and cautiously. They rocked, glanced at each other, and tried to understand the meaning of the intrusion. The pointman recognized the puzzled looks, but understanding or explanations were not necessary or part of the routine, compliance was. The message was not subtle but it was apparent: do what you're told and you won't be dying tonight.

Steele stared at the family. All the peasant farmers in the Delta seemed to be cast from the same mold. The woman's hair was black, straight, and hung to the middle of her back, while the man and boy had short-cropped hair. All wore the black pants and white silk work shirts of farmers and the clothes on their backs were probably the only ones they owned. They were all barefoot, unable to afford even sandals, but able to squat for hours on their hardened, calloused feet. Their hands, even those of the boy, were equally hard and calloused from carrying water to the chickens and water buffalo, gathering firewood from the marsh, and stooping, planting, and harvesting rice in its never ending cycle.

Warren Steele understood poverty, welfare, and missed meals, but these poor bastards had nothing…a one-room shack with no electricity, showers, toilets, or running water. They captured rain water to drink in ceramic barrels, but washed their clothes and dishes in the same canals that their flock of ducks swam. This country and people were barely out of the Stone Age, hundreds of years behind the United States technologically. He had no use for how they lived, their customs, or their country, but he respected the people. They eked out a bare existence every day while maintaining their pride without complaint. Their physical and mental toughness were inbred and they endured like generations of ancestors who had inhabited and worked the same land. They survived in a hostile world and Steele hoped to do the same.

Hearing muffled voices outside, Warren Steele turned and watched Lieutenant Roberto Gomez and Spec. 4 Clarence Sufficool, his radioman, duck through the low doorway.

Lieutenant Gomez, a small but wiry man with exceptionally straight posture, reflected confidence and control as he entered the room. He removed his helmet, looked at the family, and then turned toward Steele. "Everything alright?"

"Yeah. I didn't spot any weapons and the bunker is clear. Everything is fine, except one thing, sir," Steele said, pointing. "There are extra bowls on the table and more cooked rice than they can eat. They may have been expectin' some friends."

The lieutenant nodded his understanding. He spit on the floor, a visual demonstration of his contempt, and then stared at the Vietnamese. His eyes did not leave them when he spoke to Steele. "Join Brooks outside. I'll handle it."

Before Warren Steele closed the door, Gomez' face had changed, becoming even harder, and the pointman wished that he could have stayed for the show. Clarence Sufficool held the radio handset, calling in the coordinates of their night-hold position, but felt the opposite. He preferred to leave, but Gomez would not allow it. Leaving would have been considered a sign of weakness, an unacceptable behavior, and an acknowledgement that Gomez was not in control.

Sufficool removed his radio and knelt next to it, adjusting the volume and intentionally focusing on the equipment. He didn't make eye contact with the people and kept his back toward Gomez and the Vietnamese. In his mind, he was alone in the room and in this self-imposed isolation he could tune them out of his world. He held back any words of appeal to Gomez, but he understood what was coming and he felt a surge of shame in his role as a silent partner. Over the past month, he'd watched the riddle of the oppressed oppressing the oppressed---a black man observing a Puerto Rican terrify the Vietnamese. It was a brief encounter of minorities designed to establish power and a pecking order, but both the upcoming scene and his silence bothered and disgraced him each time.

Gomez had no idea what it was like to live in Montgomery, Alabama, but he acted like some of those folks. Those actions and those memories were not easily forgotten. As an adolescent, Sufficool had experienced the turmoil, the oppression in Montgomery, of being blasted, soaked, and rolled by a fire hose and bitten, torn, and scarred by a police dog when all he wanted was to stand in line for a bus ride. Now all he could do was watch the scene again. There were no police, dogs, or fire hoses, just differing beliefs and the same helpless people. His mother would have been ashamed that he wasn't speaking up, not taking a stand, but it was a different time and place and Sufficool believed that he could not change the system or stop this officer.

Lieutenant Gomez scanned the hooch, remembered living in a shack like it in San Juan, and then focused on the family. Like Steele, he too didn't know if the people understood English and he couldn't care less. They always understood one message. Tossing his helmet aside, Gomez slung his M-16 and removed his pistol from its holster, pointing the gun at the man's face and backing him against the wall. Eyes widened as Gomez caressed the pistol against the man's jawbone and then made a "cross" with the barrel, touching his forehead, his chin, and both cheeks. He then pushed the barrel into the side of the man's nose. With his left hand, Gomez clutched the man's throat, holding his head in place like a balloon ready to be popped.

The men stood inches from each other's face, separated by the weapon, both feeling, smelling, and hearing each other's breath. The Vietnamese man breathed rapidly, following the pounding of his heart, while the officer inhaled and exhaled slowly, his heart and mind calm and controlled. The woman sobbed and the man, looking deep into the soldier's eyes, understood that the lieutenant would have no qualms in shooting him. Gomez figured his message, their silent joint covenant, had been received loud and clear and then, staring coldly, removed his grip from the man's neck, put a single finger against his own lips, and whispered "quiet".

Gomez turned and pointed the pistol at the woman and the boy she held. He was aware that Vietnamese women pinched their children to make them cry and scream and alert any VC in the area, but that wasn't going to happen tonight. He looked at the boy, whose hands visibly shook, and watched his mother turn his head and hold him against her chest. She held a hand against her mouth, gagging her own cries, as Gomez raised the weapon to his lips and exhaled "shhhh."

With a sweeping motion of his pistol, he directed the family to crawl into the bunker and, when they complied, he tipped a chair in front of the opening, looked through the chair bars at his captives, and smiled.

There was a complete understanding of power and control. A common language was not needed as no doubt existed about the meaning and clarity of the communication, sent or received.

Chapter 2

Thursday, February 12, 1970---8:33 p.m.

Sergeant Mike Brooks knelt in the shadows, whispering and pointing directions to the line of soldiers as they stooped past him and circled the hut. Both M-60 machine guns were positioned toward the woodline, the bipods leveled, and fields of fire examined, while belts of ammunition were snapped together and stacked in even rows. Detonator cords were strung out and blasting caps screwed into claymore mines while full magazines of M-16 ammo were set within arms' reach.

Brooks watched the men, feeling the same uneasiness that gnawed at them, as they centered their packs in front of their positions. They arranged grenades and hand flares within easy reach while unrealistically hoping their packs would deflect any incoming bullets. Bodies flinched at the sound of footsteps, eyes jerked from side to side, and men struggled against the silence, the waiting. One hundred percent alert would not have to be enforced. No one was going to sleep, the proximity of the marsh guaranteed insomnia. With frayed nerves, the men guessed it was only a matter of time as they sat in the shadows, their backs against the hooch, and looked for any movement beyond their perimeter.

In a crouch, Brooks circled the hut and checked the men's ambush positions. Satisfied with the set-up, he sat between Warren Steele and Sergeant Howard Morrison, the leader of second squad.

Morrison glanced at Brooks, looked back at the woodline, and whispered, "You like Gomez' position?"

"Oh, yeah," Brooks said and then grinned. "Why don't we just shoot ourselves and save some time?" He stared toward the marsh, confident that there would have been fewer casualties the past month if he had selected the night-hold position instead of Gomez. "We should be in the middle of the rice paddies. Let the VC come to us."

"Yep," Morrison agreed, "but Lieutenant Gung Ho ain't going to win more medals that way. He's on a tight schedule too, 'cause Nixon might withdraw us out of Nam."

"Withdraw us?" Brooks shook his head. "It'll never happen while we're here. Withdrawal is what Nixon's father should have done fifty-seven years ago."

Sergeant Morrison nodded his agreement as he screwed off the cap of a black flask. Taking a drink, he shivered as he swallowed a mixture of whiskey and warm Coca-Cola and then held the container out to Brooks. "It'll straighten your short hairs."

The platoon sergeant laughed softly, shaking his head to the offer, and watched Morrison take another sip before putting the flask away. In the rear and on stand down, Brooks had no problem with the men drinking, but he objected to anyone using drugs or booze or even cigarettes on night ambush. It wasn't tolerated in this platoon and he would kick anyone in the ass for doing so, except Morrison.

He had learned months ago that the Texan took exactly two shots of his whiskey and Coke each night, an evening ritual that calmed his nerves.

Overweight by army standards, prematurely balding, and with a round baby face that resembled a pumpkin, Howard Morrison hardly looked or acted like a soldier. But in the field, Morrison had his act together. That wasn't always the case.

In Basic Training at Fort Benning, a drill instructor had yelled at Morrison for laughing in the Mess Hall and shoved his face into his dinner tray. The DI's action did not intimidate Morrison, it enraged him. He clobbered the sergeant, slammed his head into the table, and walked off the base. Two days later, he was arrested, drunk and stripped naked except for his boxer shorts and boots, staggering through the streets of Columbus, Georgia.

Military police returned him to the base but as he was being chewed out by the company commander and being called a "country faggot", Morrison punched him and then hitchhiked to his hometown in Texas where he proclaimed, "there ain't no assholes and, best of all, there ain't no Army assholes."

After four months and after being fired from a grocery store for setting a case of "free" beer in his car and claiming a "five finger discount", Morrison's pregnant wife encouraged him to return to the army. He did so, served six months in jail, completed additional training with honor and distinction, and was then cut orders for Vietnam.

Stories about an AWOL soldier who had hit both an enlisted man and an officer had floated around the base camp long before Howard Morrison was assigned to the third platoon. Despite a troop shortage, no one wanted him and that was a mistake. Brooks liked the good ol' boy's sense of humor and, as long as no one pushed him, a smile was ever present. Still he was a fighter, unable to ignore disrespect, willing to spit in the face of a man plummeting him, and in his own words "not worried about messing up my pretty face." Morrison may not have handled stateside training and regulations well, but his courage and leadership were evident and acknowledged in Vietnam. Only three months had passed in-country before he was wearing sergeant stripes and leading second squad.

The roar of jet engines caught Brooks' attention and he glanced upwards at the flashing lights of a passenger jet climbing out of Tan Son Nhut.

"Take us home, baby," he wished aloud.

"Don't sweat it," Morrison said, "'cause it don't mean nothin'. This ain't your daddy's war. We're not here for the duration. We kick ass, but the politicians and press won't let us win. It's a one year war for us...win, lose or draw, and we'll be flyin' home to the big PX in the sky...just like those guys. One year and a wake up from a 365 day nightmare." He paused and looked at Brooks. "Why'd you come here anyway?'"

Why?" Brooks thought about the question and the journey.

He wanted a baseball scholarship that never materialized. His hopes, dreams, and heart outweighed his talent for the game, so he volunteered for the draft, considering it inevitable. After re-thinking the illogical logic of that decision and with the selective service lottery being established, he requested that the draft board remove his name. The request was denied and, five months after high school graduation and with no student deferment, he was inducted into the army. Still, that's where he belonged.

"Why?" Brooks repeated, questioning the answer himself. "A draft notice and the 3-P's...Pickett, Pershing, and Patton. My family fought with all three...I could have gone to Canada or jail, but my chances of getting killed were *less* here."

Morrison seemed satisfied with the answer. "Well, you're carryin' on the family tradition. Now, it's the 4-P's...Pickett, Pershing, Patton, and Peckerhead."

Brooks smiled. "My dad served with Patton's Third Army at Saint Vith, Belgium, during the Battle of the Bulge. A company of GIs were surrounded, so he volunteered to deliver ammunition and artillery shells to them. On three night trips, he drove his truck through the German lines. All it would have taken was one bullet hitting the high explosives and it would have been over. But he was lucky. With the supplies, the GIs held the line and did not surrender. For that, he was awarded the Bronze Star."

"When it really meant something."

"Yeah...when it meant something. I wasn't going to let him down and I wasn't going any place but here."

Watching the running lights of the Freedom Bird fade away, Brooks imagined the GI's cheering at the takeoff, staring at the round-eyed stewardesses wiggling down the aisle, and relaxing for the first time in twelve months. They'd passed the ultimate rite of passage and that survival granted them the right to breed the next generation of warriors, to carry on the tradition of fighting the next war. They had lived and they were going home.

Family history and his curiosity of this strange war didn't permit any other destination or escape. But there was more. Lieutenant Gomez' battle philosophy seemed right in step with what his father had endured with "Old Blood and Guts" Patton---his guts and our blood.

Brooks stopped, reflecting on Morrison's remarks, and for some reason remembered the quote, not of President Nixon or Johnson or Kennedy. It was Ho Chi Minh who had said, "For every one of yours we kill, you will kill ten of ours. But in the end, it is you who will grow tired." The words rang true…the country, the politicians, the demonstrators, the soldiers, and he were growing weary. They were fighting a war that no one now wanted and yet they were deserted and despised for doing so. The battles had drained all of them and had demanded more sacrifice than any were willing to give. Troops were going home and all Brooks desired was survival and peace.

Only four years had passed since he had even heard of Vietnam or had watched the black and white images of war on his family's RCA television. Hell, he was only sixteen-years-old at the time, and even now he couldn't care less if these people were communists, capitalists, anarchists, or pacifists. All represented nothing more than ideas, simple thought processes from simple creatures. None of them had threatened his country or him, yet he had been leading men, trying to kill these people for whatever purpose, and they had in return tried to kill him.

If freedom was an issue, he didn't understand. In basic training, the draftees were corralled in an auditorium and prompted by their drill instructors to chant "Die Ho Chi Minh, Die Ho Chi Minh" over and over. The order came at the conclusion of an orientation meeting and he had joined the other soldiers in the yelling, chanting loudly and joyfully as if this one death would solve all problems and miraculously end the war.

That was the extent of their political training as to why this war was being fought. Someday, somewhere, someone would have to explain exactly why they were fighting. The rationale for World War II seemed clear and freedom was worth fighting and dying for, but was freedom the issue in Southeast Asia? The only freedom lost, in his mind, was that of millions of young men inducted into an unwanted fight without a clear reason for doing so. Was that an infringement of their freedom and their rights? He had served seven months in country and had no better understanding of the political importance of this country even now. If this country was of value to the Chinese, the Japanese, the French, and now to the Americans, it was beyond his comprehension or reason. The only dominoes falling were the foreigners trying to control this country. Personally to Sergeant Mike Brooks, the war in Vietnam was indeed a countdown of 365 days, a day-to-day test of survival, and it was madness.

After watching the treeline for nearly an hour, Mike Brooks' eyes blurred and distorted his vision. The trees bent and swayed like heat waves, while clumps of mud appeared to be human heads watching from afar. Brooks rubbed his eyes and then twisted and adjusted the two bandoliers of full M-16 magazines tied to his waist. Sweat rolled off his chest and wet his shirt down to his trousers. He, like most of the soldiers on line, wore no underpants. He had learned that tip in Non-Commissioned Officer, "shake and bake", training. The garments were burdensome, hot, and the men did not want to rip off another piece of clothing to tie a compress on a wound or to dig out a burning chunk of white phosphorous.

To the dismay of the older sergeants, Brooks' hair and moustache were longer than approved military standards and he wore the first two buttons of his shirt open, exposing his barrel chest and two necklaces---a circular leather peace symbol and a twenty-four carat gold chain and medallion.

Brooks lifted the gold medallion which was a gift from his Vietnamese girlfriend, Huong Van Nguyen or "Butterfly" to Brooks. It pictured a dragon twisting and snarling and, on the reverse side, Vietnamese letters spelled "Good Luck".

Having a woman in Vietnam, someone who cared and someone to hold, was indeed good luck and his relationship with her was vastly different than with other women of his past. After being cheated on and used, he had resigned himself at a young age to being alone. It wasn't a feeling that he despised, but rather one that he held as a source of freedom and independence. Somewhere, sometime, he read and copied down the words, keeping them on a ragged scrap of paper still tucked in his pocket, of painter and poet Maynard Dixon's poem, "I Am". Thinking back, he repeated the memorized words in his mind:

"Now I go out alone to ride the free hills,
Bare-breasted and stark,
These hills that make no concealment;
Where no woman is with me, no woman shall ever be;
Where stern and alone I face the thing that I am,
Where I face the void of all that I fail to be,
And knowing my fear, shall be not afraid of that fear.

Now I put out my hand, touching the sky of evening...
Reaching, reaching between the stars, and it seems
There could be no time at which I did not exist
And no time ever at which I shall cease to be---
While here alone in my manhood-self I am."

Brooks thought of the words, which no longer rang quite as true. His attitude had been changed by nothing more than a smile on the face of a beautiful woman and the blink of her eyes. He no longer wanted to be alone and, deep inside, felt his luck had been especially good since meeting Butterfly. For the first time, he had found a woman who was special to him and she had become his good luck.

Now, as he rubbed the medallion and thought of her, he could not know that their luck and the destiny of the platoon would be drastically changing in time.

Chapter 3

Thursday, February 12, 1970---9:12 p.m.

Inside the hooch, Lieutenant Roberto Gomez placed candles next to the tipped-over chair, symbolically blocking the entrance of the bunker and creating an overnight cell. The Vietnamese family laid side-by-side in the dirt like dogs in a kennel, forced to stay in captivity. The three stared through the bars, cramped and hungry for freedom, finding it difficult to breathe. Dust choked their throats and they desired both water and the right to stand. Watching the lieutenant arrange his equipment on their plank bed angered them as they twisted and turned in a vain attempt to be comfortable on the floor of their mud mausoleum.

The mother whispered assurances to the boy, but the father said nothing, ashamed that he had accepted this treatment without fighting back, ashamed to look into his son's eyes. He had accepted disgrace rather than death and this feeling, and that choice, would gnaw at him for the rest of his days.

They had not uttered a word in Vietnamese or English to the American officer, but their eyes revealed their thoughts. How dare these men come into their home, threaten them, and cage them? Instead of being liberated, they were held captive in their own home, in their own country. Why would they do this and still expect loyalty?

Why would anyone expect that they would support anyone other than their own countrymen against these invaders? This family and hundreds like them could only hope the war would end soon, the Americans would leave beaten and bloodied, the nightmare could be forgotten, and they could return to their rice and their lives.

Clarence Sufficool had tied his hammock between two roof support beams and was swinging gently, recalling his training as an electrical lineman back in Alabama, as he monitored the radio. He preferred the company of the grunts outside, but when it rained or mosquitoes swarmed, he enjoyed the luxury of being inside. Still, it was odd sharing the room with Lieutenant Gomez. They were so different. Like all of the members of the platoon, he had known Gomez for only a month, but their uniforms and the radio signals were their only bonds. They were bound together by a radio, an elastic cord, and a handset. Gomez controlled everyone, but Sufficool felt like a marionette to Gomez, talking for him as he pulled the strings and dancing through the system as needed. His voice was Gomez' voice, his actions were Gomez' actions. There was not any normal conversation, no discussion of home or hobbies or sports, and never any laughter. He had never witnessed Gomez laughing nor did the lieutenant appreciate his sense of humor. His ability to amuse kept him out of lots of scrapes in Montgomery, but with Gomez, he wasn't free to be himself, wasn't free to laugh. So they worked together in silence, the solemn puppet and his master. It was all business to Gomez…military business.

Lieutenant Gomez sat on the hard plank bed and watched the Vietnamese family lying in the bunker and remembered his own boyhood in San Juan, Puerto Rico. Those were unpleasant memories; memories that held him captive and pulled him back. Back to the hunger and the pain that had always been part of his life. But he had always been a survivor, a scavenger, and he had become hardened in his youth. Hate molded his body and mind to that of a Spartan and he used the pain by redirecting it to others. Those traits and his admiration of the soldiers and their uniforms, medals, and money captured the dreams of a poor boy and that led him to the military.

When Puerto Rico became a commonwealth and Gomez came of age, he joined the army and served the last few months of the Korean War. He arrived as a private, but with his courage under fire, his ability to kill without remorse, and his uncanny luck to remain untouched while casualties mounted around him, he left Korea as a field commissioned second lieutenant. After the cease-fire, he reverted to an enlisted man but immediately applied to Officer Candidate School and was re-commissioned. With his years of service and record, he believed his nationality was the only reason that he had not been promoted to captain. At age thirty-five, he was old for a first lieutenant and he resented it.

Lying back on the bed, Gomez knew this night would be no different than all the others. His sleep habits had been predetermined in another time and another war. He'd doze but never sleep peacefully. Past wounds did not keep him awake. That was not the reason, he didn't have any. His restlessness came from certain sounds---soft footsteps or the initial "thump" of an M-79---ingrained to immediately awaken him. Now, as he held his pistol on his chest and closed his eyes, he dreamed of opportunities and success that the military brass could not overlook.

At 10 p.m., Sergeant Brooks again crept around the hooch, reminding the men of their guard duty time and their relief. The men nodded and pulled their camouflaged nylon poncho liners out of their packs. In the Delta with its flat terrain, sounds carried easily and objects could be seen for long distances. The mode of operation was simple: digging foxholes or lying on shifting air mattresses created noise and the silhouette of poncho tents could be spotted by an observant enemy, so the men laid in the dirt and mud with no protection except the surrounding dikes.

Howard Morrison folded his blanket lengthwise, spread it on the ground, and then squirted insect repellent around it. "Makin' me a bug fortress," Morrison whispered to Warren Steele. "No critters should be hoppin' over that line."

Morrison looked forward to sleeping indoors again, away from the mosquitoes humming and circling his head and away from rats running over bodies in their nightly searches. He scooted in the dirt, trying to find a low spot in the ground for his hips and a raised area for his head. Inevitably, he always seemed to find a depression in the ground on the nights that it rained and he would awake soaked and muddy in a pool of water. He lay fully dressed between the blanket halves with his boots sticking out and longed to be next to his wife, holding her warm and soft body. Instead, he retrieved his rifle and held it close to his chest, a plastic and steel object of comfort and security, and then flipped the liner over his head to escape.

Sergeant Brooks took the first watch for second squad, sitting in the shadows near the radio, thinking and enjoying the peace and solitude. He relished the quiet time, leaning back like an old man satisfied with the stillness and time alone, as he scanned the area. The moon's rays still did not penetrate the woods, but it cast a glow onto the rice paddies, illuminating the land and creating shades of yellow and black. No village stood nearby, just the distant and isolated huts of Delta farmers that appeared to be tranquil oases. In another time and place, he imagined working the fertile soil with a wife and children and living a simple life, needing no more than this.

After re-checking the claymore mine detonators, Mike Brooks heard the distant pop of gunfire and saw red U.S. Army tracers flying through the night and green Viet Cong tracers returning. The sight and sounds reminded him of fireworks at a Fourth of July celebration. He wondered whether Americans or ARVNs were engaged in the firefight as the bullets streamed across the horizon, back and forth until they burned out. The sounds of the fight were faint and the view of the tracers' flight was partially blocked by a nearby tomb, erected in the rice paddies and holding a body above the high water table.

The tomb was elaborate and encased someone of importance, but the unknown dead from the past didn't matter to him. Still, Brooks imagined being enclosed in the tomb of a soldier, a premature burial in a zippered plastic bag, while he gazed into the blackness and struggled to free himself. It was a vision straight from Edgar Allan Poe's dark tales and he hated the thought of being enclosed dead or alive. Yet in this place, death could come so swiftly. He remembered a night when a VC sneaked between their platoon and another American unit that had unknowingly set up their night ambush positions less than one hundred meters apart. The VC fired his AK-47 rifle at their platoon, turned and shot at the other platoon, and then crawled away as the Americans began shooting at each other. One soldier was struck in the forehead and killed instantly before someone noticed the same colored tracers and radio contact halted the "friendly fire".

"Friendly fire"...what sickening words... and Brooks understood there's no such thing that exists. There's nothing friendly about it. It's a mistake and it only brings unintentional death. He had attended the ceremony honoring the fallen soldier, but his platoon members did not want any outsiders there, especially their friend's killers. They were angry, rightfully so, and no words of comfort mattered or existed to ease the pain.

Thinking of the incident, Brooks' mood had turned solemn until he watched two rats scampering up the mound that was Morrison's sleeping body. Morrison stirred, but the rodents lingered, standing on this raised stage and surveying their domain. Brooks was amused, observing the rats pace inside the perimeter of Morrison's "bug fortress".

He could have told Morrison more in their conversation, but he kept thinking of his father and the photographs of him in his army uniform. He was so young, so proud, and yet he was older than most of the guys now serving in third platoon. Growing up, his dad rarely spoke of the war and only repeated one message: "Never lie, never steal, and never start a fight…but if you get into a fight, you finish it". His father and he had lived by that philosophy and he wondered why the government didn't follow the same code.

His mind was filled with sporadic thoughts of his parents and sister and Butterfly and home until he saw it. A light flickered and glided south, ten meters inside the woodline, and Brooks snapped back to reality. He lifted his starlight scope, but the moonlight and a lantern held in someone's hand radiated and intensified the light. He blinked rapidly until his eyes adjusted and he concentrated not on the lantern, but on what the person carried in his opposite hand. Partially concealed by the body, it could have been a weapon, but he was unsure.

Lowering the scope, Brooks set his M-16 onto his lap and whispered into the radio handset. "31, this is 32, over."

The voice of first squad's guard, Frank Nelson, returned. "This is 31, go ahead."

"Movement on this side," Brooks said, recognizing the husky voice of the former casino dishwasher from Reno. "Anything over there?"

"Negative. How many dinks on your side?"

"Possibly one," Brooks said, concentrating on the light.

"Are you going to fire him up, Mike?"

"No, but hang loose."

"Roger that. 31 out."

Brooks reached out and squeezed Howard Morrison's shoulder, scattering the rats and immediately ending his sleep. Morrison gasped and, with one motion, gripped his rifle, shoved off the poncho liner, and sat up. "Gooks?"

"Maybe."

"Aw…man. I lose more hair and sleep 'cause of them."

Brooks pointed toward the light. "Take over while I tell Gomez."

Bending low, Brooks walked through the doorway of the hooch and stood there momentarily, noticing the candles burning near the bunker and Lieutenant Gomez sleeping on the plank bed.

The slight creak of the door awakened Gomez and he recognized Brooks' form. "What's wrong?"

"Movement."

Gomez swung his boots to the floor, pointed the pistol at the caged Vietnamese as a reminder, and then nudged his radioman. "Cool…time to go to work."

Within minutes, Brooks, Sufficool, and Lieutenant Gomez laid prone in the dirt, near the scattered bodies of sleeping soldiers, while the officer studied the situation through Brooks' scope. The field of vision glowed and the lantern, now placed on the ground, acted like a theatre footlight. It illuminated the body, probably a man, but Gomez couldn't see any weapons nor could he determine why this person was outside, broadcasting his presence to anyone watching. Still, whoever was out there was violating the 10 p.m. curfew in a free fire zone, where anyone could be shot with no questions asked.

Gomez lowered the scope, blinked to regain his night vision, and faced Brooks with his eyes reflecting his decision. "We'll recon by fire, do a 'mad minute' on his sorry ass before the gook ditty-bops away."

Brooks reacted, feeling his jaw tighten, angry at himself for waking the lieutenant and putting the platoon in this situation.

"I alerted you as ordered about the movement, but why fire?" Brooks asked. "He's probably just a civilian headin' for the outhouse. We'll pinpoint our location to any VC around and waste ammo that we may really need later."

"We will recon by fire," Gomez repeated. "It's our duty to kill anyone out after the curfew. One gook or one hundred and one…I don't care. Besides, if he's dead...he's VC. Now, pass the order."

Brooks threw down a handful of dirt. He'd only served a few weeks under Gomez' leadership but he should have known. The lieutenant was a stubborn, kill happy bastard and it was unbelievable that he had survived the Korean War and was on his second tour in Vietnam. He seemed to go crashing into trouble without any consequences to himself. He always came out unscathed. No physical wounds, no Purple Hearts, but there was no immediate explanation for his mental state.

Gomez questioned the hesitation. "Are you deaf or are you waiting for me to tell you again?"

"Will we at least change night-hold positions?" Brooks asked, rather than respond to the lieutenant's remark.

"Negative."

Gomez felt his anger increase with each of Brooks' comments, knowing that he was killing communists when this sergeant was in grade school.

"If we stay here after the ambush," Brooks explained, "you're inviting the gooks to kick the crap out of us. One B-40 rocket from the woodline would do us a job. We've had eleven wounded and six dead in the one month that you've been in command. Let's not have any more."

"We've also shot thirty-one VC in the same time," Gomez countered. "We're not here to make new friends, just to kill old enemies."

"That's fine but not at the expense of our own men."

Gomez' eyes widened, dark and unblinking, and his eyebrows pushed the wrinkles up on his forehead as his face flushed. "Damn it, Sergeant, shut up and follow my orders. Follow them or I'll relieve you of your duty. I'm done talking and I'm through debating the subject. This is not a fuckin' democracy." He checked the light again and then glared at Brooks. "Wake up the men. He's violating the curfew and we're going to blow him away!"

Brooks said nothing further. He had tried, but his arguments had been ignored and someone was about to die. This wasn't a battle, not even a firefight; it was an execution by a long range firing squad. The person was not a threat to twenty armed soldiers, but they were going to kill him for breaking curfew and being outside with a lantern. It didn't make any sense…humans killing humans…for nothing. The government had taught Brooks the proper methods of how to kill, but they had failed so far in teaching him how to enjoy it.

Chapter 4

Thursday, February 12, 1970---10:52 p.m.

Lieutenant Gomez eased back the bolt of his M-16 and double-checked if he had chambered a round. He already knew the answer. The brass casing shined and he slid it back into the darkness of the barrel. It was time.

Like a worker in a slaughter house, he understood and accepted killing as part of his job. Compassion, mercy, or even a thought as to the morality of it never entered his mind. Killing was simply a part of his chosen profession and he did it well.

Switching off the safety, Gomez shifted his prone position and held the rifle stock firmly against his cheek, adjusting his arms until he was comfortable. The shot was unobstructed, no more than one hundred meters and, even with open sights, he felt confident that one less VC would be violating the curfew and would soon be permanently dropped to the ground. Aiming at the man holding the lantern, he breathed deeply and, as he released half of the air, he tightened the trigger pressure and anticipated the weapon's discharge.

A fraction of a moment before Gomez fired, Sufficool interrupted with an unexpected message. "Don't shoot! First squad's radioman says gooks are headin' our way."

Gomez grabbed the starlight from Brooks and swung it around. He counted nine VC coming into view, all carrying AK-47s, walking in single file along a dike near the tomb. They were halfway between the hooch and the woodline, even closer than the claymore mines, and that was a shame. He could've killed all of them with one click of the detonator, one squeeze from his hand, like the wrath of god manifested in a fiery explosion. Still, he could not believe it and he presumed his good luck would soon have the opposite effect on nine men.

Lowering the scope, he ordered Sufficool to again pass the word to fire after his first shot and then handed the scope back to Brooks.

Gomez stared at the targets, his eyes readjusting from the scope's light, and then spoke softly. It was a quiet message, spoken like a prayer, even though he knew his sarcasm was both a cliché and a lie. "This is how to 'win the hearts and minds' of these people."

Brooks ignored the comment and lifted the scope while Gomez tightened his grip on the rifle. Again breathing deeply and releasing half of the air with a hissing sound, textbook-style for marksmanship, Gomez aimed at the first man in the column and squeezed off the first shot.

The bullet "popped" and ripped into the lead man, striking his neck and severing the jugular vein. The VC hunched up in reaction to the bullet's impact and then dropped on top of the dike, the shocking power of the projectile immediately extinguishing his life. As the man fell, Lieutenant Gomez glanced toward Brooks with a slight smirk on his face, as if waiting for congratulatory praise on the shot.

No reaction was offered, but the platoon members followed orders. They fired a heavy volley while the remaining VC dove for the ground. Three men were hit in midair, while the others scrambled along the backside of the dike and crawled behind the raised grave.

The first volley of shots quickly declined in intensity and was replaced by the slow, individual popping of weapons on semi-automatic. The men, who fired on full automatic, zipped through their eighteen rounds and hurriedly reloaded.

The five remaining VC fired short, low bursts in return. Their AK rifles "kracked" with their distinctive sounds, zinging bullets over the heads of the Americans, no more than two feet above the ground, punching holes in the rain barrels sitting against the hooch, and splitting the bamboo sidewalls. Inside, the frightened Vietnamese family clung to each other, listening to the battle's roar, feeling the bullets impact smacking their hard mud enclosure and now thankful to be hunkered together within their bunker. Outside, some soldiers jumped into the canal for protection and better firing positions, now ignoring the putrid smell of the stagnant water.

Mike Brooks lifted to one knee and fired three shots. He rolled onto his back, extracted the empty magazine, and pulled out a full one from his waist bandolier. He shoved in the clip and yelled past Gomez, who continued to fire, to Sufficool. "Have you called in gunships?"

"Negative, Gomez' orders."

"How about illumination?"

A whistling-sound, approaching from the southeast, answered Brooks' question. The shell whined louder and louder and finally screamed above them. The round banged and then popped and a white flare flickered to life, increasing in intensity and brightness as it descended, rocking and gently floating down under a small parachute.

The radioman smiled and chanted, "Light from heaven to you...compliments of 'Cool."

Warren Steele steadied his rifle. It would happen again. As expected, one of the VC stood behind the tomb, jumping up like a mechanical target in a shooting gallery, and fired his AK. Steele aimed and returned fire, but the bullets hit low, shattering the corner of the grave and throwing chips of white stone and a fine dust into the man's face. AK bullets belched back, thudding into the dike and hurling dirt clods into the air. Steele dropped flat, listening to the sounds of the firefight, and felt the rush of adrenaline pounding through his body. He hated the waiting and the suspense before the first shots, but those bursts of fire and lead filled him with an exhilaration that he craved as much as women and heroin.

Turning onto his back to reload, Steele saw the new man, Pfc. Cunningham, holding his knees to his chest and lying next to his M-79 grenade launcher. Covering his ears to deaden the noise of his first firefight, he squeezed his legs together to control his bowels.

"What the hell?" Steele said, crawling to Cunningham's side and glancing at the weapon. It was perfect for lobbing rounds over the tomb's protection. He slapped the top of Cunningham's head and screamed. "Move up and fire, asshole, or give me your 79!"

Cunningham grabbed the weapon before Steele took it away. He slid a grenade round into the breech, closed it, and crawled alongside Steele to the dike. Peeking over the mud wall, AK bullets whizzed by him and he dropped the weapon and ducked. Holding his hands over his ears, he again curled into a ball and yelled, "They'll kill me!"

Steele slapped Cunningham's hands and then pressed the hot barrel of his M-16 onto the nape of the man's neck. Cunningham screamed and jerked, thrashing his arms and pushing the weapon away, but Steele shifted the barrel and pushed harder, pinning Cunningham's neck down. The stench of burning hair and skin rose while smoke floated out of the barrel and the skin blistered and sizzled like bacon tossed into hot grease.

When the skin oozed and was branded with the red imprint of the flash arrestor, Steele shoved the muzzle next to Cunningham's ear. "Now, start shooting or I'll blow your head off before the gooks even get the chance."

Tears flowed down Cunningham's cheeks and urine wet his crotch, but he sprung above the level of the dike, fired the M-79 without aiming, and dropped to the ground. He looked at Steele and then loaded another round.

The pointman thought about his motivational technique and then grinned. "Now, have fun."

Lieutenant Gomez grabbed the radio receiver-transmitter handset from Sufficool and called first squad. "31, this is 30."

"30, go ahead."

Gomez pressed the sidebar button. "Pass the word to flank your men to the right of the grave in two minutes. Out." He tossed the handset to Sufficool and faced Brooks. "Second squad will flank to the left. We'll put those gooks in a cross fire."

"They aren't going to lie down and die for us," Brooks said. "Call in a gunship and we'll keep them pinned down until it can waste them."

Gomez blurted out the words. "In Korea, no gunships helped us. We took every bit of land away from those chinks by ourselves. Twenty of us can surely blow away five more gooks. Now, damn it, pass the message!"

Gomez eyed his watch for the allotted time and then stood, running and yelling, "Let's go!"

The two squads of men ran forward, spreading out and trailing their leader. They shouted, whooping wildly, reminiscent of a Civil War charge and followed Gomez while the machine gunners blanketed the tomb with heavy covering fire. Chips of stone, dust, and sparks radiated from the grave as the bullets chewed up the masonry and covered it with jagged edges and pock marks.

The VC pressed back against their cover, feeling the pounding impact of the bullets, and listened to other lead whistling and screaming over their heads. Watching the flanks, they had no choice but to wait out the barrage and reload their AKs, knowing the two lines of soldiers were advancing.

Gunsmoke hung at ground level, a smelly man-made fog, and flares hissed and floated downward, casting shadows of the men as they dove behind dikes. Crawling forward, the Americans separated into better firing positions and began flanking the tomb.

When the machine gunners ceased fire, worried about hitting their men, one of the VC stood and sprayed the area just wide of Lieutenant Gomez. The bullets slammed into the dike and Gomez ducked, ordering the machine gunners forward with the command of "Guns up!"

Steele adjusted for his first low shots and fired an eighteen round burst on automatic, returning fire at the VC. The rifle rose up with the recoil, but seven bullets smashed into the man, splintering his teeth and driving a bloody hole into the middle of his face.

Falling onto his back, the four remaining VC shouted in rage and terror and accepted their own fate as they stared at the body. Their friend was gone and had left no identifying marks. This was a stranger with a red mask, a corpse with no face. They looked at the close-up results of the Americans' work and understood that only minutes remained of life. Hate swelled within them and they swore aloud, committing themselves to kill as many of them as possible.

One of the VC grabbed his only Chi-Com grenade and spotted a soldier crawling over the rice stubble with his butt too high. Yanking the igniting string, he waited until three seconds before detonation and threw the explosive.

Men scattered, diving over connecting dikes and yelling, "Grenade!"

Cunningham swung an arm over his head but that was his only reaction. He froze from fear as the grenade sailed above him and ignited in mid-air with a loud "whomp", driving hot blades of metal downwards. Shrapnel ripped into his right hand, back, and legs and, in that flash, the fingers between his thumb and little finger had disappeared, leaving only three stubs and severed finger arteries squirting blood with the rhythm of each heartbeat.

Cunningham's screams alerted Doc Tyson and he was already running behind the line of soldiers when someone yelled, "Medic!" Tyson's response was automatic, a reaction that could be likened to a startled mother lunging for her falling child. Logically, his movement was one of a fool, but he was there, running to his call.

Howard Morrison saw the movement, not of Tyson, but of the VC aiming at the medic. The two men fired simultaneously, with Morrison's shots traveling high and the VC's bullets dancing around Tyson's feet. The medic dove forward and landed next to Mike Brooks, who was reloading.

"Hey, those guys are pissed," Tyson said, grinning and shoving his glasses back on. "I think I'll try a little crawling."

"Good idea."

As Tyson crawled away, Brooks rose to one knee and shot twice. He squeezed the trigger again, but the M-16 didn't fire. Ducking down, he pushed the magazine release button, yanked out the clip, and found it nearly full. His rifle was jammed, even with loading only eighteen rounds instead of twenty in the magazine. He twisted the rifle sideways and saw the spent cartridge stuck halfway in and out of the chamber with the bolt wedged against the casing. He tugged once, but the shell did not budge. Glancing toward the grave, he saw the enemy aiming at him.

Shots rang out and Brooks flinched, watching the VC topple backwards with holes in his neck and upper chest. Brooks turned toward the sounds of the shots. Morrison nodded as two of the three remaining VC jumped to their feet and, in a reckless, panicked manner, charged the left flank. Their charge only lasted a few steps before both were cut down in a hail of bullets.

Doc Tyson scrambled to Cunningham's side when Lieutenant Gomez yelled, "Follow me!" and waved his arm, sprinting toward the grave where the last VC remained. Hearing the pounding footsteps, the VC swung his AK around just as Gomez dove and fired. The bullets straightened the VC up, pinning him against the grave, and then, as if the tomb had drunk enough of his blood, it let him slide into an awkward sitting position.

The VC's head drooped, his black hair hanging to his knees, and his muscles shivered and twitched. Gomez shot him again, eliminating all doubt that he was dead, and watched the body lean to the side, now fully relaxed. The lieutenant paused, glancing at the scattered bodies and his own men, as all firing ceased. He cautiously walked forward through the rice stubble, visually confirming all were dead, and grabbed the AK-47 rifle, the best of prizes, away from the VC's grip. He then watched Steele claim another rifle, setting off a search of the bodies for valuables. Gomez looked at the AK, admiring its style while smoke still curled out of the barrel and disappeared like a white snake vanishing into the night. Blood, still warm and thick, coated the stock and Gomez wiped it away on his trousers. He held the weapon above his head, shaking and displaying it as he yelled, and then lowered the weapon to his shoulder. Warmth from the VC's cheek still clung to the rifle's stock and Gomez pretended to fire until he noticed his soldiers' changing behavior.

It was a feeling he knew well…firefights could be the ultimate rush, the ultimate high. The men's senses were now at their absolute peak and nothing in peacetime could match these feelings. The running, the shooting, and the killing had long ago become an alluring sirens' song for him, calling him not to destruction but to destroy, and he loved the feeling. With the adrenaline flowing as well as the blood, Gomez knew the young men could acquire a taste for it, just as he had. Adolescents with weapons were a lethal combination for one's body and soul and Gomez nodded approval like a teacher whose students' finally understood the concept. The killing seemed to increase the soldiers' awareness of the sanctity of life and they were uplifted by surviving while others had died. The scavenging seemed to validate the thought…they had taken their lives and now they would take their possessions.

It had always been that way. Possessions were always acquired, no taken, from the weak and that was perfectly acceptable in Gomez' mind. It had been a good night's work--nine dead VC and only one American wounded. It was the type of night and carnage that would harden his men's hearts and change them into the type of soldiers, the type of students that he wanted.

Scrambling for the rifles and looting the bodies, it exhibited the meaner side of their conscience that had lain dormant from their childhood. As boys, many had toyed with the sadism of holding a match to a spider, sprinkling salt on snails, or tying cans to a cat's tail. As boys and now as young men, human law did not exist and the dark side of their souls swelled like an erupting boil, spilling over and infecting others in the upheaval.

Warren Steele reached into the pants pocket of one of the dead and felt the blood seeping out. He didn't react. He could always wash away the blood on his hands and checking out the bodies did not bother him. He slid his hand along the boney pelvis and could feel the man's testes, veiled by the wet cloth. Steele felt the urge to castrate him and shove the sac into the corpse's mouth as a warning to other VC, but the image of slicing off the testicles escaped when he touched something of more interest in the other pocket. They were wet and crumpled but he recognized the feel and he extracted it...Vietnamese money...twenty Dong bills. He wondered what the others had found, but the AK that he had claimed plus the eight bills he counted equaled a very profitable and satisfying night. He straightened the money, wiping the blood onto his shirt sleeve, and let the idea of castration flee as he neatly folded and transferred the notes into his own pocket.

The money reminded Steele of the time when he and Sergeant Morrison had barged into a hooch, looking for an alternate day-hold position, and surprised two Vietnamese men, squatting, counting money, and separating it into piles. One threw his hands up to surrender while the second slammed his shoulder into the hooch's wall, squeezed through the bamboo, and ran. The VC's daylight run was cut short by bullet holes drilled into his back. Still, the incident reinforced the idea that following a routine could get one killed. All four men had reacted in shock and surprise with the simple opening of a door, but the biggest surprise came later.

The captive was identified as the local Viet Cong Finance Minister and Tax Collector, making his scheduled rounds and carrying the Vietnamese equivalent of one thousand dollars. The capture prompted the company commander to helicopter into third platoon's day-hold position. The colonel squatted next to the prisoner, his hands tied behind his back, for photographs and to display the holstered pistol that the American officer claimed as his own. The money, however, was never mentioned, had mysteriously disappeared and, under Morrison's insistence, was split among members of the platoon.

Tonight, that would not happen. Steele tapped the bills in his pocket. No one knew of this and he would not be sharing the Vietnamese money with his fellow soldiers. It would be his secret that the dead man had bequeathed all to him, unknowingly and unwillingly contributing to his stash of beer and drug money.

As the other soldiers scavenged, Mike Brooks and Howard Morrison strained to hold Pfc. Cunningham, who screamed and kicked in a vain attempt to relieve the pain as Doc Tyson feverishly wrapped the jagged, spurting fingers. Cunningham pushed with all of his power, struggling not to be pinned and wanting only to cradle his hand and centralize the pain. He shook his head, his mind twirling in a dizzy, suspended state, and felt as if it were detached from his body.

He gazed at his burning hand, the bandages covering the permanent "hang loose" appendage while mumbling and moaning and calling himself, "a two-fingered freak".

Doc Tyson tied off the compress on the fingers and noted the odd-shaped burn on the neck as he checked the shrapnel wounds to Cunningham's back and legs. With Morrison and Brooks' help, Doc Tyson raised the back of Cunningham's shirt and lowered his trousers, stripping him in the field. Rice stalks poked at the front of his body, jabbing like a bed of nails into his chest, legs, and groin. Tyson worked quickly and noted that the wounds to the back were minor, unworthy of even bandaging, while the fatty tissue of the buttocks was punctured with several jagged holes. The holes only slightly bled and none of the wounds were of major concern. The shrapnel would burn and ooze, but Doc refocused on the missing fingers as they dressed Cunningham.

The severed fingers alone would prevent the FNG from returning to the platoon and, based on his observations, the medic felt that was a good thing. Cunningham did not have the personality, courage, or mind set to be an infantryman. Inside this circle of soldiers, Doc Tyson alone was their healer, their surgeon, and their executioner. Twice, he had sentenced men to a future death. Two times, he had patched up men too well and within weeks the same soldiers had been shoved back into the platoon, where they had been killed. Cunningham could have been the third execution.

Tyson extracted a morphine syringe from his aid bag and pushed the needle into Cunningham's arm. He squeezed in only half of the pain killer for two reasons: the amount would calm the man without pushing him further into shock and the distant thumping of blades could be heard.

"The dustoff is coming," Sufficool yelled, relaying the message from the medevac helicopter to Lieutenant Gomez, who switched on his hand-held strobe. The white light pulsated and flashed brightly, identifying their position and beckoning the Huey helicopter to approach.

The chopper's running lights blinked as it skimmed the treetops, half-circled, and then dipped, flying barely above the fields. As it slowed, the pilot switched off the red and green lights, raised its nose, and set down the skids. The helicopter roared and vibrated heavily while a white cross, painted on its nose, glowed above the words, "You Call...We Come."

Doc Tyson and Mike Brooks wrapped their arms around Cunningham's waist, while he hooked his arms around their necks. They walked slowly with the moon, flares, and pulsating strobe creating a visual illusion that made them appear and disappear, appear and disappear, with the beat of the light. Blood dripped through the bandages, raining drops onto Brooks' pants and boots, while Cunningham's shirt and pants rubbed against the uncovered shrapnel wounds and he jerked and limped with each step, craving only escape from his pain and from this land.

The prop wind created a whirlwind of dirt and debris, blasting the men back as Lieutenant Gomez switched off the strobe light. Leaning forward into the blowing dust, the three men staggered to the helicopter where the crew chief pulled Cunningham up and onto a litter.

The soldiers jogged clear of the blades and Doc Tyson signaled a thumb-up "all clear" to the warrant officer, who half-saluted and accelerated the engine. The medic considered flashing the "hang loose" sign, but figured Cunningham would not appreciate the gallows humor. Holding onto his bush hat, Tyson lowered his head into the dust as the chopper shook and strained to lift its skids off the soil. Rising up, the nose dipped and then no longer awkward, the machine gracefully skimmed the checkerboard paddies, leaped higher into the moonlit sky, and headed for its infirmary home.

The soldiers stood together and yet felt alone as their adrenaline slowed and their thoughts evolved into a mixture of opposing emotions. They were thankful to be alive, indifferent to those that they had killed, and saddened by Cunningham's wounds. Still, they felt a strange envy of him, knowing that he would be departing the country with his life.

Standing in the field like a silent and solemn congregation, the soldiers listened to the helicopter fade away until the hush of the night was broken by only the fizzling of an illumination round, smoking and weaving a ghostly trail as it floated down. After it struck the ground, the men waited for another shell to whiz over their heads and bring the imitation light of day, but none was fired. The last flare flickered and faded and darkness veiled the platoon.

Chapter 5

Friday, February 13, 1970---7:02 a.m.

The morning sun peeked over the horizon, casting a pink tint on the sleeping soldiers, and its rays sparkled and shined through the dust already stirred up by both ill-tempered water buffaloes pulling plows and a multitude of smoking motor scooters on dirt roads.

Time had passed and the previous night's chaos was not reflected in the calm of the morning. The last two guards ended their watch and then woke the other soldiers, who stretched and yawned and began the rituals of the dawning of a new day and the necessities of life. The light was always a welcomed sight and for the men of Bravo Company, third platoon, life continued as usual with another day and night scratched from their assigned time in Vietnam and their mental calendars. For some, last night was simply history, a footnote in a page of life. The firefight's results did not disturb them and certain details were already erased from their minds. They thought little of the bodies lying meters away and most slept better knowing that nine VC could no longer harm them. They were alive and safe and that was all that mattered. In the Delta, the equation was mostly true: light equaled safety and safety equaled happiness.

Besides Lieutenant Gomez, Daniel "Doc" Tyson was the oldest platoon member at age twenty-three. A graduate of the University of Idaho with a major in anthropology, he worked as a state archaeological aide until the draft notice summoned him from the dirty excavations to the mud of Southeast Asia. If he had to go, traveling outside of Idaho and exploring Vietnam appealed to his curiosity. He had worked year round and, with help from his dad's truck driver wages, became the first in family history to graduate from high school, junior college, and college.

His curiosity and his willingness to try anything pushed Doc Tyson to step forward. His intensity, inquisitiveness, and a desire to experience all aspects of Vietnamese culture led him to the two planks that extended above the canal and which served as the Vietnamese family's toilet.

It was a miniature pier capable of holding one person of Vietnamese size and weight and business was conducted by squatting at the end of the pier. Shoving the C-ration toilet paper into his shirt pocket, Tyson held onto the two support studs, which secured the planks above the water.

When his morning business was completed, Tyson rose, holding one of the posts to stand, and seemingly pulled the trap door lever of this bathroom gallows. The pier cracked and collapsed and sent him straight down into the canal, where he stood stunned and waist deep in the water. He stood there, unmoving and frozen in his own stupidity. Cursing loudly, he reached down into the sewage, pulled up his pants, and waded out.

The rest of the platoon had been drawn to the sounds of the crack, the splash, and the shout and all laughed at the morning entertainment, pointing at the so-called educated man and wondering what in the hell he was thinking.

Morrison laughed, but the medic's foolishness made him think back to his own mistake. On a night mission, he had crept under a hooch's overhanging roof and sat with his back against the wall, watching the perimeter until he felt the tapping on his hat and shoulder. It was puzzling. He couldn't figure out how he was being pelted with raindrops, dripping through the porch's roof and he leaned forward, extending his hand to touch the non-existent raindrops on a nearly cloudless night. He cautiously stood to investigate and discovered that it was not raindrops striking him. He had been sitting under an open-bottom bird cage, which held a large parrot and hung from the dark underbelly of the hooch's roof. In anger, he began shaking the cage, forcing the parrot to squawk and flap its wings until platoon members forced him sit down and be quiet.

Morrison continued to chuckle as he struck a match, lit a marble-sized ball of white C-4 explosive, and held the lid of a can of beans and franks over the intense flame.

"Beans for breakfast? How do you eat that?" Steele asked with a smile. "Morrison's preparing some incoming. It'll curl your hair."

Some soldiers dragged their packs away, pretending to know the outcome, and laughing and pointing as Morrison mixed the beans and overzealously licked the white plastic spoon.

"Just like mom used to make," Morrison said, winking. "But, she was a lousy cook." He stirred in some Tabasco sauce and then wolfed down a giant bite, licking his lips and pretending the taste was delicious. "I'm eatin' four cans and then really curlin' your hair." Morrison rubbed his own thinning hairline. "Wished that'd work for me...baldin' at twenty-one. I'll be hairless before I get out of Nam."

Brooks watched and smiled, thinking Morrison may be right, as he jiggled his P-38 opener and bent the lid back on a can of peaches. Drinking the juice, he watched the men gathering and packing their equipment, inventing breakfast menu items from their C-rations, and Warren Steele pulling out a camera from his pack.

"Picture time?" Brooks asked, already knowing the answer and wishing that he had an updated picture of the platoon. He didn't have any group photos that included Cunningham and he wondered who would be missing from the next one. In time, he'd forget how the FNG even looked, his memories of Cunningham's face fading like an old photo. He would remember only the agonized cries of pain, the blood dripping onto his trousers, and the image of their last walk to the dustoff helicopter.

Steele answered the question, holding up a Kodak Instamatic camera. "Yeah…time for some souvenir snapshots. Somethin' to show the grandkids. You want me to take your picture with Luke the Gook and his friends?"

"No." Brooks shook his head. He didn't want his picture on the same roll of film like an epitaph of the dead and the thought made his Baptist church upbringing flash through his mind. "We took their lives, but I'm not proud of it."

Steele's smile vanished. "I'm just doing my job."

"And that's exactly what you should be doing," Lieutenant Gomez said, walking up to Steele and looking at the scattered platoon members.

None were truly educated, most were barely out of high school, and none represented the upper echelon of society…poor boys from thousands of little towns, with no power or voice, being shipped to the slaughterhouse. The politicians wanted the war fought, but it was a cause unworthy of their own sons' blood. They preached patriotism and warned of the surging tide of communism, but they were hypocritical. Honor, sacrifice, and devotion to duty were only empty words to them, spoken for elections, but not believed. Gomez thought differently and lived the code. He was proud to be a U.S. citizen, Puerto Rico born, but a U.S. citizen and willing to do whatever his country wanted. If his country asked him to kill other people because of their differing beliefs, he was obligated, maybe obsessed, and he would do so without hesitation, remorse, or apology.

"I'll check them out with you," Gomez said, focusing his attention back on Brooks. "Don't let Sergeant Perfect bother you. Brooks judges everyone but himself. He's a dreamer in a world of nightmares, but he's changing and he's afraid of it." Gomez looked deep into Brooks' eyes. "Think about it…I used to be like you."

Brooks watched Steele and Gomez walk into the field and wondered why all of the men of peace, the dreamers of a better world---John and Bobby Kennedy, Dr. Martin Luther King, even Gandhi---had been murdered. Assassinated to silence their words.

And what did his high school history teacher say? Brooks tried to remember. None of the students guessed correctly when asked how many wars the United States had fought in. Including Indian wars, the number was fifty-three with seven major wars between the Revolutionary War to the undeclared Vietnam War. Plus, seven hundred U.S. military bases were established in one hundred and fifty foreign countries. Could that be true? How many of the wars were for righteous causes and how many stemmed from greed? Were all of the bases necessary or another form of imperialism? Brooks shook his head, not knowing the answers. He thought of "*The Ugly American*" book and character, the arrogant savior of the world who knew what was best for others, and then remembered Gomez' words, which lingered and gnawed at him.

It was true, he was a dreamer and he was changing. A malignancy was growing within him and he felt powerless to stop it. His mind twisted in a duality of thoughts, contorted into a Jekyll and Hyde, and both sides struggled for control of his soul. He had seen the dead too many times before and now grotesque faces stared at him in the night, shattering his dreams with their shattered faces. As life slipped from the bodies of the dead, so had his feelings died and there was no going back.

His innocence had been smashed with his first kill and the spilling of that virgin blood was one that he could never forget. Certain sights or sounds triggered the image of the VC running toward the hooch's door. As the man spun to shoot again, Brooks stopped him with a burst of automatic fire that dropped the VC screaming and rolling, pressing down on the holes in his stomach. Brooks stood above him with tears clouding his vision until he heard the cries from inside the hooch. Opening the door, he found the other results of his bullets. A mother rocked her bloodied daughter, whose smooth complexion was now jagged and wet. When he saw her eyes roll up and heard her last breath, Brooks burst out of the hut, weeping and running and trying to escape the nightmare. But, he could not. It was one that he would never escape.

The image and death of that little girl always haunted him. With her death, his own uninhibited childlike joy had died and a cancer of his soul was unleashed, growing and sickening him and leaving only a horror that he could never shake. He could disguise it by becoming harder, but the cries of any child brought the memory screaming back, flooding his eyes with tears.

At present, he felt no sorrow and no joy over the bodies lying in the field. "Better them than me" was always the prevailing philosophy. He wondered how many would weep for these soldiers, but he and the rest of third platoon would not feel any sorrow. He only felt apathy when he thought of the nine corpses. Nine less creatures could no longer harm him and, if he didn't look at the bodies, he could pretend that they weren't human…they were nothing more than gooks, not men. He could dehumanize the decaying corpses in words and thoughts but, deep in his heart, it was a concept that he simply did not believe.

Chapter 6

Friday, February 13, 1970---7:38 a.m.

Lieutenant Gomez flipped the corpse of the lead Viet Cong onto its back, sending a swarm of flies upwards, buzzing and circling until the head stopped rocking. The insects landed again on the open wounds of the neck and crawled freely into the nose and mouth, laying the eggs that would hatch into maggots. It was a fitting end Gomez felt for the weak, the unfit. In death, the corpse would be the perfect incubator, warming and housing the immature eggs until maturity, and the perfect nourishment, feeding and fattening the grubs until they could fly away.

Warren Steele squatted next to the man that he had killed. The smell of decay already hung in the air, while flies and ants devoured chunks of flesh and crawled into the brain cavity where only human thoughts and electric impulses once passed.

Steele gazed at the man with no face and remembered how a mortician reconstructed his stepfather's head with wax after he leaned a shotgun against his chin and pulled the trigger. The mental image did not bring about sadness…sadness was never an outcome of that death because Steele had always hated him. He'd always been a user. He was a man who only wanted his mother for her welfare check and spread legs. He was a man that had molested his sister

Trixie at age fourteen, destroying her virginity and her innocence, while pushing her out to the streets where she was forced to marry early to escape. But, the marriage was not her salvation or her escape.

After three years of neither happiness nor bliss, her estranged husband walked into the Baptist church service, raised a .22 pistol to the back of her head, and fired a single shot as she sang. She was not killed, but the bullet instantly created a seventeen-year-old vegetable, a quadriplegic paralyzed from the neck down.

Before leaving for Vietnam, Steele visited her, brushing her hair and wishing he could change the past. But he could not. She solemnly sat in her wheelchair, hunched over with her head hanging and the support straps digging into her ulcerated skin, unable to escape or run, staring only with a twisted face that silently screamed, "Why?"

Warren Steele blamed his mother for not protecting her children and his stepfather for his sister's fate. Good riddance to a man that had beaten him with a piece of hose and who had made drunken, failed attempts to sodomize him and his two brothers. Still, it was his sister that saddened him. The man had taken everything from her. A normal life, her dignity, and her chance for happiness were lost in a stepfather's lust and a husband's warped rage. If he could have foreseen her future, he would have killed both of the animals himself. So, screw them, Steele thought, may they both rot in hell. He respected the men now lying at his feet and rotting where they fell more than those human parasites.

Steele shook his head as if to escape the demons of the past. He pulled on the shoulder of his shirt and bit the threads that attached his Ninth Infantry Division patch, a camouflaged daisy pattern, nicknamed the "flaming asshole". Snapping the filaments loose, he ripped off the emblem and set it into the man's concave face, watching the patch wiggle and quiver as insects crawled beneath it.

"Now, that's what I call effective propaganda," Gomez said, walking up and borrowing the camera.

Steele grabbed the man's calloused feet and dragged him away from the other corpses. He stood behind the body, set one boot on the dead man's bare chest, and held his M-16. Smiling, he pointed at the emblem and the man's missing face until the picture was snapped.

Gomez nodded approval and then took the liberty of photographing the other dead, documenting the event. With childlike curiosity, he examined the twisted and awkward ways their bodies had fallen until he noticed a distant vehicle, trailing a cloud of dust.

Handing Steele the camera, Gomez began walking toward the hooch. "Come on...we'll get other pictures 'cause I plan on killing a lot of gooks." The lieutenant paused and looked back at the dead. "Yeah, a lot of gooks."

Lieutenant Gomez slipped on his pack and helmet and lit a Camel cigarette as he kicked the chair and melted candles away from the bunker entrance, releasing his prisoners.

As he walked out of the hooch, the Vietnamese family crawled out, their clothes blanketed with dirt, and they followed in silence. Stepping into the morning sunlight, they squinted as they observed the results of the firefight.

Incoming bullets had snapped the dry bamboo on the walls of their hooch, leaving small sections broken and dangling, while their dwelling was surrounded by the litter of the battle. Brass shell casings, C-ration cans, empty hand flare canisters, and shattered water barrels lay everywhere. But only one object, one body, concerned them.

The young boy noticed it first, pointing in shock at their water buffalo lying dead in its pen. Its legs had been shattered by incoming VC rifle fire and it toppled, falling like a massive tree cut at its base, directly into the hail of bullets. The animal's head and horns hung on the last rung of the fence, the dry tongue protruded from the side of its open mouth, and intestinal gases gurgled and inflated the carcass.

The father walked forward and sank to his knees in despair, his hands shaking at the loss. His wife and son stood next to him, crying as they patted his shoulders to offer comfort, while he petted the animal's black neck and prayed for life to return. He was unaware of the human bodies lying in his fields, left unburied as if they were offerings laid at the foot of his ancestor's shrine, but their passing would have been secondary to the water buffalo.

The Vietnamese man sat in the mud next to the water trough, pulled his knees to his chest, and continued to rock. He no longer focused on the dead buffalo or the soldiers' talk of the unidentified VC. They represented the past, an unchangeable past, and his mind jumped ahead to a questionable future. The thoughts spinning through his brain were inconceivable to the Americans, inconceivable except to his family or other peasant farmers of the Mekong Delta. Clutching his head as if to control the future, the father quietly wept, knowing his family would face starvation next season without an animal to pull the plow and break the soil for planting.

The man continued to sit near the pen, oblivious to the scattered, uninterested line of soldiers departing for the truck until Lieutenant Gomez grabbed his shirt collar and pulled him to his feet.

"Time to talk about the extra supper bowls, Papa-san," Gomez said, tilting his helmet back. "You didn't think I'd forget, did you?"

The man looked confused and didn't seem to understand why the officer had yanked him up, but he spoke his first words, a standard answer in his limited English. "Me no VC."

"And me no care," Gomez said in a mocking response, leaning forward and pointing. "You're a lying little bastard."

"Me no *bic*."

"Bullshit. You understand me just fine."

The lieutenant removed the lit cigarette from his lips and placed it into the Vietnamese man's mouth, sharing it for some unknown reason. "Your dinner guests didn't quite make it, did they? But don't worry. You won't have any visitors for a while."

Clarence Sufficool stood next to the officer, listening to his arguments. A spokesman for the defense did not exist. No contraband or weapons had been found in and around the hooch, but the extra supper bowls and cooked rice was adequate evidence for the court of Gomez, who acted as prosecutor, judge, and jury. The radioman anticipated Gomez' next move, the sentencing, and predicted that if the family were not Viet Cong sympathizers now, they would soon be changed to the communist persuasion.

Gomez put another cigarette in his lips, lit it, and then stared into the man's eyes. The lieutenant inhaled deeply, his lips curling into the slightest smile as if to threaten the little man to act. No reaction occurred until Gomez administered his version of swift justice, justice that no higher authority would question. A body and weapon count of nine guaranteed his acquittal.

Reaching up to the thatched roof, Lieutenant Gomez flipped his lighter and set fire to the straw.

The Vietnamese man no longer restrained his emotions. He reached wide-eyed for Gomez' rifle, but the lieutenant anticipated the reaction and slammed the M-16's stock across the man's cheek, knocking him to the ground.

Gomez looked down at him. "You want to turn the other cheek or do I have the religions confused?"

The lieutenant waited, but heard only the boy's cries, the woman wailing, and the popping and crackling of the burning hooch. Thick smoke billowed upwards and specks of ash sprinkled down on the lieutenant, who felt the warmth of the fire and smelled the charred scent as he followed the line of soldiers walking away.

He did not care about the people or the tears shed over the loss of their meager possessions. He knew his business and the proper way of handling a war. He'd strike fear in other Vietnamese by leaving his brand. The dead buffalo was an unintentional bonus, one that he would remember, but the burning hut, the spilling of blood, and the stench of nine bloated, twisted bodies would serve as a warning to all others.

Chapter 7

Friday, February 13, 1970---8:23 a.m.

Lieutenant Gomez hopped into the truck cab with the driver while the men crowded into the open bed of the deuce-and-a-half. Standing in the back, Mike Brooks enjoyed the ride as the cool morning breeze blew against his face. He stared at the fields and flat terrain and the scene reminded him of his home in California. His grandparents had migrated there from Missouri during the Great Depression, leaving behind their foreclosed farm, but not all of the problems. Grandpa had started drinking, saddled with the entire farm debt and the inability to pay after his bankrupted partner committed suicide. But the new start near the town of Marysville seemed fitting. Named after Mary Murphy Covillaud, a survivor of the Donner Party, they travelled west for new opportunities and, like Mary, stopped along the banks of the Yuba River, the "gateway to the gold fields".

The land was rich from thousands of years of uncontrolled flooding and, like the scattered Vietnamese hooches, Mike Brooks' father made his home on the flood plain. The original structure was a surplus World War II army officer's bungalow from Camp Beale, the same size as a hooch, but with indoor plumbing. Sold at auction for $75, the building was moved onto the property and remodeled until it looked like a house.

It had always been a home, a loving home, located on a dirt street where other ragamuffin boys played and laughed and enjoyed the freedom of being kids. They pretended to be cowboys like Roy Rogers or frontiersmen like Davy Crockett, portraying characters with honor, fighting for the weak and the right causes, without killing and certainly not shooting from ambush. Looking back, he would never have imagined how time and reality had changed him and his boyhood dreams.

As a boy and a product of dirt farmers, Mike Brooks had previously witnessed death only as a necessity of life. He remembered his father slaughtering a beef with a well-placed shot between its eyes, dropping it to its knees with a sleepy, bewildered look. He also recalled watching his sweet grandmother cradle a hen in her arm, gently stroking its feathers. Then, before it could panic, she twisted its neck with a sharp, circular swing. Holding its head in her hand, the decapitated chicken ran blindly, bouncing and flipping to the delight of the youngsters.

Both memories were imprinted into his own mind, but he knew both of the animals had served a purpose...they insured food on the table and survival. Those actions and deaths could be justified like Mary's ordeal with the Donner Party, but Brooks kept wondering about the human casualties that he had witnessed during his tour of duty. He thought of his boyhood heroes, the roles of both killer and those killed, and the righteousness of the cause. Still the more he thought about the dilemma, the more he became bewildered.

Forty minutes after leaving its pick up point, the truck bumped and rumbled past other destroyed hooches, outlying "boom-boom" shacks, and into the town of Rach Binh, which sat adjacent to the base camp of the same name. Dust swirled and coated the soldiers as they held up their hands and flashed the "V" peace sign to the Vietnamese standing alongside the road.

Mike Brooks watched the civilians with the same curiosity as the people eyeing the soldiers. It was a very different world. Children lined the streets and smiled, waving and hoping the GIs would toss down chocolate bars. A black wart-like growth, the size of a half-inflated football, hung from a woman's face and she begged, one-eyed, from behind the thick mass. Teenagers sold bottles of Coca Cola and pineapple sliced lengthwise with a stem handle. Toddlers, naked from the waist down, crawled in the soil and explored a new world. Women squatted, washing clothes in the canals alongside their flocks of ducks. Motorcycles sped by as an old farmer walked, balancing two wicker baskets half-filled with rice on a pole that bounced on his shoulders. In the middle of the town, women bartered over displays of fly-speckled fish, vegetables, live poultry, and the delicacy of boiled, half-hatched chicken and duck eggs. Older women squatted flat-footed under their pyramid-shaped hats, chattering and arguing, while red betel nut juice soothed their decaying teeth and drooled out of their mouths.

The largest building outside the base was the White Dragon Bar, which contained the only generator-run refrigerator and the only indoor toilets in town. The GIs hung out there, relishing its pleasures, and it became a rite of passage for man-boy soldiers who were still unable to legally drink back in the states. Liquor flowed there and the young men experienced the pleasures that this Sin City East offered. Now, as the truck neared the bar, any thoughts of the previous night's carnage had vanished and were replaced by the soldiers' dreams of carnal pleasures.

Three mature bargirls, dressed in slinky *ao dai* dresses, sat on a bench in front of the "White Dragon". The dresses were flashy, bright green, blue, and red-colored silk, and these women did not wear the traditional pantaloons. They had no intention of hiding their legs. The dresses were split up the sides, revealing their legs to mid-thigh, and the altered plunging "V" necks exposed their upper assets. Old wrinkled women on the streets chattered words of disdain at the disgraceful behavior, but the young women ignored them and were only interested in the oncoming truck, filled with potential customers.

When the truck driver spotted the women, he honked the horn, while the soldiers cheered and cat-called and the women stood, waving, mimicking kisses, and yelling, "Oh, Baby" in their sweet, broken-English voices. All laughed as one woman held her hips and thrust her crotch, another pressed and lifted her breasts, and the third wiggled her behind. In seconds, the women had displayed exactly what the soldiers wanted to see and they hoped their advertisement would coax the men to return to the bar, the adjoining building for a spa and massage treatment, or other luxuries of the night.

Howard Morrison waved and joked, "Look, the village school teachers."

Clarence Sufficool smiled. "They do give great anatomy lessons."

As the vehicle drove past the building, another woman ran through the doorway and into the road, waving and yelling, "Brook-see!"

"Butterfly!" Brooks yelled and waved. He loved seeing her and wished he could jump down and be with her.

The other men stared at the young woman. Her loose-fitting shirt and pants contrasted sharply from the bargirls' dresses, but her work attire still could not hide her figure. Her brown eyes, straight teeth, and long black hair highlighted her beauty and captured the men's attention. Still, her face did not mirror the tragedies. Five years before, she had watched the retaliatory results of her parents speaking out against the communists. It wasn't the voices of her father and mother that she remembered, it was their screams. In front of the entire village, armed Viet Cong guerillas tied her parents to the ground and systematically disemboweled them. Now, as she waved and smiled at Brooks, she was not only happy that he had returned safely, but she also hoped that these soldiers had slaughtered more VC.

Squealing its brakes, the truck rounded a corner and stopped in front of the Ninth Infantry Division's "Go Devils" base camp arch and entrance. Sufficool watched the gate guard stand and then glanced over to the headquarters building. Sitting on the roof, five soldiers relaxed as they sunbathed and drank beer in the late morning sun. A pyramid of empty cans were already stacked high, a symbol of hierarchy to those viewing from below.

"Brooks," Sufficool said, pointing. "Look at the REMFs."

As the gate guard swung the roadblock in and the truck rolled forward, Brooks yelled, "Attention!" Those men seated on the side benches stood and raised their fists. "Ready," Brooks commanded, "Salute."

Simultaneously, each of the men raised their middle fingers to the Rear Echelon Mother Fuckers as the truck drove past.

Chapter 8

Friday, February 13, 1970---11:25 a.m.

The layout of the Ninth Infantry Division base was simple, but erected to be efficient. Alpha, Bravo, Charley, and Delta Companies' barracks formed the perimeter buildings of the compound, while headquarters, the chapel, aid station, and the mess hall sat securely in the center. Green sandbags were stacked high on the outer walls of the barracks, making the dwellings safer and easily adaptable to fighting. All of the buildings were rectangular and, with the exception of the dirty-white church, none were painted. Built as temporary housing for a temporary war, the rough lumber siding had long turned dark brown with the passing of years, the alternating monsoon rains, and the pounding equatorial sun.

The perimeter was surrounded by a twelve foot chain link fence, bunkers with machine gun placements per side, two observation towers on opposite corners, multiple rolls of concertina wire, and claymore mines stacked vertically on poles. The claymores were strategically located next to an encircling moat and pointed in all directions for an effective field of fire. Although the encampment had not been tested by sappers or an outright attack for two years, the close proximity to the village of Rach Binh required extreme caution and these measures provided more than an adequate defense and killing field.

Stopping the truck in front of Bravo's third platoon barracks, Lieutenant Gomez walked toward the officers' quarters while half of the men jumped from the truck and the others handed down their packs and rifles. One by one, the men shuffled past the painted "Wild Ones" sign on the wall and into the building, adding more dust to the creaking wooden floor. The interior was dark and housed only three long rows of bunk beds, pictures of wives, girlfriends, and pinups, *Playboy* magazines, and the lingering smell of burning diesel fuel and human waste originating from the outhouses behind the barracks.

The soldiers glanced at Cunningham's empty bed as they tossed their equipment on their bunks and headed for the mess hall. No additional thought was given to the new guy or his injuries. They were alive and surviving a firefight always enhanced their appetites.

After eating cold pancakes, drinking a quart of chocolate milk, and showering outside in the sun-warmed water, Mike Brooks walked to the headquarters building.

"Could I speak to you, sir?" Mike Brooks asked, looking through the screen door.

Lieutenant Gomez glanced up from his desk. "Yes, come in."

Brooks stepped inside, removed his bush hat, and stood directly center of the desk. Besides an "in" and "out" file, and three pens stacked side-to-side, the desk and walls were void of any pictures, memorabilia, or any connection to people or places. The lieutenant's desk served only as an instrument for writing and for separating himself from others.

Gomez disliked looking up at anyone and the thought of someone looking down on him annoyed him even more.

"Sit down, Sergeant." He waited for Brooks to unfold a chair and proceeded to the point. "What do you want?"

"Have my marriage papers been approved?"

"No, they haven't come back and I wanted to talk to you about that," Gomez said, studying Brooks' face and watching for the change that his next comment would bring. "They haven't returned because I haven't sent them."

"What?" Brooks uttered in disbelief. His face twisted with the news and his voice rose. "I filled out the forms nearly a month ago. All they needed were your signature for them to move forward. I'm getting short and it takes weeks to process them."

Gomez nodded. "I know. If I sent them right now, it would be difficult getting them back before you DEROS. The government can work in slow and strange ways." Gomez stopped, purposely letting Brooks wait and wonder while he lit a cigarette and then blew smoke toward him. "If you don't stop bitchin' about my orders, I'll never sign or send the damn papers."

"I told you last night why I disagreed with the fake 'bush," Brooks said, trying to reason. "You were lucky that those gooks came ditty-bopping along. It gave you a real body count."

"Are you finished, Sergeant?"

"No, no I'm not," Brooks stuttered. "When I first came to Nam, I accepted all orders with no questions asked. But now, I question. You could've called in a gunship and killed all of those gooks last night without Cunningham losing his fingers. Too many men are going home in body bags and I don't want to see anymore and I don't want to be in one. This war's ending and I plan on going back to the world alive and have Butterfly with me."

"Then make a decision. Shut your mouth and receive your marriage papers or question my orders and lose them."

Brooks slammed his fist onto Gomez' desk as he stood. "We'll fight when it's legitimate. If it's not, count on me to speak up. We won't get our shit blown away for nothin'."

"Calm your ass down, mister! Who the hell do you think you're talking to Sergeant?" Gomez voice raised, emphasizing the word "sergeant", and then leaned forward, unafraid and accepting the challenge. "You're missing the point. I don't care if you marry your bargirl, but you better learn who's in charge."

The lieutenant pulled a sheet of paper out of his desk. "Maybe I haven't made myself perfectly clear. Let me demonstrate…this is what will happen to your marriage papers if you keep challenging me."

Gomez slowly tore the paper in halves, fourths, and then eighths. Holding his hands up, he let the bits of paper sprinkle down onto his desk. "Understand now? Your marriage plans just got ripped apart." Gomez leaned back with a smirk, watched Brooks' face redden, and then changed the subject when there was no response except the quiet anger. "We'll stand down tonight and eagle flight tomorrow. But I want you thinking of just one thing. Think about never seeing your girlfriend after your tour ends if you don't get the marriage papers approved."

"I'll get them. I'll go to Captain O'Brien or Colonel Balfrey, but I'll get them."

"Hell, Brooks, they'll send your butt right back to me since you're in my platoon. I know you personally and they don't. They know that most draftees want to marry their first piece of ass."

Brooks thought about responding, but he was finished talking. He wondered if Gomez had a heart or any feelings as he shoved open the screen door and walked out. He wanted so badly to punch the lieutenant, but figured he was probably right. The other officers would tell Gomez to make the decision regarding the submission of the required marriage forms. It was a dilemma and Brooks was unsure how to resolve it.

Standing momentarily in the street, his thoughts were broken when Lieutenant Gomez yelled out to him. "Admit it, Sergeant Brooks; I've got you by the balls. Now, make the right choice."

Howard Morrison jumped down from his bunk as soon as he saw Mike Brooks' face and how he slammed open the barracks' door. "Problems with Lieutenant Gung-ho?"

"Yeah," Brooks grunted. "I'd rather be stabbed in the front then stabbed in the back, but I'll tell you later."

He surveyed the barracks, noticing the men preparing for the evening's ambush. They talked of women, girlfriends, and wives, of R&R to Hawaii and Bangkok, and of home, while they worked and tapped their feet to a cassette player, blaring the last words of Steppenwolf's "Born to be Wild" and the beginning of "The Pusher". The men cleaned their weapons and, despite two portable fans oscillating, the smell of solvent and oil hung in the air as they listened to the song's lyrics: *"I've seen a lot of people walkin' 'round with tombstones in their eyes, but the pusher don't care if you live or if you die."*

"Goddamn, goddamn, the lieutenant man," Brooks said, changing the song's chorus, and then announced, "We eagle flight tomorrow and stand down tonight."

"Screw the eagle flight," Sufficool said, pushing ammunition into his magazines. "I'd rather go on ambush."

"I agree, Cool, but we don't have any say."

"Oh, what the hell. It don't mean nothin'." Cool tossed the clip onto his bunk. "I'm going to let the girls in the village shake my snake and whip my weasel."

Steele smiled. "Cool's dick is the only thing that's not going to stand down."

Morrison wrapped his arm around Brooks' neck in a mock hold. "Let's go to the White Dragon…we owe it to ourselves."

The conversation immediately ended when a horn blared outside. The men sprinted to the door, yelling "Mail Call!" as the soldier-mailman climbed into the truck's bed and motioned for five replacements to step aside. Reaching into a duffel bag, he grabbed a handful of letters, called out names, and tossed them to outstretched arms.

The five soldiers stood beside the mailman and glanced away from the stares of the veterans. All five were recently drafted, by law compulsory military conscripts, and their faces expressed their awkwardness and fear, like newly-arrived slaves on the auction block being gawked at by potential buyers. Imported to Vietnam only days before, the replacements' bright green uniforms and polished boots contrasted with the faded cloth and scuffed boots of the vets. The winter weather of the United States showed in their pale, sweaty faces while Vietnam's climate reflected in the veterans' dark tans. The military had shaved their hair, replaced their clothes, stripped them of their freedom and identity, and they appeared to be clones of one another, identifiable from afar by only their mothers. There had been no time to personalize their uniforms or grow their hair and they looked like a set of uncomfortable male quintuplets.

While the veterans were focused on "mail call", the replacements most recent and vivid memories of army life were of "cadence calls" in basic training. Their drill instructors had yelled and intimated them, having them march and repeat the lyrics:

"Now you'll be away from home...
Jody will have your girl alone.
You'll be goin' off to war
And she'll become a little whore."
"Sound off...one, two."
"Sound off...three, four."

Or making them hold their M-16s in one hand and grabbing their crotches with the other hand and then repeating:

"This is my rifle.
This is my gun.
This one's for fighting
This one's for fun."

The marching, the little rimes, in retrospect were nothing more than silly games. But as soon as the passenger jet opened its doors and the oven-like blast of heat hit them, they were welcomed to a red-faced, scorching hell and some of the veterans were more than willing to welcome them into the initiation, the torture, and the intimidation that they too had experienced.

"Look at the new meat," Steele said, pointing at the five men and picking up where the drill instructors had left off. "Which one of you cherries is going to take my place walking point?"

The replacements did not answer and pretended not to hear.

"Morrison," the mailman read and tossed down a perfumed, pink envelope.

Howard Morrison ripped open the letter and pulled out a picture of his wife Kay, holding their baby daughter Alicia. He kissed the picture and then held the photograph above his head. "Look at the two prettiest girls on earth."

"It's a shame," Doc Tyson joked, "that the little one has less hair than you."

"It'll grow," Morrison said softly and proudly. "It will grow."

He walked away, not thinking of the possibility of other mail, and focused on reading his wife's words in privacy. The joy, stirred by looking at her, was replaced by sadness as he stared at his daughter's face. Now eleven months old, he doubted that she would even remember him.

Warren Steele watched each letter with envy, hoping for one, and then focused on the replacements, toying with them. "What are you fuckin' new guys going to do when that first gook aims his AK at you?"

The recruits glanced away, jittery as schoolboys confronted by a bully.

Clarence Sufficool looked at Steele and said, "Cool says 'be cool'. You're scarin' me to death." He smiled at the replacements and remembered standing on the same truck five months before. "You've already got their dicks a quakin' and a shakin'. Besides, it's not the VC that they have to worry about…it's the whores." Cool thought back to the strange stories that he had heard when he first arrived in-country and he chanted:

"Razors in their pussies
Crushed glass in your booze
Screw 'em or drink 'em
And you're goin' to lose."

The recruits smiled at the poem as Sufficool changed his tone and reassured them with a nod and the words, "you'll be okay." He knew the comment wasn't true, but they would learn that lesson soon enough.

When the last letter and "care" package of cookies and crackers were tossed down, the soldiers grumbled and walked away, envious of those that received mail, until only Steele and the postman remained.

Steele stepped up on the running board. “Nothing for me again?”

“Sorry. Maybe tomorrow.”

“Damn it. You’ve said that for two months.”

“I know, but I just deliver the mail. I can’t make them write.”

Steele walked away, swearing and staring at the ground, and knowing that the five replacements were watching his departure. The same feeling existed when he had been separated from his classmates, suspended and embarrassed again. He could still hear the muffled laughter or the sighs of relief when he was gone. No one cared and he should have known better then and now. He had hoped that his mother or wife might have written, but his hopes were wasted. They couldn’t care less and he should have known. The mail, like any sort of affection, was sporadic at best. His mother had shoved him out long ago and now was no different. Expelling him out of her mind or her apartment were nearly the same. Long ago, he had been pushed into the night while she drank and moaned and acted out her pleasures, breeding four bastards. Four babies had come out through her vagina, but a hundred men had come in. It was a simple fact and Steele had known it for a long time. If an accidental pregnancy between lovers begat a “love child”, he was no more than a “fuck child”.

Chapter 9

Friday, February 13, 1970---7:15 p.m.

Mike Brooks and Howard Morrison shouldered their rifles, flashed their picture identification cards at the guard, and weaved through the barbed wire maze in which personnel entered and exited the base. They stopped to see if the GIs had written any new graffiti on the gate. The officers didn't like the remarks, but the messages continued to appear.

Three new comments had been added and Morrison read them aloud:

"Killing for Peace is like Fucking for Virginity"...
"364 days to go. It seems like I just got here"---
"You did, you dumb shit."...
"Half the Vietnamese women have VD...
The other half have TB...
So, just fuck the ones that cough."

Morrison glanced at Brooks with a big grin. "Your girlfriend has a little cough, doesn't she?"

Brooks laughed at the comment and shoved his friend. The insights were always amusing and he continued to smile until he looked down the streets of Rach Binh. The town was depressingly still and scars of the war were always present. A young Vietnamese man sat in the dirt and rubbed the stump of his missing leg, feeling the phantom nerves shoot through the amputated limb. His face was blank, unsmiling, and he worried not about his future, only what the night would bring. He leaned back against a boarded-up store front and waited and watched. A bloated-bellied child, filled with the emptiness of hunger and ravaging parasites, led his water buffalo past the soldiers, tugging on its halter as the animal snorted and tossed its head. An old woman squatted behind a basket of dried fish and shriveling vegetables, some as wrinkled as her face, and shooed away flies, hoping for a last sale. As usual, young healthy Vietnamese men were conspicuously absent from the streets and, on this night, the town seemed to be transformed into an infirmary of the old, the sick, and the wounded.

Aromas of boiled rice and fish lingered in the light breeze and carried the jukebox sounds of The Animals' "House of the Rising Sun" roaring down the street from the White Dragon. Morrison tapped his belly to the beat and hummed along as Brooks looked at the bar and listened to the song. The lyrics cried *"it's been the ruin of many a poor boy and God I know I'm one"* and, as Brooks walked, he wondered if he indeed was one.

The allure of the bar, its vices, and its dark attractions had already snared him and kept pulling him back. He was like all the others. Young men, naive of the sins of the world and predicting that they'd never reach old age, greedily drank from this cup of life and rejoiced in their youth. They wanted to taste it all, live to the fullest, and knew time was not to be wasted or taken for granted in the violent world of this country.

After countless fights and three fatalities, the base commander had ordered the bar off-limits for one month and soldiers were forced to stay on base and patronize "The Morgue", a make-shift saloon created out of a small building that had previously served the same purpose as its name. Empty beer cans hung like wind chimes from the ceiling of The Morgue, while a Jefferson Airplane poster and glowing black lights decorated the walls. Without any women, the bar served its purpose of getting men drunk, but stayed in operation only long enough to note that as many incidents had occurred when the men were confined to the base. The only difference was the object of their fights. On-base, boredom, stress, and racism sparked violence, while off-base jealousy erupted over the bargirls. After further thought, the commander re-opened the White Dragon to the GIs, but assigned the military police to monitor the bar during the evening hours.

Checking their weapons with the MPs, Brooks and Morrison smiled as they looked at the lighted front of the White Dragon. The face of a fierce dragon, belching smoke and fire, was painted on the domed front wall. Between two windows, the scaly white body, sharp claws, and enormous wings curved over the front of the building and covered the entrance. It was a monstrosity outside and inside.

Opening the door, both men appeared to walk into the serpent's abdomen as cigarette smoke billowed out. Sawdust covered the floor and white candles, stuck in empty beer bottles, flickered and dripped. A black and white porno film starring a white woman and a German shepherd played silently against the wall. Soldiers laughed at the adlibbed jokes, pointing and barking and howling, while Christmas lights hung from the ceiling and a black light illuminated a Jim Morrison poster. Three slot machines twirled, occasionally clinking, and cans of beer popped and blended with the laughter. The jukebox music was loud, but had now slowed as Bobby Vinton sung "Mr. Lonely" and soldiers chimed in on the verse: *"I'm a soldier, a lonely soldier, away from home through no wish of my own."*

The management, an old mama-san with both missing teeth and a prominent gold tooth, had questionable connections, but adhered to the English philosophy that a *"fool and his money are soon parted".* Their strategy for musical selections was simple: Play fast music early to encourage a fun, drunken evening and then play slow, sentimental songs, encouraging soldiers to drink away their personal loneliness. It worked every night---a dozen couples now danced cheek-to-cheek as the soldiers gripped the women tightly, hoping to feel more of their bodies, while the bargirls distantly gazed and wished the night would end.

Morrison scanned the booths for an empty table while Brooks watched Butterfly. Gomez had called her a bargirl, but she was not. Nor was she a whore as he presumed. She did serve drinks, cleaned the bar in the morning, but sent most of her wages to her younger brothers and sisters. Unaware of Brooks' arrival, Butterfly circled the room, picking up glasses and wiping tables clean. Her black hair hung over her white shirt and she wore black pants. Black, white, black. Very simple, but very beautiful. She moved so gracefully and this grace and her beauty were the inspirations for the nickname he had given her. She, however, first took offense to the name, knowing how other women behaved, and Brooks had to explain his use of the term "butterfly."

In some booths, Vietnamese women, dressed in low-cut dresses slit up the legs and pulled up to their thighs, snuggled against the soldiers while the drunken men kissed the women's necks and caressed their legs. The soldiers stared at the women's breasts, shoved up and patted for more appeal, while the women whispered and coaxed the men to buy more drinks, of which they'd receive a percentage. If a soldier became a "cheap Charley" or couldn't afford any more liquor, these "butterfly" girls fluttered over to another man who could.

Approaching the bar, Butterfly saw Brooks and rushed to him. He pulled her close, feeling her breasts against his chest as he kissed her. Their desires soared, but she pushed away, looking into his blue eyes. "Me go work now... you see me when I off?" As he nodded, she picked up her tray. "Me luv you."

Brooks smiled and his face blushed. "I love you too."

"She's quite a woman," Morrison said, shifting his eyes back to Brooks and grinning. "Just think. After you're married, she can fix a beautiful roast dog for Thanksgiving dinner."

Brooks laughed. "And I'll save a special piece for my Texas buddy." He playfully shoved Morrison toward a now-empty booth. "I'll get the beers."

Howard Morrison hurried to the table, passing Specialist Four Richard Wade, a company cook, and two other REMFs. Wade unconsciously tapped his fingers as he stared at Butterfly and wondered aloud, "Why is she with that grunt?" His friends did not answer as he twisted his torso back towards them. He smiled and raised his eyebrows, "Maybe she needs some real lovin'."

As Butterfly walked by, Wade grabbed her arm, stopping her. "Let's talk about the first thing that comes up."

Butterfly looked confused, puzzled by the sophomoric comment.

Wade looked at his friends, who smiled at the innuendo, and then back to Butterfly. "Why don't we get something straight between us?"

The two men laughed aloud, but she still did not understand the meaning.

"Me no understand."

"Okay…why don't you sit on my face?"

Butterfly did understand this remark. Same line, different soldier, and she had memorized a suggested reply. "Why? Is your nose longer than your dick?"

Wade's friends laughed at the unexpected response, while his face flushed and he pulled her to his lap, knocking off a half-dozen glasses from her tray.

The MP sitting by the back door hall exit did nothing. He glanced up and then returned to reading a magazine. Two other MPs looked up when the glasses shattered, but immediately turned back to the bargirls who whispered in their ears. As directed, the military police did not interfere in these matters, only fights between soldiers. Grabbing a woman in the White Dragon was a standard operating procedure, a nightly occurrence, and a problem that the mama-san would handle if needed. It was not an MP issue.

Butterfly pushed against Wade's chest. "You numba ten GI."

"No, I'd be your number one GI lover," Wade said, grabbing her hair and yanking it back until Butterfly's eyes watered and she stopped resisting.

Mike Brooks had just picked up two mugs of beer when he heard the glasses break.

Walking to the booth, he stood next to Wade's side and stared at him. "Let her go."

Wade looked up at Brooks. "I know that I'm just a little 'ol Spec. 4, but I'd run along if I were you."

Brooks' expression was blank and his eyes shifted only when Morrison stepped next to him. "I said let her go."

"Is that an order, Sergeant, or is this a private matter?'

"It'll be our little secret."

Wade smiled. "Good. So either leave or I'll twist this little gook's head in a circle and then kick your ass."

"Hurt her, Richie," Brooks said, "and your friends will be cooking you up for tomorrow night's special dish of 'Dead Dick stew.'"

Wade smiled. "Was that supposed to be funny?" He then violently shook in jest. "I'm shivering." He laughed, looked to his friends for approval, and then sipped his beer as he held Butterfly's hair. Lowering the mug, he tossed the remaining beer into Brooks' crotch. "That'll cool it off, lover boy."

Brooks didn't react and he didn't budge. He stood passively, holding the two beer mugs, while Wade's friends chuckled and Morrison's anger rose, wondering what the hell was wrong with his friend.

"You're an asshole, but maybe I should leave." Brooks looked down at his wet trousers. "One second..."

"Good idea," Wade agreed as he watched Brooks swallow down one beer.

"You know that it's Friday the 13th and I predict you're going to have some very bad luck," Brooks said, throwing the second beer into Wade's face.

Wade spit and cursed until Brooks smashed the first and then the second mug on the man's head. Wade shoved Butterfly onto the glass-covered floor, standing as he grabbed his bleeding scalp, but he felt surprised and lost. His head rang and his mind clouded, pounding and spinning in an unfamiliar haze.

Butterfly scooted back as Brooks grabbed Wade's head, pulled it down, and drove his knee into the man's face. The blow straightened him up and brought him close to unconsciousness. Wade's vision doubled and he was falling when Brooks kicked him in the groin and dropped him writhing onto the floor.

One of Wade's friends stood to help, but Morrison's fist slammed into his nose and sent him sprawling. Pushing away, the other soldier slid against the wall with his hands up and waited for the MPs' arrival.

Morrison looked at Brooks. "You're a cold bastard. I didn't think you'd back down." He then glanced at both Brooks' soaked pants and the broken glass. "You do need to do something about that urinary problem. Plus..." Morrison looked puzzled. "Was that second beer mine?"

Mike Brooks grinned, but said nothing. He had known all along what he would do and wished he could have done the same to Gomez. Maybe part of the anger directed toward Wade was the pent-up rage from his earlier conversation. Still, his reaction was as subtle and simple as knowing when to pull a trigger or blow the claymores. He had struck this enemy with a clear objectivity and had thought only of the most opportune time to inflict the heaviest damage. Smashing the mugs on Wade's head was coolly calculated for maximum effect.

Morrison knew both MPs and, as they arrived, he stepped between them, turned them toward the bar, and cautiously put his arms over their shoulders. "Let me explain over some drinks."

Stepping over Wade's body, Brooks stooped down to Butterfly and brushed the hair from her eyes. Slivers of broken glass protruded from her pants and were stuck in her feet and the palms of her hands. He lifted her carefully and carried her away, kissing her forehead as he set her on the bar. He pinched out the glass, dabbed the trickles of blood with his shirttail, and then, like a lady in waiting, kissed the back of her hand.

Butterfly wrapped her hands around Brooks' neck, locked her fingers, and kissed his cheek. Tears streaked down her cheeks, but the tears were of joy, not pain.

Chapter 10

Friday, February 13, 1970---9:07 p.m.

Warren Steele didn't like the MPs any more than the Los Angeles cops and he felt a certain uneasiness when he checked his M-16 with the military police. Giving up your weapon or even unloading it in a war zone didn't make sense. The VC certainly weren't going to wait until everyone loaded their weapons and he sure didn't trust the MPs to protect him. Regardless, giving up his weapon was the ticket to enter the White Dragon.

Stepping into the bar, Steele felt a similar nervousness the night before as pointman, but tonight's anxiety was different. Fear of death had vanished and was replaced by the fear of being caught. He nodded to Brooks and Morrison, stared at the bargirls' attributes, and watched Doc, Nelson, and others playing poker. One member of the platoon conspicuously absent from the bar was Lieutenant Gomez. The officer rarely socialized with his men and closed, crowded places seemed to bother him. Steele couldn't explain it, but the officer always positioned his back against a wall and he would always intently watch the people, his eyes darting quickly, alert and vigilant in his observations.

Weaving through the crowd, Steele bumped into Sufficool, his arm draped around the neck of a pretty bargirl, and the RTO insisted that he learn the finer movements of a new dap handshake. Steele tried, thinking it was a loud version of the hand game "rock, scissors, paper". He screwed up the snaps and slaps but always properly completed the double beat of the fist to the chest. Cool laughed at Steele's attempts at black power before he kissed the girl and staggered back to the bar. Steele smiled, but it wasn't his buddies, liquor, poker, or even the girls that he wanted tonight. He was interested in only the South Vietnamese officer standing alone.

Major Van Tri Quan acknowledged Steele with a nod as he leaned against the bar and watched the bargirls. As a boy, Quan cursed the whores and wondered why Vietnamese women would sell their bodies to the French and then to the American military advisors. Now, he not only understood the women, he admired them. They were con artists and he watched with interest as they perfected their craft. Some sat on the soldiers' laps, gently rocking their bottoms, while other women stole bush hats or shoved their hands into the GIs' pockets, running after they grabbed anything of value. Both methods worked and the soldiers chased them into the trap. The bargirls immediately turned inattentive men into pursuers and, in minutes, they'd charm the soldiers into buying them expensive, watered-down, non-alcoholic "Saigon tea".

As the men drank beer and booze and lost their wits, the women maintained their composure, continually using their sex, their only marketable product, to separate the GIs from their money. Quan understood that concept and promoted it. As a member of the *Binh Xuyen* forces, he helped control the gambling, prostitution, and heroin distribution in the Mekong Delta.

Steele and Quan stood behind the White Dragon within minutes of seeing each other. In the shadows and near a moss-covered pond, the major handed over seven glass vials and Steele opened one, licking his finger and dipping it into the heroin. He sniffed the powder, but it properly had no odor. Impure heroin was gray in color and smelled like vinegar, but this was pure white. He sucked his finger and frowned at the bitter taste.

"This is good shit."

"You betcha," said the major. "That's numba one scag."

Warren Steele nodded. "How much?"

"Twenty dollars, MPC."

"Too damn much." Steele tipped back his hat, exposing the scar under his eye. "One thousand piasters."

"No deal," Quan said. "In Saigon, black market traders give four hundred piasters for each MPC dollar. No American dollars, me take heroin back."

Steele stroked the glass vial with his fingertips and longed for the high. "Fifteen bucks."

"Deal," Quan said, waiting for Steele to pay him. "Maybe in short time, me get much more heroin."

Steele handed over the money. "How?"

"Me hear rumors in Saigon on Tu Do Street. Maybe changes in government in Cambodia. Maybe better smuggle routes from 'Golden Triangle'." Quan walked toward the tavern, talking over his shoulder. "Maybe change. Maybe beaucoup heroin."

Steele leaned against a banana tree and snorted the heroin from the open vial, first one nostril and then the other. His eyes and nose watered as he slid down, sitting on the ground. His skin felt warm and flushed. He closed his eyes and felt the soothing rush of euphoria, a call to both a world of peace and the paradise of oblivion.

Having previously smoked two joints of Cambodian Red marijuana this night, Steele's head already buzzed. The joints were manufactured to look exactly like cigarettes, including filter tips and a bright red package, with one major difference. The marijuana was first soaked in liquid opium before it was processed and the smoke was an incredible high. It was nothing like the cheap crap back in the world, a literal crap shoot as to whether one could even get high on that weed. But after a few tokes on Cambodian Red, your mind was flying off to Never-Never-Land and his brothers at home would love that journey. Still, as he stared at the heroin vial, he knew the white powder, this scag, smack, horse, or call it whatever you like, was the purest and the best. In his mind, Cambodian Red was a trip around the block, but the heroin was a trip around the world.

Steele's mouth dropped open as if to inhale the dullness that now blurred his mind. Fumbling out a pack of filtered Marlboro cigarettes, he set one on his leg and removed a safety pin holding a string of red beads circling his bush hat. He moved in slow motion, carefully digging out half of the tobacco. He stopped momentarily. His eyes and mind were heavy and dull and he held the cigarette and vial close to his face, pouring the remains of the heroin into the roll. He covered the tip with a pinch of tobacco and squeezed it closed. He'd have to hold the heroin cigarette tight, so none of the powder would slide out, but he could exhale the odorless smoke in front of anyone without detection.

Steele glanced at the empty vial and thought how fuckin' fine the scag was. It was a ticket to another world, a world of happiness. If the heroin were diluted down to only five percent with quinine or milk sugar, he figured his fifteen dollar investment would be worth one thousand dollars in any major U.S. city. Out-fuckin'-standing. He stood and stretched, feeling drowsy and thirsty, but euphoric. His legs bent, unsteady and off balance and specks of light spun in the darkness, twirling around his head. He breathed deeply, trying to gain control, staggering and then walking properly to the front of the White Dragon to collect his rifle.

His sober act worked well and the MPs handed back the weapon without question. Steele smiled broadly as he focused on each step, walking a straight line away from the police and back to the base camp. Proud of the con and his acting ability, he felt at peace. Even in his marijuana-opium and heroin haze, his mind was still able to focus, spinning not just from the drugs, but with thoughts of riches and plans of wealth.

Chapter 11

Saturday, February 14, 1970---2:03 a.m.

When the White Dragon closed, the MPs ushered the soldiers into the street. Those men sober enough to do so had claimed their M-16s and walked toward their barracks while some drunks refused to leave, demanding more drinks and more time with the hostesses. The MPs ignored the demands, much to the relief of the bargirls, piled the extra rifles into their jeep, and headed back to the base, leading the drunks swearing and weaving behind.

Mike Brooks was an exception. The MPs knew of his engagement and, for an extra twenty dollars, conveniently forgot that he was inside the tavern. When the front door was locked, Butterfly took Brooks' hand and led him through the back hallway to her bedroom. All of the bargirls lived in Rach Binh, but Butterfly slept in a converted storage room. A single window faced east and, with no curtains, the light from the rising sun served as a clock to wake her each morning. The walls were unpainted bare wood, with nothing on display, and the room held only a bed and two rickety bar stools. The bed was formed by a pair of discarded military cots, pushed together. The sagging springs were overlaid by a piece of plywood and the two holey mattresses were covered by a pair of camouflaged poncho liner blankets. The bar stools served as night stands and each held a flickering candle, dimly lighting the room and giving it the smell of smoking wax and perfume.

Butterfly lit a stick of incense over a candle's flame, wedged it between two wall boards, and switched on a transistor radio, a gift from Brooks that she kept on a stool. The radio was tuned to the military network and Del Shannon's "Little Town Flirt" played. They embraced, swaying to the song's beat, as Butterfly kissed Brooks' cheek, neck, and open mouth.

There had been an immediate attraction to this man, from the first moment he had walked into the White Dragon as a stranger. The moment, however, did not last. Brooks looked around the bar, searching for a platoon member and, when he did not spot him, turned around and left. The room had been crowded and Brooks had not even seen her. Butterfly promised to approach him if she ever saw him again and, two days later, to Brooks' delight she kept her promise.

Butterfly never imagined she would love a man other than one from Vietnam, but this American was not only handsome, in her mind, he was different from all others. His personality combined gentleness and strength, intelligence and ambition, but there was more. Just like tonight, he could protect her and she felt safe with him. She loved him, but she was realistic. She neither complained nor talked much in Vietnamese or her limited English and she neither lingered in the past nor longed for the future. She lived each day with only one desire since her parents had been murdered. She wanted out. Out of the war and out of the country. Brooks' homeland could provide safety and freedom and she was willing to do anything to get both.

It seemed to come naturally to a young woman, a simple fact of human biology and nature. Instinctively, Butterfly knew the bargirls' trade and, although she did not take part, she had studied their skills of seduction. She wanted Brooks and no one else, but she wanted more. Slowly unbuttoning her blouse, she tempted him as the garment hung open and she waited for him to undress her. She didn't wear a bra, but her firm breasts were veiled behind strands of her hair. Her nipples remained hard and her breasts enlarged and contracted with each breath.

Brooks kissed her in a deep embrace. Her body was warm and her breath cool and sweet. He kissed her again and then slid off her shirt, tossing it on the bed. He sucked lightly on her neck and breasts and, as he slowly kneeled, he kissed her hips and legs as he lowered her pants. He massaged her with his fingertips, reaching up to her breasts and to her back and then gently clawed his fingers up and down her body.

Brooks removed her damp panties, wet from her eagerness and excitement, and he gently lowered her on the bed. He felt her fingernails tense, scratching at his back and pulling him closer. He kissed her, massaging her breasts and thighs, and felt tiny bumps rise on her skin. Her flesh titillated with anticipation, watching Brooks undress next to her, while she rocked her hips and increased her desire. As they kissed, Butterfly spread her legs wide and invited him to enter.

Butterfly moaned and their bodies tensed as she circled his lips with her tongue, darting in and out of his mouth. She dug her heels into his legs, squeezing him closer, and then arched her pelvis, kissing and coaxing him. She felt as if they had become one in body and mind and, in the total desire of her heat, she craved him. As her inner lubrication dripped warm and wet and her scent aroused and controlled him, she moaned deeply as Brooks gently slid into her.

Afterwards, Butterfly rested her head on his chest, thinking of their life together, while Brooks slept and dreamed. He saw himself entangled in a web of tightly-strung booby trap wires. He couldn't move his arms without igniting hundreds of explosives. Yet, somehow, he held Butterfly. Lieutenant Gomez tugged on her with one hand and waved the unsigned marriage papers in the other. Brooks pulled back, but saw the wires extracting the grenade pins. When he loosened his grip, Gomez yanked her away, the explosives blew, and Brooks jerked awake.

Howard Morrison chugged the rest of his beer, burped loudly, and then threw the can against the painted nose of the White Dragon. He blinked, trying to clear his blurry eyes, and then stared at the MPs and the remainder of the drunks staggering toward the base.

Morrison kicked at a mangy dog barking at him and then popped open another beer that he had stashed in his pocket. Damn REMFs, he thought as he gulped down half the can, take my rifle and try to screw my buddy's girl. Weaving through the base's entrance, he swayed along the now deserted street and, when the idea formed, he muttered, "Piss on 'em."

Very shortly, he had done just that. He urinated not in a "piss tube", but on the front door of the Headquarters Company's barracks. Morrison spun around, nearly fell, and spotted a potable water tank. He staggered to the tank, turned on the faucet, and then weaved across the street to his own barracks. The men's snoring lured him to his own bunk and he felt the urge to collapse on it. The hell with it, he thought as he swallowed another drink and dug out the two needed items.

Morrison sloshed back through the ever-increasing mud puddle, stretched the detonator cord across the porch, and tied it off on two support beams. He waited on the porch only long enough to slobber a kiss onto a tear gas grenade, pulled the pin, and rolled it into the REMF's barracks.

Howard Morrison paid no attention to the yells. Shortly after the grenade popped, he lay on his bunk, singing a soft lullaby to the picture of his wife and daughter, while across the street tear gas awakened the alcohol-dulled senses of the REMFs. Men searched frantically and unsuccessfully for gas masks, dove out of their bunks, and ran through the smoky room, searching for an escape and the safety of fresh air. Noses burned, eyes watered, and men coughed. Trying to rub off the irritant and in the speed of their exit, the REMFs never saw the trip wire and, as Morrison snored loudly, they splash-landed in the mud.

Chapter 12

Saturday, February 14, 1970---8:25 a.m.

Sergeant Howard Morrison zipped up his flak jacket and looked at the artificial poppy, sticking out from the elastic band on his helmet. His wife had purchased the red paper flower from some local VFW members and had handed it to him with a kiss and with instructions that he was to return it to her when he came home safely. He smiled, thinking of the promise, and gently put on his helmet. His head still pounded and the annoying whine of the two idling Huey helicopters didn't help. He would have preferred sleeping off the hangover, but that wasn't an option. Squeezing in between Mike Brooks and a new replacement named Pat Graves, an Oregon logger with a slender build and an infectious smile, Morrison sat on the helicopter floor and dangled his legs out above the skids.

As a joke, Clarence Sufficool reached over Morrison's shoulder and held an open beer can under his nose. Morrison grabbed the beer, took a sip, and then smashed the can on his helmet, showering Pfc. Graves with beer and foam. He tossed the can out and leaned back, but felt his stomach roll when the helicopter vibrated under the increased speed of the rotors and the pilot coaxed the machine upwards.

Pfc. Graves' face quickly turned as white as Morrison's when the chopper banked, more than one hundred feet up, and he seemed to be looking straight down at the base camp and the town of Rach Binh. Heights frightened him and, on his first helicopter ride, Graves had mistakenly waited to climb aboard the helicopter and was relegated to sitting on the opened-door edge. He didn't want to embarrass himself by grabbing Morrison's waist, but he clutched the center bar and prayed he wouldn't fall.

Within minutes, the helicopters had climbed to sixteen hundred feet, leveled off, and flew parallel as the soldiers waved and snapped pictures of their buddies in the opposite craft. Graves calmed himself and glanced at the veteran Morrison, sitting in the open doorway, his head nodding as he lightly dozed and enjoyed the ride.

The helicopter rose and dipped with the air currents while the breeze brushed coolly against Sergeant Brooks' face. Wiggling his feet, he leaned forward and looked down at the changing variety of the land. From the air, the scene was beautiful. Heat waves rippled upward from the dry rice paddies. Streams and rivers meandered and reflected the shadows of the helicopters. The flat, checkerboard fields flowed smoothly away from the hooches, but were stopped abruptly when they hit the walls of dense vegetation that paralleled the waterways. The swampy marshland reminded him of the woodline they faced two nights ago and unfortunately that was their destination.

After only fifteen minutes of air time, the slicks slowed and dropped in altitude. Brooks hooked his arm around the door's edge and stretched forward. His helmet rocked with the wind, but he saw a treeline dotted with artillery craters. Artillery, he thought, was the ultimate phallic symbol, screwing everything in its way. Palm trees had been sheared off, leaving only barren trunks whose bark was riddled and torn, and even those that had escaped held dead branches that reminded him of the mother cradling her lifeless daughter.

The helicopters' landing zone was a grass meadow, paralleling the woodline, and Brooks hoped the VC hadn't heard the choppers in time to set up an ambush. Inching closer, he tightened the straps of his pack while the door gunners chambered rounds. The platoon members waited and watched, hoping they would not be stepping into a trap.

The Hueys slowed, hovering above the meadow but not actually setting down, while the prop wash made the grass roll like ocean waves. The landing zone was considered "hot" and machine gunners fired, sweeping their line of fire into the woodline to protect both the helicopters and the disembarking soldiers.

Brooks jumped off the skids, feeling the pack's weight accelerating his fall and jamming his legs. His helmet bounced and he fell, struggled up, and sloshed clear of the whipping blades. Warm water seeped into his boots and soaked his uniform as he laid prone, listening to the engines fade and feeling the prop wind die. The "krack" of AK-47 rifles was not heard, so Brooks carefully stood, shouted "clear", and the soldiers followed, looking like scattered field mice cautiously popping their heads up. Spotting Clarence Sufficool's radio antenna sticking above the grass, Brooks walked to that position and found Gomez checking his map.

Without looking at either man, the lieutenant instructed Sufficool to call in their position and told Brooks to move out in two squads. On night patrol, the platoon walked in single-file as two parallel columns in the dark could be disastrous, especially with nervous FNGs and their jumpy trigger fingers. But during the day, the unit conducted "search and destroy" patrols in two squads, paralleling and trying to stay in visual contact with each other.

Warren Steele looked up into the morning sky, hoping to spot incoming Loach and Cobra helicopters to replace the departed Hueys. He loved to watch the tiny Loach helicopter's mode of operation. The pilot and co-pilot would fly the light observation helicopter just beyond the point, hovering above the trees while searching for bunkers. They'd radio back information to the patrol while darting in and out like a dragonfly, exposing themselves to the enemy and daring the VC to shoot. It was a dangerous game and the pilot and co-pilot were unbelievably gutsy. If the VC took the bait and fired, the Loach would fly away and call its silent and circling big brother, the Cobra, to finish the fight.

Steele checked the horizon again but did not hear or see either a Loach or a Cobra and knew that he, not a helicopter, would be leading second squad. The realization was confirmed when Brooks motioned to Nelson and Steele with directions and yelled, "Take the points."

Steele nodded, knowing the routine, and then watched first squad lining up and following Frank Nelson, a big kid from Reno, Nevada, who had walked point for less than a month. Steele turned his attention to Pat Graves, who was assigned to walk directly behind him, and hoped that the FNG would soon relieve him as pointman.

Kneeling, Pfc. Graves examined paper leaflets the size of dollar bills, written in Vietnamese and displaying colorful pictures and the yellow and red striped South Vietnamese flag. He picked up more leaflets out of the grass, shoved dry ones into his pocket as souvenirs, and looked up at Steele. "What are these?"

"*Chieu Hoi* leaflets," the pointman answered. "It's for the "Open Arms" amnesty program. Choppers drop them. They ask the VC to surrender and act as a safe-conduct pass. It's a great program when it works. Still the gooks love 'em...it's free toilet paper." Steele smiled as he walked off. "Better wash your hands. There's no tellin' where those have been."

Graves' face dropped. He threw the papers down, wiped his hands on his trousers, and followed. Second squad fell into a single-file column and traced the steps of the two soldiers to the treeline. Steele's forward progress stopped suddenly when he spotted a plaque nailed to a severed tree trunk. The tree was surrounded by a pool of water and the board was cracked and faded, but Steele could still read the letters and see the drawings of a grenade and a skull and crossbones.

"Damn it," Steele said, pivoting around. "Brooks! Gomez! Here's a *Tu Dia* sign."

"What's that?" Graves asked.

"*Tu Dia* means 'land of death'," Steele said, watching Gomez and Brooks slosh forward. "At least, that's what I've been told. It marks an area of booby traps or mines. It could be a trick to keep us out, but I don't want to find out."

Brooks stopped next to Steele, shading his eyes and staring at the sign. "Do you want the grenadiers to prep the woodline?"

"No grenades," Lieutenant Gomez said, studying his map. "This is a populated area."

"Yeah, this is quite a development." Mike Brooks looked around, seeing only marshland and the uplifted and scorched earth. "Does this look like a populated area?"

"Maybe not," Gomez said, shoving the map into his pocket. "But the explosions might chase out the gooks."

"Good. It might also detonate some booby traps. With the choppers and machine guns, they already know we're here."

"The gooks will *dee-dee,"* Lieutenant Gomez said, not listening to Brooks. "I'll never find them."

"You'll never find them?" Steele interrupted, his voice rising and agitated. "That's funny. I don't want to ditty-bop across a mine field. If you want those slope heads that bad, sir, you walk point."

Lieutenant Gomez' face flushed with Steele's remark as Brooks spoke up. "Let's either prep or move farther south."

"Shut up!" Gomez yelled, finished with the arguing. "We aren't shooting M-79s and we aren't moving. We're going into this woodline, here and now. We're going where the gooks don't want us." He stopped, silently swearing he'd call in artillery on their position if he couldn't get them to move. Gomez stared at Steele. "Move your ass or you'll be pointman until you're blown away or your tour ends." The lieutenant looked at Brooks as Steele disgustedly walked away. "This is your last warning. Don't question my orders."

"I curse the day that you came to this platoon, you dumb son of a bitch." Brooks leaned closer, mocking Gomez' past words. "Sir, have I made myself perfectly clear?"

Gomez' eyes widened with the remark. Yelling in frustration, he backhanded Brooks on the mouth, knocking his helmet off with the blow. Brooks' reaction was fierce, dropping his rifle and lunging at the lieutenant, driving him to the ground. Water splashed up as arms and legs pushed and thrashed and each tried to gain control. They stood clutching and countering each other's moves until Brooks grabbed Gomez' throat, clenching the neck, squeezing, shaking, and closing off the air. Gomez punched Brooks in the jaw, loosening the hold, but he had dropped to his knees and had wheezed for only an instant before Brooks grabbed his throat again. His fingers tightened like an executioner's noose, his eyes bulged, and his face looked like an enraged madman.

Lieutenant Gomez pulled on Brooks' arms, but it was of no use. Brooks was bigger, stronger, and younger and he could feel the sergeant's thumbs pushing on his windpipe and his strength draining away. He swung his arms and pulled back with his legs, trying to escape the hold, until his face lost its color, his legs bent, and his chest burned.

Brooks leaned back, curling his arms and holding most of the man's weight, as he shook him. Pressing Gomez' chin against his stomach, the head tilted away and he watched the officer's eyes blinking closed.

Morrison and Graves ran up and grabbed Brooks' arms. They tugged and yanked and finally straightened his fingers, allowing Gomez to collapse.

"Damn," Morrison said in a serious tone as he led Brooks away. "Two fights in two days…I can't take you anywhere."

"I should kill that son of a bitch before he kills us all."

"I know," Morrison said nodding, "but you're supposed to kill the other brown skinned guys."

Brooks fumed and yet he hated his own behavior. Deep down, he knew he had lost it. It was crazy, but in the moment he didn't care. He wanted to kill and yet he realized Gomez' insight was as accurate as his shooting. His mind was twisting and his character was definitely changing, regressing. But, if a man were separated from his basic needs, expect a reaction. Gomez' backhand was the catalyst, but it was simple cause and effect. Try to kill him, starve him, snatch away his food or water or woman, and then watch him. His eyes stare, glaring with hate and jealousy and rage. His voice barks and his fists ball and the humanity and civilization within disappear…both as thin a veil as oil on water. His own behavior was witness to that fact and stopping the transition seemed to be beyond his power and control.

Lieutenant Gomez quickly regained full consciousness. Bending over, he coughed and his throat burned. He stood with Graves' help, wiped off his rifle, and stared at the soldiers watching him and Brooks. Graves had never seen anything like it, but neither had the other men.

In his anger, Gomez considered shooting this mutineer. No one had ever challenged him like this, but it might be in his best interests to forget the quarrel. His superiors might agree with Brooks and Steele's suggestions and, despite Brooks' attitude and comment, he shouldn't have hit him first. As for the counterattack, Gomez considered himself lucky. He'd never strike Brooks again. What he would do was questionable, but one thing was certain. Somehow, somewhere, he'd fix Brooks and he'd make that white bastard sorry that he ever put on a uniform.

Chapter 13

Saturday, February 14, 1970---1:38 p.m.

Warren Steele waded through the ankle-deep water, which smelled like open sewage, and moved a palm branch aside with his rifle. A small foil brown bag from his C-rations covered the M-16's muzzle and was twisted and tied in place, preventing mud from being accidentally shoved into the weapon. It was a precaution, but he could shoot through the foil without the worry of having a plugged barrel explode.

Sweat covered his face, soaked his flak jacket, and dripped into his eyes, which shifted in a half circle and then concentrated on where his next step would land. He hated looking down. He could be killed without seeing it happen, without realizing the danger that could be directly in front of him. He should have requisitioned a sawed-off 12 gauge shotgun for the eagle flight. With the scatter gun, he could simply react, pointing and firing from waist-level and letting the double 00 buckshot do its work.

Steele was calmer in the light of day, but like all the men, he despised eagle flights. Missions took place in a hot muddy hell that was exhausting and dangerous. The soldiers enjoyed the helicopter rides, but on the ground, the heat sapped their strength, the air seemed to evaporate before they could breathe, and the men panted like emphysema patients, laboring and struggling under the weight of their packs, helmets, and flak jackets.

The Mekong Delta was formed at nearly sea level in elevation and streams ebbed and flowed with the ocean's low and high tides. The soldiers would cross chest deep streams and find leeches plump with blood attached to their legs, while later the same area was nothing more than a mud field. Mud, heavy and thick, added to their weight and sucked some men down to their crotches, holding them in place as they fought, unable to escape until others helped pull them out. How and why the VC would want to stay here was beyond belief, except they had an edge. They could hear brush snap, water splash, and radio transmissions whine between squads. Eagle flights were a helluva way to get killed and walking point was like taking a stroll with the Grim Reaper.

Steele remembered one eagle flight when the tiger scout Nip was walking point and he was following, with Doc Tyson trailing him. Nip suddenly dove to the ground and others followed his lead, but for no apparent reason. Lying in the swampy water, all questioned what was happening as Nip spoke loudly and rapidly in Vietnamese. Nip stood slowly, his M-16 raised, and all watched as a VC, soaking wet in black shorts, appeared and stood atop a dirt mound with his hands raised. Nip's weapon was still pointed at the man as they conversed in Vietnamese. Papers stuck out from the man's waist band and, as he lowered one arm to reach for them, Nip fired a full magazine into the man, turning his face red and suspending him for a fraction of time in midair. The shots were totally unexpected and the platoon hit the ground as the unarmed man collapsed.

Steele and Tyson were both in shock, having just witnessed a cold blooded murder, no farther than fifteen feet away. They stood in silence as Nip changed magazines and checked the body and papers. The only words spoken were to Doc Tyson. After reading the papers, the tiger scout calmly said, "Him *bac si.* Him doctor. Same-same you" and then proceeded on the patrol.

Doc Tyson felt a new appreciation for life on that eagle flight. He had watched Nip before on day-holds, catching minnows in the canals by wading through with a net, uncovering palm branches and swatting mice and later cooking the fish and mice in a stew. He was hardcore and a survivor and Nip could have easily have killed him if he were on the "wrong side". This ex-Viet Cong was tougher than hell and was willing to bring hell with him. He was a survivor like many others, willing to grub out an existence in the worst conditions and willing to die for the cause. As such, Nip placed little value on his own life and even less on others.

Steele wished that Nip was here now, walking point instead of him, when reality hit and his leg tightened and he jerked away, stumbling and intentionally falling backwards. Below the water's surface, leaves and twigs laid in a concave pattern. Pushing aside the foliage with his rifle barrel, he saw the sharpened points of a punji pit and remembered seeing a soldier step into one. The bottom spikes did not penetrate the steel-soled boot, but they threw the soldier off-balance and into the feces-covered side spikes. Within days, the man's foot had swollen three times its size and doctors amputated it.

Steele wiped his face with the green towel hanging around his neck and unhooked a concussion grenade. He turned to Graves and pointed at the bamboo stakes. "New Meat, relay it to Cool to give first squad a sit-rep. I'm going to blow this."

When second squad backed up a safe distance, Steele yelled, "Fire in the hole!" He dropped the grenade, ran, and in seconds, the grenade exploded, catapulting water, bamboo fragments, and mud upwards.

Walking forward, Steele glanced at the destroyed pit and looked ahead. A brown and brackish stream barely flowed and banks of mud were exposed as the water lowered with the ocean tide.

"Steele," Graves passed the message. "First squad radioed that Nelson spotted a bunker."

The message surprised Steele. He hadn't seen any signs…no tracks, no trail, no discarded mackerel cans. He had not seen or smelled anything that would have alerted him and that fact alone worried him. "Where's the bunker?"

"It's in front of them…across the stream."

Sloshing forward, Steele jumped off the bank and sank to his knees. He struggled toward the water as the surrounding mud swallowed him to his crotch and squeezed his legs like soft plaster casts.

First squad's pointman, Pfc. Nelson, stepped slowly. His boots and trouser legs were coated in mud, as if he had been dipped halfway into a heavy milk chocolate. The vegetation facing the stream bed was stomped down and it looked like a miniature amphitheatre with an above ground mud manhole at center stage. The thick mound reminded Nelson of one of those large African ant hills he'd seen in a picture book, but he was sure the raised manhole was a "spider hole", a one-man fighting position.

Nelson visually searched for a tunnel exit nearby but did not spot one. By the evidence, he guessed some VC may have been here until they heard the choppers and machine guns fire. Several empty sardine cans, a crumpled empty pack of Kool cigarettes, and a half-eaten bowl of rice were scattered in the area and whoever was here had made a hasty retreat.

Two trails led away going deeper into the swamp and Nelson figured an ARVN patrol could have come through looking for VC and chased them away. Kneeling, the pointman listened, examined the area, and smelled the air like Steele had told him. There was nothing out of the ordinary. He noticed only the same raw sewage smell of the stagnant water, mud, and decaying vegetation.

Nelson looked back at the members of first squad, standing in line on the opposite side of the muddy creek and waiting to advance. He considered dropping a concussion grenade into the hole but time would not allow him to retrace his steps back across the mud to secure a safe distance from the explosion. He chose instead to move forward.

Slowly, Nelson approached the spider hole, leaned over and looked into the darkened pit. The septic smell hung in the air and it was as if he were staring down into an exposed manhole. His eyes adjusted but he quickly realized the hole was not empty. A frightened man stared back, pointing his rifle muzzle upwards. Nelson's eyes widened and he gasped, but the pointman had no time to react and his fate was sealed in a heartbeat. His only words were, "Oh God no," as his face reflected the shock. He tried to react, but three bullets slammed into his chest and his upper body fell head first into the hole.

The members of first squad dove to the ground when the bullets cracked and second squad flinched at the sounds, while the soldiers trailing Nelson yelled, "Medic!"

The unexpected shots were followed immediately by yells for help and Doc Tyson hated the call, knowing how quickly a man's life could change, standing one moment and dying the next. It was calm to chaos, with precious lives changed forever, all in a heartbeat. All he could do was respond, never knowing what to expect but always expecting the worse. He sprinted towards Nelson's position, his pack, aid bags, and silver crucifix bouncing as he ran.

Further down the creek, Warren Steele also reacted to the shots. He reversed directions and crawled back to Pat Graves' outstretched hand, helping him out of the mud.

More shots and shouts echoed from first squad. "Coming your way!"

Brush crashed across the creek as two VC sprinted, dressed only in shorts, in a race for their lives. Mike Brooks ran up while Steele fired, surprised to see the VC so close. The rifle slipped in his muddy hands and the bullets splashed at the lead man's bare feet. Brooks and Graves shot and rolled the second VC while Steele swung back, blasting at the lead man and emptying his magazine. The VC stumbled and fell and Steele believed that he had hit him. He released the empty clip just as the VC scrambled up and ran again.

"Get him!" Steele yelled.

Brooks and Pat Graves fired high, emptying their magazines, while the man sprinted toward a wooded area, splashing water and throwing bits of grass chest high as his feet pounded down. Hurriedly changing magazines, Steele pulled the bolt, released it, and aimed. Last chance, he thought as he centered the VC in his sights. In the chaos, he remembered to lead the target and swung the weapon until a bush blocked his sight.

Steele jumped up and ran parallel with the stream. The VC was nearly to the safety of the undergrowth when Steele kneeled and steadied the M-16 against a stump. Twenty more meters and he'll get away, Steele guessed as he aimed. Hoping that one bullet would hit the target, he fired on full automatic. The rifle raised and vibrated with the burst and Steele lost sight of the VC.

"He's down!" Graves yelled, reloading.

Steele trotted further, both looking for an easier place to cross the stream and watching where he had last seen the man. Graves' comment worried him. The VC may be down but not dead. Maybe he was crawling away.

Staring across the stream, Steele searched for movement but saw none. He glanced down the bank and spotted two uprooted trees that bridged the creek and gave him an easy point to cross. The shooting made his adrenaline and heart pound. He didn't want the VC to escape and with the excitement of the moment, the excitement of the kill, his legs pumped faster.

Yet it was the same thoughts, the same intensity that made him miss the slight tug of a wire, hooking around his boot as he ran. He had jogged only five meters before the booby trap exploded, ending his pursuit and flipping him into a bloody somersault that dropped him chest first into the banks of mud.

Chapter 14

Saturday, February 14, 1970---2:14 p.m.

Doc Tyson knew it was bad when he saw only the lower half of Nelson's body hanging out of the spider hole. It was a bizarre scene, half of an upside-down man. Tyson had never seen such a sight and never even considered that the VC could still be in the bunker when he and another soldier pulled the tightly-wedged body from the hole.

Immediately upon freeing him, they dragged him a few feet and laid Nelson gently on the ground. He was unresponsive. His face was muddy and wet and he did not move. With a faint whooshing and gurgling sound, trapped air escaped from his lungs as Doc watched Nelson's eyes roll back. Three holes had penetrated and exited the flak jacket, but blood did not flow from the wounds. The heart no longer beat. The medic was certain he was dead, but the exhaled air had given hope and he began breathing into the soldier's mouth and pounding on his chest in a futile attempt to bring back life.

Between breaths, Tyson gave instructions to pull the portable litter from his pack and to call in a medevac. He had heard the other shots, but continued to administer CPR until he heard Mike Brooks yell "Medic!"

Doc swore loudly, standing and gathering his equipment and instructing members of first squad to carry the body across the streambed and back to the landing zone. He looked at Nelson a final time, his body lying flat and unresponsive, and knew that he could do nothing more for him. Nelson now needed a man of God, not a medic, and Doc Tyson could only hope to help others as he turned away.

The medic ran toward the other shots and the call for help while Brooks searched for Steele. He spotted the blood-speckled M-16 first, lying on the smoky pathway, and then the silent, unmoving body. The concussion had blown off Steele's helmet and he lay belly down in the mud with one side of his face submerged.

He's dead. Brooks was positive of that fact until he jumped into the mud and saw red bubbles foaming in the corner of Steele's mouth. Shrapnel had cut his lip and blood oozed into his open mouth, gurgling and popping as he exhaled.

Mike Brooks crawled to him and twisted his face clear of the mire. Steele reacted to the touch and raised his head unaware of where he was or how he got there. His mouth and throat felt clogged with mud and he coughed and spit and clawed at the salty mixture of blood and grit. After cleaning out his mouth and wiping his eyes so he could properly breathe and see, Steele's mind became clear and the pain suddenly erupted. He thrashed his legs as if in a seizure and felt the burning of the shrapnel.

Brooks wiped off Steele's face with his towel and then turned when he heard Tyson's splashing approach. Waving his arm, he yelled, "Doc, over here!"

Doc Tyson stripped off his aid bags and jumped down, struggling through the mud. With Brooks' help, he turned

Steele onto his back, re-checked that his airways were clear, and dragged him to the edge of the bank.

Tyson breathed rapidly, still panting from his run. He shoved his glasses up and looked at Brooks. "Nelson's dead." Tears welled in the medic's eyes. His throat closed as he swallowed heavily with the words. "I couldn't save him."

Mike Brooks swore aloud, his eyes turning moist, and wondered if prepping the woodline would have mattered. He shrugged off the thought. It didn't matter now. Time did not exist for regrets or inaction. He scrambled up the incline and, lying on his belly, grabbed Steele's shirt. He pulled him upwards as Doc pushed on Steele's waist, driving his own legs further down into the muck. Releasing his grip, the medic crawled up while Brooks slid the body onto the bank and twisted Steele onto his chest.

With his medical scissors, Tyson cut Steele's pant leg up the back and released a reservoir of blood. The medic spotted a throbbing artery and shoved his hand over it, applying pressure. He could feel the warm blood, squirting and pausing, squirting and pausing into his palm, pulsating with each heartbeat. Then it struck. It was a recent, growing feeling for Tyson that had evolved from being immersed in months of ripped flesh and blood. He felt ill. New medics may have felt the urge to vomit, to gush out their stomach's contents like the fluid pumping beneath his hand, but Tyson didn't feel that way.

His illness was not physical, it was a sickness deep in his heart and he questioned the purpose of being there. Nelson dead, holes in Steele's body…for what? This piece of mangled ground? It must have been the same question that soldiers in war had always asked themselves...was the cause worthy of the cost? Maybe they were a different breed, more courageous, or maybe their devotion to duty far exceeded his patriotism. But how could they not question as they were slaughtered at Gettysburg, Belleau Wood, Tarawa, D-Day or a hundred other battles? Why would they not question? They lost thousands of brave men and he was questioning the validity of the cause with only one dead and one wounded.

Tyson looked around at the swampy marsh where the enemy barely grubbed out an existence and he did not believe it was worth one man's life and certainly not a thousand. Glancing at his bloody hands and muddy uniform, he longed to return to Idaho, to swim in the cold waters of Lake Pend Oreille, and to cleanse himself. He shook his head. That life was now a distant dream and he continued to work.

Doc pulled a compress from his helmet's elastic band, shredded open the plastic wrapping with his teeth and lifted his hand. With the pressure released, the artery squirted onto his glasses and face. He shoved the bandage in place and then removed it, probing the wound and clipping the artery closed with hemostats.

After tying the compress over the wound and the hemostats, he wiped his face and examined the other wounds. Steele was lucky. The pointman had been knocked unconscious by the concussion, but with the one exception the wounds were superficial. The flak jacket and helmet had protected his upper body and head. Tyson had seen much worse. He hated the badly wounded, those men whose guts were riddled and exposed or whose chests sucked and bubbled. It was the two extremes that he handled best, either the dead or the slightly wounded, since neither cried in anguish nor gushed in blood.

When Pat Graves returned with five soldiers and a poncho to be used as a stretcher, Brooks patted Steele's shoulder, stood, and cradled his rifle. "Doc, I'm going to look for the gooks."

Tyson glanced up. "Be careful."

"I will. I don't want you working on me."

Brooks turned and walked to where two uprooted palm trees that had been Steele's destination crisscrossed the stream bed. As he watched for other booby traps, he remembered hearing of two other dinks that Charley Company had pinned down the previous week. When a tiger scout shouted in Vietnamese to those NVA, asking them to give up, the two demanded the opposite…the company must surrender to them. The response was humorous to the soldiers of Charley Company, but the VC's insubordinate reply stuck in their memories. The two men were tough little bastards until their dying time.

Stepping across the tree bridge and onto the opposite bank, Brooks walked a few yards but seemed to be transported into another world, a world where another two VC's dying wish might be to kill him. He walked further in his search and whirled to his left when he heard an indistinct sound. His hands tightened, his body stiffened, and his heart pounded. Now he knew how Steele felt on each mission. Swallowing heavily, he kneeled and searched the grass for booby traps. Seeing none, he crept forward and was irritated by the splashing and sucking sounds made by his footsteps. Brooks listened to his own breathing, rapid and open-mouthed, and then flinched at a sudden groan. Pointing his rifle at the grass curtain that surely hid the VC, the urge struck him to shoot blindly, but he stepped forward and then instinctively jerked back when he gazed down at the man.

The VC shivered, smelling of fish and swamp water, and his body and hair were soaked and sprinkled with bits of grass. The man rocked and moaned and clutched his leg where two of Steele's bullets had hammered him above the knee, leaving a gaping wound that looked like a butcher had not finished slicing off a roast. He breathed irregularly, his chest rose and fell quickly and, under the midday sun, his face not only dripped in a cold sweat but looked pale and ghost-like from the shock.

Mike Brooks motioned for the VC to slide sideways and he checked for weapons. He saw none and then retraced the crumpled grass trail to where the other man lay dead. He was a young man, no more than eighteen, and he laid on his side with his legs and arms strangely twisted and his skin a pale yellow. Brooks wondered if either of these men had killed Nelson or set the booby trap on Steele, but he would never know and the answer no longer mattered.

Brooks had seen enough. When he returned to the wounded VC, he put out his hand. The young man hesitated and then accepted the gesture, grabbing hold. Pivoting, Brooks bent his knees and helped his former enemy climb onto his back. The man was lightweight yet he felt the strong grip and boney fingers digging into his shoulder and neck. But there was both a cause and a rhythm. With each of Brooks' steps, the loose chunk of the man's leg flapped and bounced and the man winced, unknowingly sinking his fingers into Brooks as a reaction to the pain.

Walking back to the stream bed, Brooks shouted to Doc Tyson. "Here's another customer."

The medevac helicopter had departed with Nelson's body by the time Doc Tyson and Sergeant Brooks set the VC down next to Warren Steele and among the resting soldiers.

"Brooks, one question," Lieutenant Gomez said, chewing a bite of cold C-rations and looking at the VC. "Why'd you bring him back?"

Brooks imagined saying, "Shut the hell up", but ignored the question, feeling like he couldn't do anything right.

Gomez really didn't expect nor want a response, especially after their earlier altercation. He only wanted to play mind games and, as an afterthought, was pleased to see the prisoner. A proper interrogation privately conducted might yield information that could work to his benefit.

Doc Tyson checked on Warren Steele and offered to open a C-ration can for him. The pointman refused, not wanting to eat, and preferred to watch the prisoner.

The medic checked the compress on the VC's leg and then handed him an opened can of C-ration spaghetti. The prisoner leaned back, surprised at the offer. These soldiers shot him and now they were feeding him. It was a strange situation, a strange war, but he eagerly accepted the food and gobbled down half the spaghetti before looking up, tomato sauce dripping from the corner of his mouth.

"This guy's not VC," Tyson said. "He's fuckin' Chef Boyardee."

The platoon members laughed and that too startled and again surprised the prisoner. He watched them, watching him, and he had relaxed enough to offer a quick smile. Despite the *bac si* bandaging his leg and giving him food, these soldiers had killed his friend and he hoped that this waiting game was not just a prelude to his own death. He wondered if he too was a condemned man, enjoying a last meal as he waited for a life or death decision by his audience.

The soldiers sat in the meadow in a semi-circle and silently watched the prisoner, center stage and the star of the show with Warren Steele at his side. Two players in a mission that had ended in a stalemate: one dead Vietnamese lying in the swamp, one dead American flying to a more ceremonial disposition, and the two wounded men on display, one white and one brown. But it was the little shirtless man, with his leg ripped below his black shorts, who was the center of attention. A representative of an enemy that the Americans fought but seldom saw alive. He was a rare specimen of the breed, a phantom that had been captured and held like a moth in a glass jar.

Still, despite the side show attraction, the soldiers' interest waned and they soon turned their attention away and continued resting, eating, and lowering their trousers in an uninhibited search. Some found plump, blood-filled leeches on their legs, butts, and in their crotches and were amused when they touched a burning cigarette to the parasites. The slimy leeches spewed their hosts' blood as they dropped and that entertained the soldiers until they focused on an incoming Cobra gunship, diving toward the woodline.

The co-pilot sat directly behind the pilot and the sleek machine resembled a green shark with its streamline body, high tail rudder, and rocket pods. A gaping red mouth with sharp white teeth was painted on its nose and the machine could attack, tearing and shredding and devouring with open jaws. The Cobra was a killing machine and the soldiers' minds were temporarily distracted from Nelson's death as they watched the gunship expend its rockets and cannons and listened to the loud chainsaw-like buzz of the mini-guns firing up to four thousand rounds per minute. As the gunship blanketed the marsh with more destruction, it was questionable whether more enemy soldiers had been killed, but the power was impressive and the display held everyone's attention except one.

Dried mud clung to Warren Steele's hair and he picked at it while staring at the prisoner and waiting for an opportunity. When the man looked away, Steele leaned across and smashed his helmet into the man's face, whipping the VC's head sideways as he reached for his M-16. "You gook bastard…I'll kill you!"

"Stop it, Steele!" Doc yelled, running up and yanking the rifle away. He then dragged the VC back and then refocused on the pointman. "What the hell are you doing?"

"Finishing the job." Steele stared at the prisoner and then looked at the medic. "He hasn't bled enough for me."

Doc Tyson stared back, shaking his head. "Well, I've had enough blood today."

"Doc's right," Cool agreed in a subdued voice. "And here comes your dustoff."

Cool dropped the handset of his radio and popped a purple smoke, tossing the canister downwind as Warren Steele leaned back and listened to the whirl of the incoming helicopter. He turned onto his side but no position relieved the burning pain shooting through his legs. The wounds felt like miniature volcanoes spewing heat from the lead that lay beneath the surface.

Chapter 15

Saturday, February 14, 1970---3:20 p.m.

In less than twenty minutes, the medevac helicopter landed at the Third Field Hospital in Saigon and Warren Steele was rushed through admissions and into the X-ray department. The remainder of his muddy trousers was cut away for a series of X-rays and his wounds were cleaned as the pictures were developed.

Lying face down on the exam table, Steele lay awake, his senses back intact, and he watched the doctor examine the X-rays. Leaning closer to the pictures, his stethoscope hanging around his neck, the doctor counted twelve pieces of jagged lead, matching the puncture holes blanketing Steele's legs, the side of his left knee, and his buttocks. More than a dozen more tiny pieces of shrapnel showed up on the X-rays.

Warren Steele studied the doctor and was reminded of the stocky physician that treated his mother at the free health clinics. After two miscarriages and bearing four children from three different fathers, the doctor persuaded her to have her tubes tied. No more children, no more brothers or sisters, but she had complained about another case of gonorrhea before he left for Vietnam.

"Nothing to worry about," the doctor explained, snapping back Steele's attention.

Leaving the X-rays hanging in front of the lighted screens, he picked up a syringe and began injecting anesthesia near the wounds. "It's a cliché but you have the million dollar ticket." The physician talked as he worked and even sounded like the clinic doctor. "I've already tied off the severed artery and removed the hemostats on your leg. Thankfully it wasn't a major femoral artery or you might not be here."

He looked carefully at each of the shrapnel entry wounds and then pushed down on a wound with a gloved hand, checking the effect of the anesthesia. "Does that hurt?"

Steele shook his head.

"Okay, let's go to work," the doctor said.

Adjusting the lamp, he began debriding the wounds, removing the shrapnel and cutting out the dead tissue with his scalpel. He worked meticulously for thirty-five minutes on the legs and buttocks and then turned Steele onto his side to work on the knee.

"Son of a bitch! Nurse! Come here!" the doctor yelled out to the nurses' station and waited for her arrival. The doctor held a compress against the knee and explained, "I cut another artery when I was debriding the wound."

Steele had not felt any pain, but the doctor apologized profusely, upset with his lack of skill and annoyed that the soldier had another artery severed. He muttered to himself for several minutes, but with the nurse's assistance, he closed off the artery and finished debriding the wound.

After twenty more minutes, the doctor stopped the process. He re-checked each wound, satisfied that he had removed all of the contaminated flesh, and began wrapping

Steele's legs with gauze. "Again I'm sorry about the slip. Just didn't see the second artery under the dead tissue. Because of the knee, we'll cast your leg for a week, let all the wounds drain, and then I'll stitch you up as needed. You'll be transferred to the Sixth Convalescent Center in Cam Rahn Bay for physical therapy."

Steele twisted around. "Can I go back to my unit?"

The doctor glanced up with a puzzled look. "Should I check your concussion again? I've received requests for home, Hawaii, or Japan, but never back to a base camp." The doctor taped down the gauze. "You can return after I sew up the wounds, but no combat duty. You'll need therapy on that knee. Expect it to be very stiff when the cast comes off. As for the tiny pieces of shrapnel, they're like blemishes, they'll burn but eventually work their way to the surface." The doctor removed his latex gloves and tossed them on the medical tray. "You still have another piece of shrapnel lodged behind your knee cap, but you'll have to live with it. The probing and removal would do more damage than the shrapnel."

The doctor looked at the nurse and then rubbed Steele's shoulder. "The nurse will administer a tetanus shot and then cast your leg. You're going to have a hell of a time going to the bathroom for a week, but..." he said, smiling, "we'll get you some help."

Walking toward the door, the physician looked back at Steele. "Remember, it's your decision about going back to your unit, but let me warn you. Shit can happen, just like me slicing the artery. You have a million dollar wound...you may be able to go home or at least relax on the beach at Cam

Rahn Bay. Anything can happen here. This whole county's a war zone and, if you stay, you may come back in a body bag."

Saturday, February 14, 1970---5:17 p.m.

"Colonel Balfrey!" Warren Steele hollered, with a tone of surprise and excitement, when he spotted the gray-haired brigade commander walking by the open doorway. The colonel, a lanky Texan with West Point posture, stopped and walked into the open ward, which housed Steele and eleven other wounded soldiers.

"You're Lieutenant Gomez' pointman, aren't you?"

"Yes sir...Spec. Four Steele...I'm sorry for yelling."

"No, I'm sorry to hear about the other pointman and seeing you here," Balfrey said, watching Steele nod in agreement over the loss of Nelson. The colonel quickly changed the subject and tapped Steele's exposed cast. "So what happened?"

"I screwed up...running, shooting, watching...I just didn't see the booby trap wire," Steele answered, feeling awkward. "But I'd like a favor, sir, a job until I DEROS." He glanced at his cast. "I'm done humpin' the boonies."

"When do you go home, son?"

"In August, sir. I've been a pointman for seven months. Five more months left on my tour," Steele said, "but I know the brigade mailman jets out March 1st. Could I have his job?"

Colonel Balfrey shrugged his shoulders. "No one has asked me and Lieutenant Gomez has bragged that you're a damn fine pointman. So, why not? I'll have a Purple Heart for you and that's the best qualification. See me when you're ready." The colonel stopped and pulled out a pad and pen from his starched and pressed fatigues, writing himself a note. "Anything else?"

"Negative, sir. Thank you!" Steele said, saluting and grinning, but nearly oblivious to the colonel's departure.

Steele's thoughts were already spinning as he leaned back in the hospital bed. But one thing stood out----he'd never walk point again. Never be in harm's way again nor anguish over his questionable existence. He was a grunt no more and this realization was a mixed blessing, knowing that he'd be separated from the platoon and those men that had been as close as his real brothers. Yet, he would have power…the power to turn heads and spread legs…power that he would attain because, with Colonel Balfrey's approval, the mailroom job closed the loopholes. The wounds that he had predicted and had dreaded so long had finally come and now the question of his survival was answered. His million dollar wounds were not his ticket home, but an opportunity right here in-country. The burning pain in his legs was his rebirth and these wounds were going to net a lot more than the proverbial million dollars. In his calculations, he'd be a wealthy man by the end of his tour…a very rich and powerful man.

Chapter 16

Saturday, February 14, 1970---5:29 p.m.

"Talk!" Captain O'Brien shouted as he slapped the Vietnamese prisoner with a force that whipped the man's head sideways and added redness to the welt previously inflicted by Warren Steele. The prisoner furiously tugged on the ropes, binding his hands and feet to the chair, and then after deciding that he could only fight with defiance, spit blood and saliva onto the officer's fatigues.

"You little bastard!" O'Brien yelled and jabbed a walking stick into the man's stomach. He scraped off the spit from his shirt and shoved it onto the man's face. "Talk or you die." He turned to his Vietnamese translator, a man only known as Tran. "Tell him that."

The former Viet Cong, an enlistee under the *Chieu Hoi* program, nodded. He repeated the message but the prisoner said nothing.

O'Brien reached into the prisoner's black boxer shorts and cupped the man's testicles in his palm. With one quick stroke, he swatted them with his walking stick and the popping sound reminded him of cracking walnuts.

The man screamed and his head drooped as the headquarters' door squeaked open and Lieutenant Gomez entered.

"Join us Roberto," the captain said, motioning with his cane. "The dink that Steele shot and I are just playing baseball…my bat and his balls."

Gomez tossed his helmet, pack, and flak jacket into the corner and set his rifle on his desk. "Nice bat," he said, pointing at the black fist carved on top of O'Brien's cane.

"I have a closet full since Colonel Balfrey made them off-limits on base and at the White Dragon." O'Brien held his up. "They do come in handy on occasion."

Lieutenant Gomez nodded and knew incidents of soldiers bashing each other with the sticks had been eliminated after being outlawed. He looked at the VC, remembered his earlier relaxed smile, and wondered how long ago the grin had vanished. "How long has he been here?"

"Not long. The chopper brought him in after his condition stabilized."

Lieutenant Gomez had not spoken to the prisoner as they waited in the meadow, but he had sized him up. His youth, the smile, his acceptance of food, and now his solitary imprisonment were all clues…information to be used. Although he'd never admit it to Sergeant Brooks, Gomez was pleased that he had brought the prisoner in alive.

"Has he told you anything?"

"Negative. Not a damn thing. Not even his name and rank. He's young, but he's not Viet Cong. He's NVA sure as hell." Captain O'Brien paused. "Any suggestions?"

"Let me think," Gomez said, rubbing his chin. "I can be very creative."

For some reason, his mind turned to thoughts of saws, hammers, and his personal favorite, pliers. A tool designed to twist, pull, and crush and an instrument capable of yanking out fingernails and teeth, crushing knuckles, or tearing off skin.

But so many methods existed: an ice pick inching closer to someone's ear or eye, hanging electrical wires from the testicles, holding a man in the open door of a high altitude helicopter, or simply shoving a man's head under water were all effective. The key was whether the prisoner believed the interrogator was willing to thrust the ice pick, attach a charged battery, throw him out of the chopper, or keep the head submerged. The methods of cruelty were only limited by one's twisted mind and imagination.

Torturers prided themselves in scare tactics and their ability to gain valuable information with few visible marks on the prisoner. Gomez remembered how he once grabbed the hair of a VC prisoner and pushed the man's face toward the twirling blur of a helicopter tail rotor. The man knew that he'd either have to talk or have his face split open like an overripe cantaloupe. He talked.

Lieutenant Gomez walked out the rear door which attached to the sleeping quarters of the officers. When he returned, he held four items, two in each hand.

"We can do this the easy way or the hard way." He held a Coca-Cola bottle and a C-ration can near the man's face and then set them on the desk and offered him both. "Ask him the name of his unit."

The tiger scout asked the question, received an answer, and then relayed the message. "Him say that he no talk."

"That's fine. He had a choice and free will can be a bitch. But I think he's about to become a blabber-mouth,"

Gomez said as he unscrewed the tops of two other containers.

Blinking and holding them at arms' length, he poured salt into a bottle of ammonia and swirled the liquid. He set the bottle down, knelt in front of the prisoner, and untied the bandages on the NVA's thigh. The prisoner's face cringed as Gomez tugged on the compresses, tearing loose the dried pus that glued the gauze to his skin. Exposing the wound, Gomez saw that the jagged edges of flesh had been sliced away. Stitches held the flap of flesh in place but a sticky yellow fluid still oozed and drained.

Gomez held the bottle of ammonia-salt mixture in front of the man's eyes and tipped it slowly toward his leg, hoping that the threat would force him to speak. The NVA said nothing and his jaw tightened while he stared at Gomez with defiance.

The lieutenant shook his head, somewhat surprised at the response. "Your choice, your very bad choice."

Never had he made a threat that he was not willing to carry out. Gomez glanced up at Captain O'Brien, but knew he had previously served two tours as a platoon leader and would approve of the tactic.

O'Brien concurred with a nod, feeling that the need justified the means.

Gomez stared back at the NVA, who remained silent even as he further tilted the bottle. Only a cold silence returned, but refusing to talk was not an acceptable option and the officer poured the mixture onto the wound.

The NVA howled, thrashing and pulling on the ropes as the solution seeped between the stitches and burned and foamed. The lieutenant dug his fingers into the man's cheeks as the NVA's consciousness faded and then held the ammonia under his nose. Tears dripped from his eyes and his head rocked and jerked until the fumes awakened him.

Gomez twisted the man's jaw and forced him to look up. "Ask him 'what unit'?"

The translator questioned him. "He say 'Seventh Division'."

"It's amazing how pain in the leg improves one's memory." Gomez looked at the captive. "Where's the location of the Communist Central Office?"

The question was changed into Vietnamese but silence returned.

Lieutenant Gomez squeezed the bottle. "Tell him that I'll pour it into his eyes."

The translator repeated the statement. When silence again was the reply, Gomez yanked the man's head back and slowly tipped the bottle toward his face. The NVA's eyes widened and he hurriedly jabbered in Vietnamese, stopping the fulfillment of the threat.

As Gomez released him, the man lowered his head with the shame that he had been caught and had failed as both a soldier and prisoner. He only hoped that his information and pleading words of surrender might stop the torture and keep him alive.

The tiger scout stared at the bewildered face of the NVA and then bowed his own head and eyes. "He tell you anything," the scout said in the soft tones of the defeated. "Anything you want to know."

Chapter 17

Saturday, February 14, 1970---6:34 p.m.

"Sit down, Sergeant!" Captain O'Brien ordered, barely allowing Mike Brooks to open the door of the headquarters building.

Brooks walked in quickly but didn't understand the captain's attitude until he saw Lieutenant Gomez sitting at his desk.

The smell of ammonia hung in the room and Brooks' eyes blinked as he stepped over the damp floor and sat near O'Brien's desk.

The captain marched up to Brooks, wasting no time. "Lieutenant Gomez says that you attacked him after failing to follow his orders."

"That's right," Brooks admitted, noticing the red scaly cheeks of the man. "But...."

"Don't give me any 'buts'. I don't want any excuses." O'Brien waited, sizing up Brooks and thinking. "Were you a college boy?"

"No, sir."

"Valedictorian of your high school?"

"No, sir."

"Any scholarships?"

"No, sir."

"So, after seven months of being here, you must think you're Audie Murphy. Lieutenant Gomez is a decorated, career military officer and now you think you're smarter than him?"

Brooks paused, knowing he was being set up. "No sir. Lieutenant Gomez is *much* smarter than me."

"Good. I'm thrilled you agree. Then, if I properly recall, Lieutenant Gomez's rank of first lieutenant is higher than a staff sergeant," O'Brien said sarcastically. "So Lieutenant Gomez, and not you, is in charge of third platoon. Do you understand?"

"Yes, sir," Brooks said. "But rank doesn't equal common sense or good judgment."

"That's enough!" Gomez shouted, thinking Brooks just didn't know when to shut his mouth.

"I did choke Lieutenant Gomez, but only after he hit me," Brooks explained. "Two days ago, Pfc. Cunningham lost three fingers because the lieutenant refused to call in gunships. Today, Nelson's dead and Warren Steele's legs and butt look like Swiss cheese. If we'd circled a '*Tu Dia*' sign, maybe Steele wouldn't be hurt and Nelson would be alive."

"'Maybes' don't count," Captain O'Brien said, countering the remarks. "You can't second-guess life. Maybe the entire platoon would have been ambushed if you had entered the marsh in another location. Taking it further...maybe you don't have the rank to question any officer. Maybe I don't feel the need to explain anything to you. And maybe we don't give a shit what you think."

Brooks started to speak when Lieutenant Gomez cut him off by standing. "Let's proceed."

"I agree," Captain O'Brien said. He lit a cigarette and looked back at Brooks. "Did Lieutenant Gomez warn you about questioning his orders?"

"Yes, sir."

"Today did you argue about an order before the fight?"

"Yes, sir."

"I appreciate the honesty. But I'm surprised that Lieutenant Gomez hasn't hit you before. You're the platoon sergeant for God's sake. You know there's no time to discuss an order in combat."

"We weren't in combat," Brooks said, shaking his head. "We win the fucking war by killing gooks, not letting them kill us. Before Lieutenant Gomez replaced Lieutenant Simpson, we'd killed as many gooks and we only had two casualties…two in four months. Gomez comes in and we have seven dead and thirteen wounded in one month." He looked at Gomez. "Not the kind of record that I'd be proud of in this war."

"The comparison isn't worth a shit. Every week each platoon has a different casualty rate." O'Brien pointed his finger at Brooks, shaking it as he spoke. "Today, you attacked an officer after disobeying an order. But I'm not going to court martial you. Instead, I'm confining you to the base for three months."

Brooks stood up, knowing that he would not be able to see Butterfly. "You can't do that!"

"Plant your ass, Sergeant!" O'Brien yelled and slammed his fist onto his desk. He waited until Brooks sat down. "I can and will do that unless you'd prefer a stay at Long Binh jail. Plus if you're caught off-base, I'll have the White Dragon fire your little Vietnamese friend. If I threaten that our soldiers can't patronize the bar until she's fired, her butt would be on the street in a minute. Even more importantly, I'll be ordering perimeter guards to blow your ass away if you're out of the confines of this base without permission."

"I'll stay put but I will marry Butterfly," Brooks insisted, his jaw tightening.

Gomez walked up to Brooks. "Maybe you could find a way to marry her, maybe after your tour is up, but right now you have a major problem…and that's me. If you bitch about my orders again, you will gripe yourself into a court martial and a dishonorable discharge. With a glorious record like that, you'd never get your marriage approved."

"I could send for her."

"Yeah, you could. But don't plan on bringing her home to mommy," Gomez said, feeling smug when he countered each of Brooks' arguments. "If it's arranged that she's classified as an undesirable alien, immigration officials wouldn't let her into the U.S. and they sure as hell wouldn't approve her citizenship."

"So you may be staying and living in Vietnam a very long time." Gomez glanced over to Captain O'Brien. "By the time you could get her back to the states, she'll look like some old mama-san with betel juice drooling out of her mouth."

"Do you have any questions?" O'Brien asked, figuring Lieutenant Gomez had summarized it all. "No? No more wise ass remarks? Then you're dismissed."

"How do you like that decision?" Gomez asked.

Brooks said nothing as he stood again. He was mute, unable to find the right words. His reason and intellect had vanished again and his instincts angered and confused him. For the second time in one day, he wanted to kill Gomez. He wanted freedom and he felt like strangling them both, choking them until their hearts quit beating and their chests stopped heaving for air.

Mike Brooks inhaled deeply, trying to regain his composure. It was no use to fight them. Their deaths wouldn't help. If he killed them, he'd never get Butterfly. He'd never see her again and he'd only rot in the Long Bien jail. Unable to look at the officers, he unclenched his fists and shuffled out the door, followed by only the laughter of his leaders.

Chapter 18

Saturday, February 14, 1970---7:14 p.m.

An orphaned Vietnamese boy awaiting surgery stood up crying and urinating through the crib's bars, while wounded soldiers wrapped like red mummies moaned in low tones. The yells and the whimpering, echoing through the open wards, awakened Warren Steele and he turned slowly in the hospital bed. Sweat beaded on his forehead and he tossed the bed sheet aside, feeling the heat radiate from the wounds, his pajama top, bandages, and cast. Antiseptic smells lingered and he wiped off the sweat as he watched the nurses making their rounds: sponge-bathing soldiers, monitoring IVs, administering injections, changing compresses, and handing out pills.

This constant flow of personnel made sleeping difficult while the throbbing of Steele's wounds made it nearly impossible. He rubbed his buttocks, tender from penicillin shots and damp from the drainage of his wounds, and then scratched his arm. A few old scars adorned both arms where he had intentionally cut himself as an adolescent, while the words "Hell Razor" were tattooed on his forearm. This play on words sat directly below a fangs-barred rattlesnake, curling around and poking through the eye sockets of a human skull and raised up between two blood-dripping straight razors.

From age twelve to seventeen, Steele lived his tattooed slogan, raising hell and serving time in both juvenile hall and the California Youth Authority. His first arrest occurred after a cop red-lighted Steele's borrowed, weaving white Ford and found a plastic bag stuffed with marijuana and a vodka bottle under the seat. The grass and booze were leftovers from a drive-in movie date where Steele got shit-faced, used another sandwich bag and a rubber band in a failed attempt as a condom, and knocked up his future wife. His second arrest happened when he bought a "nickel bag" of heroin from an undercover policeman. The judge considered Steele's age and his pregnant wife and offered him the choice of either jail or the army. Jail didn't frighten him but he chose the army for the monthly pay, medical care for his wife, and a closed juvenile arrest record.

Steele fluffed his pillow and looked around the ward. He had slept in a similar bed as a kid, but not alone. He and his two younger brothers were turned sideways and shared one bed while his sister slept on an air mattress a few feet away. Now he relished being alone, the shiny linoleum, and the smell of laundry soap rising from the clean bed sheets…much different than the stained carpet, the filthy sheets of his youth, and hearing his mother through the apartment wall, acting out her orgasmic moans for money.

The memories and the luxury of the moment vanished with the turn of his head. Out in a lighted courtyard two soldiers tossed body bags onto a truck's bed. Steele turned away from the window. He could have been shoved in one and Nelson most assuredly had been tagged and bagged. His chest heaved in disgust at how the remains of these grunts were being dishonored. Oh sure, a brief ceremony would be held. Soldiers would line up in parade-rest, thankful to be alive and thankful not to be so honored, outside the Rach Binh chapel with Nelson's helmet stacked on his bayoneted M-16, stuck in the dirt behind his jungle boots…symbols of his short life and his death.

The chaplain or a priest, dressed in his all-white gown, would pray and the battalion commander would repeat some carefully chosen words, recycled from another service, glorifying a life that had ended in the inglorious act of peering into an occupied spider hole. After the words were issued for a man that neither knew, the soldiers would be dismissed, scattering to be alone with Nelson's fleeting memory.

Steele grimaced, his melancholy feelings growing, as he watched the soldier in the opposite bed. The rumor was that claymore mines had been reversed by the VC before a firefight began and that his injuries were the result of the GIs blowing the mines on themselves. Steele didn't know the truth but the soldier looked like a flour sack, a legless grub of a man, whose nose and mouth and skull were the only parts of his body not covered by bandages. Grunting and weeping, the creature vainly gnawed at the IV tubing that dripped life into him and washed away his dignity.

This gathering of freaks was the final destination of so many soldiers and yet, in the past, he'd had never reflected on their fate. He had only seen wounded men airlifted out and then replaced by new undamaged human equipment, a simple extension of a throw-away society whereby it was easier to discard the garbage of broken bodies than to solve the problem of their destruction. These men, these bags of debris, represented the dead branches of a family tree that would never bud, never grow.

"Damn it all," Steele whispered to himself.

He twisted around and looked at a map of Vietnam hanging above his bed. I Corp started just below the demilitarized zone separating North and South Vietnam and the zones were labeled north to south, down to IV Corp. The cities and bases, Dong Tam, Saigon, Bien Hoa, Pleiku, Dak To, Chu Lai, Da Nang, Hue, Quang Tri, and even Rach Binh were marked. His unit was lucky. III Corp wasn't bad compared to the shit that the 101st Airborne and the First Cav Divisions had been hitting up north.

Lying in his bed only miles apart, Steele wondered what the men of third platoon were doing and yet he couldn't relate to them even now. Nor could he relate to Nelson or his unknowing family. It was impossible to know. He only felt relief at never having to walk point again. He had hated Lieutenant Gomez' decision, but the order that could have killed him, just like Nelson, now brought him to safety. He had just enough shrapnel to get him out of the field, into the rear area, and he'd now have the perfect job to bring him wealth.

The plan was simple. He'd buy a kilo of pure heroin each day from Major Quan and then deliver the wrapped package to the Tan An mailroom on the following day. Even if they were used, dogs could not smell the odorless drug and as company mailman no one would suspect him.

Purchasing a kilo for $1,200, he could mail it home where his wife and brothers could dilute it down to only five percent, selling it on the streets for over $225,000. Steele picked up a pen and paper from the bedside table and wrote the number. Under that figure, he wrote 150, the approximate number of days that he would work as postman, and multiplied.

Unbelieving, he stared at the number…it couldn't be right. Steele recalculated the math and smiled. In days, he'd begin his mail job and in a few months, he'd be going home to riches. He didn't trust or love his wife. He'd only known her for less than a month and only married her because of their baby boy, but his brothers would watch her and they were street savvy enough to handle the sales.

His brothers would help upfront the cash for the first deal and, in time, they'd have it all…mansions, cars, clothes, and cash. With all of those, he'd have the power to attract his main object of desire…women. And yet, they were all the same. They might pretend to love him, but soon he would be in control. He would buy and use them and then throw them away like they had always done to him. Steele looked again at the figure of $33,750,000, almost thirty-four million dollars, and whistled softly. He was going to have a golden future.

Part II

Chapter 19

Thursday, April 23, 1970---10:00 a.m.

Colonel Jeffrey Balfrey, whose mother insisted that the rhyming name would be remembered in military circles, walked into the mess hall, heard a voice bellow "Attention!", and watched the officers stand straight and tall.

"At ease," the brigade commander said, "and be seated."

He glanced at his four company commanders and each of their three accompanying platoon leaders and then adjusted his portable map of Southeast Asia until chairs no longer scooted on the floor. He noticed the smell of fried bacon and turned toward the men only after the room became silent.

"This is a very special meeting. Consider all information secret."

Sitting at tables covered with red and white checkered contact paper, the attention of the officers focused on the second generation West Point graduate, whose brow wrinkled and pushed up his scalp of neatly-trimmed gray hair. A veteran of three wars, Balfrey had landed on D-Day, June 6, 1944, on his 23rd birthday and had survived Omaha Beach, distinguishing himself in five weeks of battle until a Nazi "potato masher" grenade thrown from a French hedgerow ended his tour in Europe. Seven years later, he fought on Pork Chop Hill in Korea as a platoon leader where he received another Purple Heart and the Silver Star for gallantry in action. With the Cold War, the career officer found himself in Southeast Asia once again. He had served as platoon leader, a company commander, and now, on his third tour in the Republic of Vietnam, he was in charge of the Third Brigade of the Ninth Infantry Division.

Colonel Balfrey's fatigues were starched, pressed, and spotless, unlike those of his audience, and he snapped off a loose thread before pointing to the map. "In the past, we've sat with our dicks in our hands while the NVA haul weapons and rice down the Ho Chi Minh Trail and infiltrate Vietnam. While we wait for an attack, COSVN, the Communist Central Office for South Vietnam, sits comfortably inside the borders of neutral Cambodia. As you know, NVA troops use the 'Fishhook' and 'Parrot's Beak' areas for sanctuaries and R&R. The little pricks fight and then retreat, pump their wives, smoke opium, and build up troop strength until they're ready to fight again."

Balfrey lit a cigarette and looked at Lieutenant Gomez and Captain O'Brien. "A few months ago," the colonel said pointing, "these two officers gained some valuable information from a captured NVA soldier, which correlated with data from our agents and high altitude recon photos." He inhaled deeply on the cigarette. "Four important pieces of intelligence...first, we believe that Saigon will be attacked within a year since the communists know that control of the Delta and Saigon are keys to victory.

Second, we believe the Communist Central Office has moved from the 'Parrot's Beak' to the 'Fishhook'. Both areas jut into Vietnam like fingers and either zone could be the hand that strangles the South."

Balfrey tapped his finger on the map. "In the Parrot's Beak, the NVA forces are less than sixty miles from Saigon even though they're still in neutral territory. They could sever, control, and attack Saigon from Route 1. If the dinks do take the offensive like Tet of '68, it'd be a severe setback to both President Nixon's withdrawal program and his 'Peace with Honor' credibility.

Third, if we disrupt the flow of weapons and supplies to the south, the ARVNs will have a chance to make Vietnamization work. Lastly, the NVA in Cambodia are monitoring our radio transmissions and jamming our frequencies during firefights, screwing up our capability to call in gunships or artillery. But, we're going to put a stop to that."

Balfrey snuffed out the cigarette. "Any questions?"

The commander of Charley Company raised his hand and then stood. "Are any actions planned?"

"Yes! We 'Bad Asses' are finally going to march." Balfrey smacked the map with his fist. "We're going to kick ass and take names 'cause the President approved the invasion of Cambodia."

The officers appeared to be both pleased and surprised. "What about its neutrality?"

"The NVA violate it so why can't we?" Balfrey snapped. "But there's another reason. Prince Sihanouk wanted his neutrality, but he never had enough balls to tell the NVA to get the hell out of his country. Last month, he was ousted from power."

Captain O'Brien shot up his hand. "Do we go in?"

"Damn right we do. The ARVNs, with support from the Rangers and the 25th Infantry Division, will invade the Parrot's Beak on April 29th. The First Cav goes in the Fishhook on May 1st. They go first and that pisses me off, but we'll go in June 1st."

"Sir, what will the folks back in the world say about it?" asked the Alpha CO.

"I don't really care what they say, but they'll claim that Nixon's widening the war. The hippies will toss trash cans in front of cars, lie down in front of buses, and generally make assholes of themselves. If someone had guts enough to squash just one, they'd trample each other trying to get the hell out of the way. "Hell," Balfrey snickered," one-traffic accident could effectively stop the anti-war movement."

Colonel Balfrey turned serious, clasping his hands as if at parade rest. "Enough bullshit, this war is about to become fair. We've never had a front, rear, or flanks, but this time we can go knockin' at the gooks' front door." Balfrey's face tightened, solemn and secretive and he lowered his voice. "MACV does want the Ninth to handle a special task before the actual invasion."

"What's the mission?"

"To pinpoint the exact location of the Communist Central Office…it would be a helluva coup for the Ninth and the President and it would insure both the success and merit of the Cambodian invasion to the American people."

The explanation seemed reasonable to the officers. "How many companies do you want?"

The colonel shook his head. "None. One platoon, only the twenty men, will go."

"What?"

"What did he say?" The officers questioned each other, certain that they must have misunderstood.

"Quiet!" Colonel Balfrey shouted. "One platoon will be airlifted into Cambodia on Sunday. Their mission is simple…locate the NVA's headquarters and radio the coordinates back." The colonel hit the Fishhook area on the map. "You find 'em and we'll fight 'em. If we control Cambodia, we control the southern Ho Chi Minh trail and, if we do that, the ARVNs may have a chance when our troops are redeployed back to the world. Two men could theoretically do this job, but twenty men can be crammed into two choppers. You'll move in and out with speed."

The captain of Delta Company raised his hand. "Doesn't COSVN house up to five thousand NVA regulars?"

"Rumors only…no one knows for sure. Estimates have ranged from a low of two hundred and fifty men to a high of five thousand in the Parrot's Beak, but we don't know how many are in the Fishhook, especially if their headquarters have moved. MACV intelligence says that COSVN is mobile and widely-dispersed, possibly functioning in ten to twelve camps and spread throughout the Cambodian jungle. COSVN has been a ghost, but it may be more than one ghost. So the number of NVA will depend on which camp is located, their objectives, construction, and when the monsoons hit."

"Do you really believe the mission can be accomplished?"

"Even if it's a failure...it's a success." Balfrey paused to pour a cup of coffee and took a drink, letting the message sink in. "Even if we're attacked, there'll be time to radio back a message and you'll have served your purpose."

"Why aren't the Rangers or Recon doing this job?"

"The cold hard truth…they weren't even asked. They're too valuable for a mission of this type. The ARVNs would screw it up and the First Cav has been getting its butt shot off. It's a cold decision but Operations and I agree that losing twenty men is better than sixty and if twenty have to die...let 'em be draftees."

Colonel Balfrey noticed the uneasiness of the officers, knowing that the men in their platoons were all draftees. "If there aren't any more questions, I'll ask mine. Will anyone volunteer their platoon or do you want me to pick one?"

No one answered the question and an uncomfortable silence hung in the room. The officers did not want to make eye contact with Colonel Balfrey out of fear that they would be selected. In their minds, Balfrey's question could have been rephrased to be "are you willing to climb into your own coffin?" None of them wanted to be the last ones killed in Vietnam while others safely returned home. Balfrey recognized the same attitude from Pork Chop Hill, hearing the post-battle criticism for losing so much for so little…so many men killed and wounded for terrain that held no strategic value. Now he was asking the same: venture into hostile territory only to sacrifice their men and then retreat, turning the hallowed ground back to the enemy.

As he waited for a response, the silence in the room became painfully uncomfortable. The officers hung their heads and silently looked down. They had nothing to say and they too waited as if in a funeral home, tearing napkins into bits and nervously tapping their coffee cups.

Raising his hand slowly, questioning whether he should speak, the captain of Charley Company stood. "Sir, our platoon leaders would volunteer for a secret mission, but this is an execution."

Colonel Balfrey stared at the faces of his men and felt ashamed that his officers, his leaders, were afraid. He could see it in their expressions and hear it in their whispers. Their actions screamed out that they were petrified. Men chewed on their pencils and puffed unknowingly on their cigarettes. They had lost the temperament of war, suppressing a history of valor and the tradition of challenging an enemy in combat.

With a coaxing voice, the colonel spoke again. "I can only offer my personal thanks and the gratitude of your unit and country." He waited. "Are there any volunteers?"

Captain O'Brien looked around the silent room, knowing the officers would not want to die for what they now considered a lost cause. All the men appeared to be afraid, except Gomez. He had more courage than O'Brien had ever seen and it separated him like a gifted athlete or a brilliant scholar. He took his gift of bravery for granted and he expected others to handle their nerves in the shittiest places as he would. Most men handled combat by shielding their fears, but if Gomez were afraid, it didn't show.

O'Brien glanced at him and saw his jaw tighten with determination. He'd never seen him this tense and he touched his arm as if to control him. Lieutenant Gomez pulled his arm away and stood, facing the colonel and knowing all of the officers' eyes were on him. Little time remained to meet his personal objectives. Soldiers advance by accomplishing goals, by standing out, by being noticed, by not retreating. He would not accept failure. This war was coming to an end and troops were being withdrawn. Time was running out, but Balfrey didn't fool him. The colonel knew that there would probably be a fight and so did he. But that didn't matter. He had nothing to lose and no family at home. The army had always been the only family he needed. More importantly, he wasn't afraid of death. He'd seen plenty of it during his combat in Korea and Vietnam and because he was at his peak, his goddamn best, at those very moments. He was the best man for a job that the others were even afraid to try and this was his chance to show them how to mock danger and do something bold and dramatic. This was an opportunity to be noticed and even the generals could not overlook this.

Understanding both the risks and the rewards, Lieutenant Gomez glanced at the other officers and then stared into the colonel's eyes. "Sir, I believe in the saying 'no guts…no glory'. I'll volunteer my platoon."

Chapter 20

Saturday, April 25, 1970---11:34 a.m.

Warren Steele flinched when he pushed in the clutch and the unengaged gears grinded and jerked the mail truck. The deuce-and-a-half truck engine roared, regained its speed, and left a trail of dust.

Steele glanced at his passenger as they drove along and then tapped his left knee. "Sorry. Still hurts like a bitch."

"No problem," the soldier said, not bothering or caring to ask why Steele was in pain.

"What's your name?"

"Arthur Wellington, but people call me 'Tiny'."

"Lots of guys have had nicknames here: Slim, Curly, Moe, Tex, and Bates, but we called him 'Master'". We even had a 'Tiny', but he weighed 285 pounds and was 6 feet 5 inches. Not quite the same as you…you're a little shit."

The remark offended the soldier and he momentarily stared at the driver, trying not to show any reaction. He had heard it before, but the words still stung.

Steele had been looking straight ahead, driving, and he didn't noticed the facial change. Besides he had already sized up the effeminate little man with brown hair and soulful eyes and was reminded of past wimps in school. After gym class, he'd smear hot salve into their jockstraps and wait until the next day when perspiration re-ignited the liniment, setting off their howling and his laughter. The past jokes were still amusing, still brought a smile to his face, and they were the best part, no the only part of school that he enjoyed. Apparently he was the only one laughing. The childish pranks and some subsequent fights were followed by visits to the principal, suspensions, and then ultimately to the school board for his expulsion.

Tiny looked like all the new replacements with his bright green fatigues, ball cap, and his short military haircut. But maybe his nickname should have been "Needy". His looks, posture, manner of speech, and the New York style was so different from his own upbringing. He looked like a kid that was used to getting whatever he needed and wanted and still expected more. But there was something else. The small man reminded Steele of the mice that dashed through his mom's Los Angeles apartment, scampering and watching with nervous eyes. The soldier's head constantly moved, trying to comprehend this different world and the more he saw the more stressed he became. Judging what he had seen so far, the man was small in stature but his nerves were huge and wound tight.

Tiny would have agreed. He clenched his hands into fists, but the speedy ride was not the cause. It was the sights and sounds and experiences of this place. Back at Tan An, he and another soldier had been assigned night guard duty, walking a section of the lonely perimeter fence every fifteen minutes, and expecting to meet another soldier walking the opposite direction from his post. Tiny had refused to go and asked his partner to take his place. He was not going to walk the fence line alone in the dark with the unloaded weapon given to replacements.

The whole concept was ridiculous. He supposed that any VC watching from afar would presume that the weapons were loaded and the sentries were ready to fight. Both presumptions were incorrect. The M-16 was not loaded, he was not willing to fight, and furthermore he was not willing to walk the wire.

The completion of guard duty, his first assignment in Vietnam, had been ignored. His behavior was not discovered or reported, but he had to get out. He made a final appeal to be a clerk-typist while he waited on his transfer from Tan An to Rach Binh, but an officer laughed at the request and told him to get out of his sight. With that response, all of his options had passed. His destiny was that of an 11-Bravo MOS---the Military Occupation Specialty of a "rifle infantryman".

Tiny looked at Steele. "Any way of getting your type of job?"

"Driving truck? What's your MOS?"

"Eleven Bravo."

Steele glanced at Tiny. "Eleven Bravo…same as me…well you're screwed, blued, and tattooed. Getting that job is easy, but there's only three, make that four, ways to get out: Dead, Wounded beyond repair, DEROS, or Refuse to go to the field. I personally fall under category number two. Refusing is better than getting shot, but plan on being court-martialed, spending time in Long Binh jail, and then getting a dishonorable discharge. Only the DEROS is any good."

Steele laughed aloud. "You have what---360 days left in-country? You poor bastard. Well, you'd better get used to your surroundings." Steele motioned with his hand to the land. "You're going to spend a lot of time, a lifetime, in the bush."

Tiny watched the countryside fly by his window. He had never seen anything like this. In fact, he had never seen much outside the beauty and the security of his hometown of Kings Point, New York. He expected to see the color green like the manicured lawns of his family's home, but even that was missing as he looked at the dry rice fields. Scattered hooches dotted the fields, but these were nothing more than small shacks, structures he imagined the homeless might build to escape the rain. They were like old slave cabins set back from the estates that had been home.

The people were so different. Women squatted under pyramid-shaped hats outside their shacks while their half-clothed toddlers played in the dirt with empty flare canisters and C-ration tin cans as toys. They too squatted in the dirt, not toilet-trained and naked from the waist down, eliminating the need for diapers. They were not wiped or cleaned and he watched in disgust as children urinated and defecated on the ground like dogs. He wondered if the women had been bred in the same fashion, unashamed and in the open for all to watch. He imagined them on all fours, doggy-style with exposed and engorged tits, hanging down and swaying with each thrust, raising their tails to accommodate a circling, sniffing pack of human mongrels. The thought alone was sickening and repugnant.

The sights, sounds, and smells were of a different world as if he had time travelled to an ancient past. It was a garbage dump, a primitive world inhabited by subsistence farmers, not much different than the animals they tended and Tiny took mental notes as he watched. Women stood knee deep in water and mud, bending over and tending flooded seed gardens, separating rice sprouts by hand in preparation for planting. An old man poured a watery slop into a trough for his pigs that squealed and pushed for their share. A young woman nursed her infant son, holding him in a sling as he suckled, while she weaved split reeds into a sleeping mat. A young girl tossed vegetable scraps down to her chickens, watching them scratch and scramble for a bite.

In his mind, these people lived in squalor…no tiled showers and baths, no running water or toilets, no electricity, no lights, no television, no stereo…and he wondered how they lived like that. He hated this country already and wondered why the wealthiest country on earth would send its military to this godforsaken land. He regretted being dismissed from college and wished that he had left for Canada or any country rather than accept the induction notice. He wished that he could have paid someone to take his place in the draft like the North allowed in the Civil War. He could have been safe in a rich man's war and a poor man's fight. It may have worked then, but not now. It was too late. He felt like a prisoner on death row who had waited too long to repent and now there was no escape and he was destined to serve his time in hell.

Speeding past a hooch, Steele drove the truck through a flock of chickens. They scattered, running, flapping, and flying, but the truck bounced and Steele counted three chickens, flopping their smashed bodies in the rear view mirror.

"Dinner's served," he joked. "It's chicken-CRUSH-atori." Steele looked at the little man who neither laughed nor smiled. Changing the topic, Steele asked, "How come you're the only replacement?"

"I don't know. Most of the soldiers were sent to the First Cav." Tiny rolled down his window and watched the chickens in the mirror flipping and dying. He had never seen an animal die before. "Was that a hit-and-run and should we report it?"

"Yeah, yeah, I'll take care of it…I'll get 'em each a little casket." Steele grinned and glanced at the soldier, wondering where the army had even found this guy. But there was no response to the sarcastic answer. The comment either seemed to satisfy his concern or his mind had already moved elsewhere.

Tiny then turned to study the driver. "Back home in New York, our newspaper said that the Mekong Delta is under military control."

Steele swerved around a man riding a smoking Honda 90 motorcycle. "The question is 'which military'?"

"Ours."

"Sure…I'll believe that if you will."

Tiny held onto the door handle as he watched the fields whiz past the window and listened to the gravel pinging against the fenders. He looked sheepishly at Steele, noticing the "Hell Razor" tattoo on display below his rolled up shirt sleeves, and assumed the artwork held the answer to his question. "In Rach Binh, are there lots of drugs?"

The question surprised Steele and he looked at Tiny. "Why? You like gettin' high 'cause you're so damn low?" Steele snickered to himself at the sarcastic remark about the man's height and his perceived mood.

"Maybe." The soldier nodded in agreement. His spirits were indeed low, depressed and his bottom lip quivered as he tried to maintain his composure. He thought back and explained. "Maybe I like drugs too much…that's why I ended up here. I did too much partying and not enough studying. I screwed up royally. Maybe I wanted an escape, but I never imagined this place. Never in a million years…Now, I guess it doesn't matter."

Steele related to the answer, completely understanding why people wanted to escape some of the nightmares of life. "What flavor do you want?"

"What?"

"What kind of drugs?"

"Marijuana?"

"Yeah, if you know the right people."

"Heroin?"

"Sure," Steele said. He smiled. "It's great here. You can snort it, smoke it, or shove it up your butt if that's your style. As long as it gets into your blood stream, it'll take you where you want to go."

Tiny thumbed through his wallet counting the MPC. "I have sixty dollars and a bottle of whiskey in my duffel bag. How much heroin would that buy?"

Steele turned the corner into the town of Rach Binh. "For the money and the booze, I'll fix you up. Meet me at 7:15 tonight behind the White Dragon, which is right there," Steele said, pointing as they passed the building, clouding it with dust and giving the painted dragon the appearance of attacking through a dense fog.

"Deal," Tiny said, agreeing to the meeting and terms, as the truck entered the open gates of the base. The vehicle squealed to a stop near the infirmary and Steele pointed out the headquarters building to Tiny. Watching him depart, Steele knew that tonight he'd buy another kilo of heroin to be shipped home and the FNG would be his first in-country customer. It seemed logical. Might as well grab some additional cash here and add them to the suckers and addicts back home.

In his mind, he had been the best pointman in Vietnam and he would be the best heroin supplier back in the states…the best supplier for anyone wishing to escape their world by walking points up their arms.

Chapter 21

Saturday, April 25, 1970---12:15 p.m.

Warren Steele limped out of the aid station, feeling the jabbing pain of shrapnel permanently lodged behind his knee cap. More than two months had passed since the booby-trapped grenade had exploded and blasted fragments into his body. Still with each step, the jagged metal rubbed against cartilage and continued to throb and burn like a hot needle shoved into his skin.

Shortly before, he had laid face down on the exam table while a medic pinned his knee down and pulled his foot toward his back, bending the joint in order to tear the scar tissue. The knee had stiffened and the scar tissue developed while his leg was in a cast. As the medic worked, Steele groaned, sweating and gritting his teeth and feeling like his knee was being ripped off his leg. His eyes had filled with tears and he moaned as the tissue was stretched and torn, but he was slowly gaining the full range of his leg and maybe, just maybe, that was worth the torture.

Still, this visit had been for something more important than therapy. The wounds that had scarred his legs also affected his mind and he brooded over his profits, unaware of how his greed had planted seeds of distrust. He swore to himself knowing that he'd been foolish, so foolish to have told Tiny of his access to the heroin and thereby risking discovery of his daily shipments. He didn't know Tiny and wasn't sure he could be trusted. He'd been stupid, but if needed, he remembered a method of guaranteeing that the little man would be silent.

Back home, Steele knew an addict that had supported his own habit by reporting pushers, other than his own, to police. The authorities paid him for the information and looked the other way in his case. But the families of those arrested were not so forgiving. They threatened and forced the pusher to alter his product and, when the junkie injected his next fix of heroin, he immediately felt something was wrong. As his body began shaking, he realized that he had been given a "hot shot", a deadly mixture of heroin and strychnine.

Steele was sure that his combination would work as well as he unlatched and lifted the hood of his mail truck. It was simple. He was doing preventive maintenance, controlling the situation before it became a problem. He looked around but there was no worry. The streets of the base were relatively empty as he stepped onto the bumper, concealing the prize that he had captured from the aid station---a discarded syringe. He slipped off the needle's plastic cover, unscrewed a battery cap, and dipped in the tip. Extracting the plunger, the needle sucked up the bubbling acid until the reservoir filled.

Tucking the syringe inside his shirt pocket, the acid would be his protector, but no doubts were to exist. The second ingredient of this mixture was deadly.

He liked touching it, fingering it, and knowing that the pests of the fields even ate it. Kneeling next to the box, labeled in both English and Vietnamese with the words "Danger: Rat Poison" and a skull similar to his tattoo, Warren Steele rubbed a pinch of the white powder between his fingers and experienced a strange allure. The alkaloid was nearly identical to heroin.

Moments later, Steele sat behind the company out-house and figured, unless it was a burn day, the location and stench guaranteed his privacy. He squirted the battery acid from his syringe into an empty tin can, stirred in the strychnine, and then sucked the mixture back into the reservoir.

Limping toward his barracks, Steele tapped his pocket and felt both the syringe and a growing sense of confidence. The sulfuric acid-strychnine combination was an excellent weapon, even better than the M-16 that he carried in his mail truck, for it was silent, concealed, and instant. The poison-ous white dust still clung to his fingertips and this venom seemed to penetrate his system, preparing him to strike first as if he were pointman again. If it were in his best interests, he could easily justify his actions and eliminate anyone with just one jab. Just one push on the plunger would silence anybody who interfered with his heroin shipments. But no one, Steele swore, would ever do that and live.

Chapter 22

Saturday, April 25, 1970---2:16 p.m.

"Shut the hell up!" Mike Brooks yelled at the seventeen angry men that circled him. "I can't tell you any more than I know. Gomez told me double ammo for a three day mission, wearing flak jackets and steel pots. We lift off tomorrow morning."

Pat Graves stood near Brooks. Now a veteran of thirteen firefights and two months in the field, he asked, "Where we going?"

"My old pal Gomez didn't tell me," Brooks said. He thought about apologizing for yelling and for the sarcasm until the barracks door opened.

A soldier shuffled in, his head hidden from the half-circle of men by a duffel bag balanced on his shoulder. Dropping the bag, dust spiraled upwards and his face flushed from both the heat and being surrounded by the men. Their presence, standing near the door like an angry mob, startled him.

"Is this third platoon?"

"You got that right, dude," Howard Morrison answered.

"I'm Pfc. Arthur Wellington. My, uhh, friends call me Tiny."

No one spoke in return until an unknown voice said, "You don't have any friends here."

Tiny searched around the room for a friendly face but didn't see any. The men seemed somber and melancholy. "Who's Sergeant Brooks?"

"I am," Brooks said. "Are you the only new guy?"

"Come on, Mike," Morrison said impatiently. "Talk to the FNG later."

Tiny smiled and swallowed heavily. "What's up?"

"A mission that none of us want," Brooks said. "Let me finish then we'll square away your gear. You can have Cunningham's bunk."

Tiny nodded. The mood of this veteran platoon was gloomy and that worried him, but being an infantryman, a grunt, disturbed him even more. As he studied the faces of the veterans, something was wrong. He didn't fit here, didn't belong here, didn't know how he got here. Perhaps his father and mother had grown tired of his Ivy League freshman antics, tired of his lack of focus on his work, and tired of bailing him out with their wealth and prestige. In their desperation and annoyance, they concluded that it was time he grew up, built a resume of success, and that the army would harden him.

As he looked around, he would not believe that his parents would have wanted this, would not have knowingly thrown him here, not if they could see the men that surrounded him. Despite their young ages, they were hard and their expressions seemed to be diaries of conflicts that had aged them beyond their years. They were eighteen, nineteen, and twenty-year-old men, but they looked much older.

The war had turned them into walking corpses, jumpy and nervous, with sunken dark eyes and haunting stares. Yet, he was still different than them. His breed was one of a pedigree surrounded by poor mongrel junk-yard dogs and that alone frightened him.

Brooks twisted his gold chain and cleared his voice. "One strange thing...Gomez said we'd avoid contact."

Morrison choked on a swallow of beer and it dribbled onto his belly. "Bullshit!"

"Maybe he's been ordered to avoid firefights." Brooks scratched his head. "Hell, I don't know. Anyway, it's the same as usual at night. No poncho tents, no air mattresses, and no digging in. No noise and no silhouettes. Wake up anyone snoring…if you're lucky enough to get any sleep." He took a sip of Morrison's beer and then handed it back. "You'll like this one too. Since he doesn't want us being seen or heard, there'll be no automatic ambushes or trip flares."

"Great decision," Morrison said, throwing his beer can against the wall past Tiny's head and making him duck. "We'll just invite the VC to bee-bop into our perimeter."

Brooks looked at Pat Graves. "Pick up two flashlights, two .45s, and two machetes from supply."

"What for?" Graves asked and then paused. He held up his hand as if to halt Brooks' response. "I know...Gomez' orders."

"No telling what he has in mind," Brooks explained. "But, it don't mean nothin'. This mission is part of one big bad dream…a one year nightmare."

Howard Morrison tilted his jungle hat back. "No contact, but double ammo. No destination, but helmets and flak jackets." He thought for a moment. "How many other platoons are goin'?"

"Just us."

"How did we get so fuckin' lucky?" Morrison asked.

"I heard Gomez volunteered us."

The seventeen men grumbled and cursed. "He volunteered?" "That son of a bitch." "Why did we get stuck with him?" "That fuckin' lifer." "Shove a grenade up his ass." "Yeah, frag him."

He didn't know if they were bluffing, but Sufficool wanted no part of a fragging. It wasn't right…intentionally killing an officer and he tried to de-escalate the situation with a rhyme. "Don't ya'll get uptight, 'cause we can whip the VC in any fight. We bad...B-A-D." Cool spelled out the letters.

"Clarence is right," Doc Tyson spoke up. "Every time we hump extra ammo or expect a lot of shit, the mission turns out to be nothing. If we slack off, then the VC kick our butts as a little reminder."

Brooks studied the faces of his buddies and knew that they had already been on too many missions. Unknowingly, his observations were much like Tiny's first thoughts. Wrinkled brows and sullen tired eyes spoke of old men. They seemed shell shocked, men with "one thousand yard stares" in a war where they were always jumpy, a war that none believed held any purpose. They had been drafted into an aging process, a time machine fueled by dysentery, malaria, and the acid of worry. The war had drained their youth, muted their laughter, and stolen their innocence. They had arrived as virgins of war, but were now the old experienced whores. They'd been bred and bled in battle and had carried too many blood-soaked poncho liners to ever return.

"If everyone does their job and we keep our shit together, we'll be fine." Brooks' voice quivered as he stared into the men's eyes and felt the emotions. "Man, this platoon is like a marriage...it's until death do us part."

"Yeah," Morrison said, "but this could be a short marriage."

"And why even have a honeymoon?" Pat Graves asked. "We're already gettin' screwed."

"Piss on it…It's three more days off our calendars," Cool said, lumping the situation with all the other shitty details that faced the grunts. "It's just one more thing that the man throws at us, but we can take it. We can take anything."

The men said no more and then walked back to their bunks. Their silence was a gangrene of the soul, a quiet fear that grew as they cleaned their rifles and taped M-16 magazines bottom to bottom for faster reloading. Over and over, these men had faced the enemy, had taken chances, for two purposes only...to live and to help a buddy. Doc Tyson had run through a hail of bullets to retrieve an injured soldier. Morrison had charged a VC spider hole to add firepower. Cool held his position to call in deadly artillery support. Graves stood in a firefight, running forward and carrying more ammunition. All had run to the aid of a squad being pinned-down by VC fire.

No orders forced them. They were driven by an unspoken devotion, a silent love affair which bonded the men in the bush as brothers and which compelled them to gamble with their lives. But now they were afraid. Their minds never left the mission as their fear of the unknown scrambled their thoughts. Their inner spirits bid farewell to their families while their minds echoed Cunningham's screams, Steele's moans, and the stillness that surrounded Nelson and the lifeless bodies of others. They imagined themselves dying young, wondering if anyone would care, and they desperately searched for the comfort of companionship.

Howard Morrison took the picture of his wife and daughter from the wall, picked up his helmet, and stared at his wife's flower. He didn't have the heart to tell her that the poppy was a symbol of the poem "In Flanders Fields", a World War I epitaph written by a doctor, Lieutenant Colonel John McCrae, after he had witnessed his best friend's death. To Morrison, the flower was no more than a symbol of her love and beauty and he thought of her long brown hair and eyes as he squeezed the photograph inside the webbing of his helmet liner. He smiled at the image, staring at the picture until the loneliness moistened his eyes. He clutched Brooks' arm, remembering the ordeals of fire which were bearable only because he was there. He turned, forcing a half-smile at Brooks, the type of smile given in hospitals when there is nothing left but hope.

Morrison then seemed to recite a decree of doom. "Double ammo. One platoon. No trip flares. Gomez' leadership...I don't like this, Mike. I don't like this at all."

Chapter 23

Saturday, April 25, 1970---6:38 p.m.

Tears streamed down Butterfly's cheeks as she lowered her head and covered her face. Reaching through the barbed wire fence, Mike Brooks separated her hands and looked deep into her eyes. "What's wrong?"

"Butterfly no happy. Me no virgin. No married. Have baby."

Brooks leaned back in shock. In the darkened room and in the heat of their desires, he had not immediately noticed. Their first time together, their passion and their intimacy ignited in red flames, had also been her first time. Now his mind whirled. What the hell else could go wrong and what would his parents think?

Shock...disgrace...disappointment would be the reaction. His family would experience it all. Both of his parents had dropped out of high school during the Depression to work and both wanted him to go to college. But they would never expect or want this. As much as he loved her, his folks and even his sister would not understand or share his feelings.

He may not lose his life in Vietnam, but his parents would believe that he had destroyed it. They said little, but he understood their thoughts about race and interracial marriages. His mother had written a letter to him every day and they prayed for his safe return home, but neither would be happy if he returned with a Vietnamese wife, much less a baby. Still he couldn't control who he loved and, since Gomez' arrival, he didn't seem to have control over any aspect of his life.

"Brook-see," Butterfly said, bringing back his attention. She rubbed her still flat stomach. "Me uncle hears of baby. He wants me to return to village. You talk to him?"

The request was impossible unless they spoke on opposite sides of the wire barrier. Still, Brooks decided he no longer needed to explain himself to anyone or ask permission to love someone. He'd follow his heart and not the life his parents or her uncle desired for them.

"We'll get married, I swear it. But I can't talk to him until I can get the hell off this base."

"No can wait," she pleaded. "Me uncle, he come after me and take me away."

"I can't come!" Brooks yelled, feeling helpless and yet annoyed that she couldn't understand his confinement, his status as a prisoner of war. "Tell him to go to hell…Tell him to wait…I can't get a pass until next month."

Butterfly smashed her fist onto the fence, poking a barb into the edge of her palm. "Me never see you again. Baby from American shame my uncle. He kill baby. Maybe kill me and himself. You come…please!" She covered her face and began pleading in Vietnamese.

The high-pitched words irritated him, fueling the pressure already burning inside him until he boiled with anger. "Knock off the chattering!" He reached for her bloody hand, but she yanked it away from his touch. "I'll try in four or five days," Brooks said in desperation, trying to pacify her. "We have a mission tomorrow."

"Come tonight!" Butterfly demanded, staring into Brooks' eyes.

He was two feet away and yet she thought that he had become distant and indifferent. The barbed wire fence that separated them had become an emotional wall.

"If you luv me, you come tonight." She turned and rattled off some Vietnamese words as she ran away.

"Stop the gook talk!" Brooks shouted, feeling his face flush as red as the dust that he kicked up. Her tone of voice delivered the birth of a new resentment and he questioned why he'd even think of marrying her. He felt like casting her off like the shell of a cocoon, knowing that he could release this butterfly and be free. Still, even in his anger, he couldn't do it.

Brooks yelled to her, wanting to apologize, as she ran down the alley towards the back of the White Dragon. She did not stop, but only disappeared into the darkness. Brooks remembered Captain O'Brien's and Lieutenant Gomez' threats to court martial him and their orders to the gate guards to kill him if necessary. Thoughts of his confinement, the mission, the men, his parents, and now this pregnancy rolled in his mind until his anger exploded into a rage and he cried aloud, kicking and shaking the fence with all of his power.

Chapter 24

Saturday, April 25, 1970---6:58 p.m.

Instead of serving drinks inside, Butterfly sat behind the White Dragon, crying and reflecting on how her mismatched affair had alienated her. She loved only Brooks and she didn't think of boys in her past or men in her future. He was the first man to be given her heart and her body and he'd torn both of them apart. She felt as if she had been used, betrayed, and then sentenced to live alone in disgrace. No, not alone. Her future might hold a half-breed baby that neither society would accept nor cherish as one of its own. She could not escape her fate without Brooks and she might never escape Vietnam. She didn't know what to do, her life was in shambles and out of control, and nothing she could think of would resolve her problems.

She clutched her head, dug her fingers into her own scalp and twisted her hair, punishing herself while praying she could go back in time. She breathed deeply and rubbed her eyes, looking toward the rear exit of the bar and knowing she should return to work. She waited, unable to force herself to move. She listened to the music and laughter, but neither helped her mood. Sitting in the darkness, she stared at the back door, which was lit by only the glow of the front spotlights and the light from uncovered bulbs that squeezed around the door, surging or dimming with the pulsating mood of the generator.

Yearning, sick at heart, she rocked slowly and her thoughts focused on Brooks, the baby, and her uncle until the back door swung open and allowed smoke and Warren Steele to escape. Butterfly backed away, scooting into the shadows near a pond where frogs croaked and crickets chirped their songs of the night.

Moments later, Major Van Tri Quan marched down the stairs, approached Steele, and reached into his pants pocket. "Here are the six vials."

Steele shoved the heroin into his shirt pocket. "Let's get on with it."

Major Quan snapped open a leather attaché case and pulled out the hidden kilo of heroin, sealed in a clear plastic bag.

Steele took the bag, bounced it on his palm to judge the weight, and exchanged an envelope for it. As Quan pivoted around, Steele grabbed his arm. "Wait. You count the cash and I'll taste the scag."

"No need. That's numba one heroin."

"Yeah, but I believe in occasional quality control."

"Not necessary," Quan persisted.

"Hey." Steele put his finger up to Quan's lips. "Shut up."

Steele bit a corner of the bag and shredded a small opening. He wet his fingertip with his tongue, touched the heroin, and then tasted the white powder, expecting the bitter taste of pure heroin that he had tasted for more than a month. What he swallowed was not bitter…it was the bitter-sweet taste of heroin and finely granulated sugar mixed together. The two men looked at each other and Quan expected a reaction if caught, but not this.

"You cheating bastard!" Steele shouted as he smashed his fist into Quan's jaw and knocked him down. "I'll give you some sweetness."

Steele limped forward and kicked Quan in the ribs, crunching and separating them with his steel-plated boot. The major groaned and rolled into a ball, pulling his knees to his chest and clutching his ribs, while Steele shredded open the bag and poured the mixture onto Quan's face.

Quan coughed and sputtered, choking on the granules that sifted into his mouth and nose. He rubbed his eyes and attempted to block the downpour as Steele recited, "Ashes to ashes and dust to dust." Emptying the bag, he zeroed in on the center of the man's face, hoping to kick the nose cartilage up and into his brain.

Quan held out his hand begging for mercy. "No. No don't."

The plea stopped Steele as he considered another method of killing the man…a method that he wanted to verify. He pulled out his syringe filled with the sulfuric acid-strychnine solution, removed the needle's cap, and reached for Quan's neck. Death by injection was less evident than beating someone to death.

"I have more heroin. You kill me and no one will sell to you."

Quan's words sunk in like Steele's needle would have, pressing the point to his brain. The gook might be right. If the major were dead, he'd also kill his access to any more dope and his supply and profits would come to an immediate halt. Steele's face softened and he stepped back, capping the syringe.

"You won't hurt me?" Quan asked, still shaking and surprised at the level of attack.

"No." Steele shook his head. "Whatever gave you that idea?" He motioned for Quan to stand. "No, we're partners 'till the end. Just don't fuck with me."

Quan held his rib cage and stood, brushing the white powder from his face and hair. Straightening his back, jolts of pain caused dizziness and he hunched over, breathing in short gasps until the chest spasms eased. Slowly, he pulled out another bag from the case and handed it over.

Steele bounced the bag in his hand. "This kilo better be pure."

"First bag was big mistake. It belonged to someone else." Quan waited until Steele ripped open the plastic. "That good heroin."

"It better be good. For lying, you can go to hell...prematurely."

Steele didn't believe the excuse. The mistake was getting caught and trying to increase the profit margin. His business was not going to suffer because Quan wanted more.

Tasting the powder's authenticity, Steele was satisfied with the transaction and, despite their different ranks, he felt superior to the Vietnamese major. He stood close to the man and he looked into his eyes unblinking as he brushed away the heroin from the shoulders of the major's uniform. He then touched Quan's forehead with his finger and made the symbol of a cross in the white powder's residue. The major stepped back in pain and was dumbfounded by the scene, as Steele mocked the stance and voice of an overzealous evangelist, the kind that forced him to listen before his family was dished out a free supper at the mission. "You are now forgiven and have been redeemed."

Quan was still stunned by the response and by the puzzling words, but the drama amused Steele. Picking up the envelope of cash, he stuffed it into Quan's case and then tapped his finger on the man's chest, watching him flinch as he held the heroin next to the major's face and carried on the scene, prophesying, "Always bear this type of tithe, for next time you won't be saved." He spun Quan around, ordered *"dee-dee mau"*, get the hell out of here, and then watched him stagger away holding his side.

Butterfly had watched the strange events in horror, feeling the urge to run away and wishing she had done so during the confrontation. The beating, the inhumanity reminded her of the VC's treatment of her parents before their abdomens were slit open and their bowels spread on the ground. Their screams, their agony, all the memories rushed back and brought instant revulsion. Sitting in the shadows, there was no immediate escape from her memories or Steele and she shivered, wondering how long she would be forced to wait.

Warren Steele sniffed some heroin out of the bag and then shoved it inside his shirt when Tiny walked out the rear door of the bar. Steele called him into the darkness to complete the deal and in silence the vials were handed over in exchange for the money and whiskey. They both nodded and smiled, satisfied with the trade, but neither expected the interruption.

Shifting her body, Butterfly scooted over to better observe and cracked a twig. Steele pivoted around, wondering what had made that particular night sound and he stepped towards her, searching as he'd done for so many months as pointman.

The silhouette of the soldier stalked closer and closer and Butterfly trembled, her punctured hand shaking at his approach. Steele walked toward her, hunched over and crouched ready to spring, until Butterfly could no longer control her fear and she instinctively backed away.

Steele spotted the movement and yelled, "Come here!"

Butterfly scrambled to her feet and ran, but Steele lunged and tackled her. They rolled twice and when they stopped their feet touched the edge of the pond. Steele swung his leg over her chest and sat on her stomach, pinning her arms. He recognized her as Sergeant Brooks' girlfriend, but that hardly mattered.

"What'd you see, woman?"

Butterfly grunted and strained to pull free. "Nothing."

Steele's face stiffened and he slapped her. "Now, no games. What'd you hear or see?"

"Nothing."

Steele slapped her again, leaving a red imprint on her face and blood flowing from her nostrils and mouth.

Tiny ran up. "Please leave her alone."

"Get the hell out of my face!" Steele yelled and then waited for Tiny to retreat before his eyes again besieged hers. "I think you know the question." Silence greeted him and he backhanded her, whipping her head to the side and splitting her lip. She moaned and then inhaled deeply, sucking hard for a breath. She cleared her throat and spit a mixture of blood and sputum onto his cheek.

Steele's eyes widened. "You fuckin' gook bitch."

His arm swung across his chest like a pendulum gaining all of its power to swing the opposite direction and then he drove the back of his hand into her face. The blow splattered tears and blood as Butterfly cried aloud and lashed out, scratching and clawing at his flesh. Steele countered the attack by grabbing her throat and squeezing with all of his strength. Her air passage closed immediately and she thrashed her feet, splashing pond water and moss onto Steele. She tried to yell, but her voice only squeaked and each attempt only increased her panic and decreased her air. Her kicks slowed and finally ceased as her face changed color and her eyes shrouded Steele into an ever-darkening eclipse.

As her consciousness faded, Steele suddenly released his grip and twisted her around. She breathed deeply until he dragged her into the pond and shoved her head down. Butterfly struggled, knowing that she only had seconds to live, as water plunged into her nose and seeped into her mouth. She pinched his hands, hoping to snap his fingers loose, and tried to push off the pond's bottom. Steele only tightened his grip and pushed her deeper. Her lungs burned, feeling like they were smoldering and bursting into flames, and she could sense her life draining away as her hands slipped and her legs floated. Her vision clouded further and she could see only darkness. A darkness that would soon become permanent, even though only eight inches separated her from the surface, from air and from life. Her body and mind began to relax and her nearly unconscious state had accepted death until an intervening force beckoned.

"Please let her go," Tiny pleaded. He couldn't physically stop Steele, but he had to do something. Mustering the courage of a little boy, he cautioned, "You kill her and I'll report you."

Tiny's threat and doubts over what the woman had seen alarmed him and Steele realized that her death could also haunt him. If he drowned the girl, he'd have to kill Tiny as he could not afford a witness to the murder. It was becoming too complex, Steele figured as he yanked her head up by her hair and hauled her to shore.

Butterfly gasped and her chest pounded as Steele stood above her. "One warning, bitch." He then looked at Tiny. "The same message goes for you. If either of you tell anyone about tonight, you're dead. You understand…dead!"

Steele removed his hat, picking off bits of moss that Butterfly had kicked up off of the pond, and then dropped them onto her face. His emotions and adrenaline were slowing but he repeated his warning, "Squeal to anyone, especially Brooks, and you'll have uttered your last sound."

He then turned toward the base to remove his wet boots and trousers and was suddenly angered by his own reactions. He had always had a temper and, even as a boy, he had learned to strike first and think about the consequences later. Those instincts always brought him trouble, but tonight's actions were designed to avoid problems. Fear would insure Butterfly's and Tiny's silence and he needed fear to keep Quan honest. It was ultimately their choice to live or die, but he swore no one would interfere with his plans.

Walking back to the base, Steele's mood softened with the self-assurance that he had put the fear of death and god into all three of them. Their silence was guaranteed if they valued life and none could doubt that he would follow through on his threats. He was willing to bet their lives on it. Smiling, he pulled back the blue felt covering from Tiny's bottle of Crown Royal whiskey, opened it, took a drink, and then raised the bottle in a toast to himself…to silence, victory, and wealth.

Butterfly watched the men walk away as she coughed and spit up water. Her hands shook, trembling not from the wetness but from fear for herself and her unborn baby. She knew that Brooks would no longer be there to protect her and that silence was her key to life.

Tiny could feel his heart pound and his hands shaking. He could not believe how Steele had treated the woman nor had he ever witnessed such brutality. The violent response was unnerving, but the whole scene was their problem, not his. He wanted nothing more to do with either one of them. His words, his bluff, had luckily helped save her, but he wouldn't do it again. Steele was as mad and dangerous as a rabid dog. A certified head case that was capable of murdering them both with absolutely no remorse. Tiny sure as hell did not want that and he would definitely keep his distance and his mouth shut. Five days in-country and he never expected this type of problem. The only object he wanted, he already held in his hand and surely other people could sell him drugs.

He lifted one of the glass vials and remembered hearing about the excellent reputation of Vietnam heroin. Back in the states, he had twice experimented with a version of heroin that had been diluted down to only five percent purity, never questioning the drug's strength or its composition. He predicted that this Vietnam scag would make his mind zoom to new horizons, but he had no awareness of the drug's true strength or the fact that this heroin was nearly one hundred percent pure. Walking back to the White Dragon, Tiny stashed the vials in his pocket and decided not to immediately inhale them. He'd wait until the stress built even higher and compelled him to fly away from his fears.

Part III

Chapter 25

Sunday, April 26, 1970---5:45 a.m.

The prop wind from the two idling helicopters pushed Mike Brooks back and pelted him with sand. He leaned into the dust, counting the men and their helmets as they loaded. More than half of the steel pots were marked with graffiti. Colored hearts surrounded names like Kathy, Lucille, and Jasmine, peace signs, and FTA/"fuck the army" slogans were drawn on the helmets, while their elastic bands held plastic cigarette cases, bug spray, field dressings, and one small red poppy. But something new adorned their helmets. Several soldiers had scrawled---AB+, O-, A+---letters that matched their blood types.

In the darkness and despite threats of refusing to go on the undisclosed mission, the men were all present. Some men felt like it was the last day of their existence. But even in a dying and hated war, they faced their fears as they boarded in silence. They had complained, but they stood together, patriotic brothers in an unpatriotic war, courageous in a time of cowardice, and willing to fight when others turned away.

Neither Lieutenant Gomez nor Brooks had spoken to each other, but for once they would have agreed. These men, these draftees, had their act together and both were proud to serve with them.

The soldiers were solemn and tired and several were hung over from the previous night's stand down, but they were ready. The men had prepared their gear in advance of their drinking, but they had done more for this mission. Dog tags were tied and tucked into the laces of their jungle boots, eliminating the slightest noise of the metal disks clicking together. Men wrote what they considered might be their last letters home, words that seemed more sentimental. They carried miniature Bibles in their packs, wore their government-issued silver crosses, and prayed. Ever since Lieutenant Gomez had joined the platoon, Doc Tyson carried more medical supplies and the veterans who had known other leadership predicted it was just a matter of time before they were wounded or killed. This mission appeared to be the fulfillment of that bleak forecast.

Rumors of the special mission had spread throughout the base, but the men boarded alone. Brooks saw wisps of black smoke and smelled the odor of burning diesel and shit, their farewell bouquet.

Looking toward the darkened base, Brooks concluded that this expedition held no more respect than all of the rest. They were alone here and ignored at home. Their service was never appreciated and the soldiers themselves were the only ones who were thankful for the courage displayed. Rarely had the men ever heard praise of their bravery. At home, while most Americans carried on their normal lives, these draftees had been spit upon and called "baby killers" and "war mongers." The anti-war movement or the nation itself had never demonstrated their support of the troops, only the hatred of the war, and the emotion most often exhibited was the silence of shame and indifference.

Brooks looked at the men's faces and, as they stared back, he remembered photographs of solders of the Civil War, World War I, and World War II. All were frozen in time and all of the youthful faces seemed to reflect their pride and eagerness to fight the wars created by old men. The images held a strange fascination and Brooks was reminded of the men sitting around him. Only the uniforms had changed and any generation of boys and men could have had their faces transposed into the photographs.

They were young and eager at the war's beginning, but those faces were soon replaced by pictures of the dead, lying stiffly and contorted in the trenches and fields. Mouths were open, their valiant charges stopped in mid-stride as they yelled to frighten the enemy and muster their own courage. Brooks wondered what they had thought, what they had felt when they killed another human or when brothers fell, and yet he knew. The men and these ghosts were forever linked, sharing the same tests of manhood in different times. The experiences connected them. Not just the ordeal of battle, but enduring it all...Sleeping in the rain, struggling through the mud, vomiting from disease, scratching insect bites, living in filth, and dealing with dysentery-induced diarrhea soaking their pants, unable to change or stop the column's movement for fear of being left behind. The grunts of all wars knew the hardships and knew the sounds of weapons and of men's dying cries and the smells of blood and ripped intestine and gunpowder. These were their sullen bonds to the past and only those that had experienced it, understood it.

The shared experiences had molded the men. How could they not shape your mind and your memories and harden one's mind and soul? Brooks remembered his father's story of sitting on the frozen corpse of a Nazi soldier, using it as a hard bench as he calmly sat and ate his dinner in the snow. At that point, there was no right or wrong. One man simply sat and ate and hoped to live another day, while the other's hopes and dreams had vanished, washed away in a moment of violence.

Brooks looked again at the men. They were fighters and their families could be traced back a thousand years to warrior ghosts that had survived the test of battle. But their next test was coming. Pulling his flak jacket closed and tightly gripping his rifle, Mike Brooks wondered who would be standing at the end of this day.

The choppers had been in the air for only a short time, but Sergeant Brooks figured they were flying west. The glow of the rising sun glistened off the helicopters' tails and he had spotted the Ben Luc Bridge, the Mekong River, the Plain of Reeds, and the Hobo Woods. To the north, the aluminum-sheeting roofs of Saigon's slums reflected the sunrise. Some of the land was beautiful, pristine and untouched, while other terrain was pox-marked.

Created by thousands of exploding artillery and mortar shells, the land was a moonscape of water-filled craters which sparkled and held the colors and residue of Agent Orange. Some defoliated trees, still standing but lifeless, held the small parachutes from flares. From a distance, they appeared to be white orchids rocking with the breeze.

As they flew, their legs dangling out of the helicopter, Morrison nudged Brooks and pointed to the changing landscape. Fewer hooches dotted the land and the lush foliage of forests and rubber tree groves replaced the rice paddies. Fewer bomb craters could be seen and fingers of triple canopy jungle grew in the ravines and now jutted into the valley. Beyond the valley, the elevation increased as the mountains rose and the vegetation appeared to be all jungle.

The helicopter pilots quickly dropped altitude and switched to radio silence. They flew low and fast, following the contours of the land and skimming at treetop level. A sea of green screamed by as they climbed the hills, hoping this strategy would both muffle their sound and hide their location. The grunts smiled for the first time, with the wind rocking their helmets and wildly flapping their trousers, and they loved the ride. It was cool and fun and some imagined being back home, riding in a convertible with their lady on a beautiful day. They enjoyed the thought until the prop wind caught scattered wisps of clouds and tossed the mist onto the troops, baptizing them into a new type of warfare and refreshing them with a rebirth of resolution.

The choppers adjusted course, flying southwest of An Loc, and then shifted again to the west. They continued to fly low, barely above the top of the now ever-present jungle, and the troops yelled above the roar of the helicopters, pointing at vegetation that none had ever encountered and questioning the mission's objective.

As the airspeed slowed, Brooks gave the unneeded reminder to "lock and load", to secure a loaded magazine and chamber a round, as he leaned out and spotted a small plateau below the crest of a steep hill. The meadow was surrounded by rainforest and appeared to be the only area capable of landing. The LZ looked like a perfect ambush site, but the men hoped for the best as they scooted about the floors of the choppers, preparing to exit. They noticed the musty smell of dampness and rot being held captive by the jungle, but thought the landscape was as beautiful as the Garden of Eden and just as capable of sheltering its serpents.

The door gunners were ordered to go in "cold", not firing to maintain a quieter approach, when the helicopters suddenly dipped and hovered above the meadow. The soldiers jumped off the skids and the grass sliced their hands and faces as they dove for cover. They listened for shots and watched beads of dew vibrating with the choppers' gusts and sparkling against the dawn's reflection. In less than two minutes, the machines had spewed out its human cargo and left only the lingering smell of fuel and the fading hum of their engines.

The huge trees loomed down upon the meadow as if the men were gladiators, standing in an arena and awaiting their fate with a simple thumbs-up or thumbs-down. Left by the choppers, these twenty men were now isolated and alone and there wasn't any immediate back-up. Their only support was through their radios and Brooks didn't like that. Radios could fail. Mountains could block transmissions, batteries could weaken, or the NVA could interfere with the signals.

The sudden hiss and crackle of Cool's radio made Brooks twist around and he spotted the antenna, sticking above the grass. Lieutenant Gomez sat next to Cool, checking his map and wondering if he had made the right decision. Still, it was too late to second guess and he felt confident that this would be a memorable mission, one that would bring him the captain's bars, glory, and success. All doubts had vanished as he watched Brooks approach and listened to Cool relay the coordinates of their position back to the firebase. It was time to go to work.

"We're now on radio silence and on our own." Gomez said. The comment was directed more to himself than to either Cool or Brooks.

Brooks looked around and checked his watch, thinking of the air time and direction of flight. "This is Cambodia, isn't it?"

Gomez nodded as he stood. "We're to pinpoint the Commie Central Office."

"My idea and the military's idea of 'seeing the world' differ somewhat," Brooks said in a matter-of-fact manner, waving for Pat Graves and Tiny to advance and take the point and drag. "Will this be our pickup point?"

Lieutenant Gomez tipped his steel pot towards his eyes. "Affirmative…on Tuesday morning." He checked his rifle safety. "Now," he said, walking toward the edge of the meadow, "let's stop the cluster-fuck and get the hell out of this clearing."

Zipping up his flak jacket, Gomez waited until Graves and Tiny stood in front of him and then he pointed to a small animal trail, wet from the rain, climbing to the west. "You're looking for a very large bunker complex and you'll know it if you see it."

A very large bunker complex was not what he wanted to find, Pat Graves thought, as he re-checked that he had chambered a round and then forced a worried smile at Brooks.

"Rub your medallion for me. I'll need all the good luck I can get." Graves paused, thinking. "Better yet, polish it for me."

Gomez said nothing, but remembered in Korea that soldiers would tap the top of his helmet for good luck. He didn't like them touching him and the superstition didn't work for them, but deep down Gomez hoped that Brooks' medallion would help on this particular mission.

Lieutenant Gomez glanced at each member of the platoon, knowing that any observers would not be able to determine rank and responsibilities. Spec. 4 Sufficool would stand out with his radio, but the other men's status was defined by their actions and the weapons they carried...M-79 grenade launchers, M-60 machine guns, or M-16s. In the Delta, Gomez guessed that the VC maintained a killing preferential order: officers first, followed by medical corpsmen, and then radiomen. Although they'd be pleased to kill any American soldiers, killing them in that order assured no direction, no medical response, and no immediate help. It was a theory, put into practice, of letting them bleed and die in confusion.

Besides the black first lieutenant's bars on his shoulders, nothing distinguished Gomez as an officer. He, as well as all of the veterans, proudly wore the cloth Combat

Infantry Badge above their pockets, except Doc Tyson, whose shirt was adorned with the Combat Medical Badge. All had earned their distinction months before, surviving their first firefight and entering an exclusive brotherhood. Months had passed since their status as virgins of war had ended with exploding projectiles and a hail of bullets. All had experienced the bond of shock, fear, and pain and they were battle tested and bloodied…all except the "cherry", the new replacement.

Now, as Gomez watched Pat Graves take the point and Pfc. Arthur "Tiny" Wellington climb the hill behind him, he wondered about the future. He had never backed away from a fight, never shirked his duty. In fact, if he were honest with himself, he always wanted to fight, always wanted to be in control. It seemed to be in his breed, in his character, and years of war had only tempered this spirit. But to his confusion and on this occasion, he was struck by the hope that the new man would not earn the badge on this particular mission and that he would indeed remain a virgin.

Chapter 26

Sunday, April 26, 1970---6:27 a.m.

Pfc. Pat Graves stared at the jungle forest ahead and it reminded him of Oregon's Blue Mountains where he had hunted deer and elk. He was at peace and free in those mountains, but not these. Time would tell but he already felt suffocated and, in a short time, he could be the hunted, not the hunter.

Moving up the hill and into the shadows, Graves looked back at the men forming the single column line behind him. His hope, as well as theirs, was that he would not lead them into an ambush. He felt the burden of their safety and fear mounted as he walked into the jungle, silently reciting the 23rd Psalm: *"Yea, though I walk through the valley of the shadow of death, I will fear no evil."* Others had added the sacrilegious line *"because I'm the meanest son of a bitch in the valley"*, but that wasn't his belief. His religion comforted him, but his fears still grew as he climbed and repeated, *"For thou art with me."*

Tiny's feet dragged behind Graves, heavy not only from the red mud clinging to his boots but from the fear that bogged him down. In this country, his nickname was appropriate. He was miniscule and inconsequential to the other soldiers. None of the veterans, besides Sergeant Brooks, had spoken more than a few words to him in the last two days. When they did speak, he wasn't called Arthur or even Tiny. He was now named FNG, Fuckin' New Guy, Cherry, or New Meat. They had little use for him on base and even less out in the bush. He walked directly behind the pointman for only one reason…if the NVA sprung an ambush, all of the veterans were behind him, and sacrificing him and Graves would give them a chance to live.

The thought of being a sacrificial lamb terrified him until his mind was distracted by a simple sound. His heroin vials had clinked together, enticing his desire, and he wished the magic powders would exorcize the demons that devoured his courage. He craved one vial to settle his screaming nerves and one to rescue him and carry him away from the terror of his first mission. But now, he could only touch his shirt pocket and follow Graves.

Howard Morrison watched Pat Graves and the FNG---Tony, Tiny, Tommy, or whatever his name was---climb the hill and wondered why they were even taking the cherry on this mission. Still he knew the answer. The new guy was a draftee like all the rest, was a trained soldier of the U.S. Army, and he met all of the current qualifications of an American draftee----he could walk, talk, and chew gum at the same time and furthermore he had an operating set of ears, eyes, legs, and arms. Morrison smiled, amusing himself. The FNG was a fine specimen of the American fighting man.

Stepping into line, Morrison took one last look at the picture of his wife and daughter and then mumbled to no one in particular, "I'm gettin' too short for this shit."

The quiet words had been an attempt at humor, an uplifting of spirits, but seemed only melancholy. Walking up the hill and past Mike Brooks, Morrison nodded his feelings of reassurance, tapped his fist against his heart, and then he and Brooks touched fists. Simultaneously, they mouthed the word "Brothers" to each other.

Sergeant Morrison wasn't sure how the other men felt, but he could already feel a slight tingling in his legs from the pack's weight and the incline. As he climbed, he removed his helmet and held it in his hands. He plucked the small poppy from the headband, knowing the bright red color would be illuminated during the day amid a sea of green. It was not a color associated with the jungle and he could not chance having it be seen. Staring at the poppy and remembering his promise to safely return it, he kissed the flower, stuck it inside his helmet liner with the picture of his wife and child, and trudged up the hill.

One by one, the soldiers followed the pointman. When it was Mike Brooks' turn, he entered the single file column, walked out of the meadow, and into the jungle, a primeval rainforest. Vegetation climbed, wet and green and tangled, to three distinct levels and created a triple canopy that either shaded the men or cast dark ominous shadows. The men clambered up, bending, dodging vines and limbs and creeping forward and the column soon disappeared. Swallowed by this green monster, it smelled of death and decay and seemed offended by the light. The jungle closed in, as if to entangle and prey on them, and Pat Graves occasionally swung his machete to clear a path. He looked up. The domed and interlinked branches of the trees held moss-covered vines and he imagined it as being the boney crescent of Satan's mouth preparing to devour them.

The men, unused to the steep mountains and heavier packs, breathed heavily and strained to climb the slippery trail. Some fell, rolling and banging elbows and knees, and silently cursed as no one dared to speak aloud. The men imitated the man in front of them and all imitated the pointman. When Pat Graves stopped, the column nervously froze in place. When he crouched down, they squatted, pointing their weapons to opposite sides of the trail, while their eyes darted, searching for clues, and they strained to hear above their pounding hearts.

Near the top of the hill, Pat Graves signaled for a break while Brooks watched the line of men and realized that none were prepared physically for the mission. Their loaded packs and the extra M-60 machine gun ammo, crisscrossing across their chests, weighed them down. They were flatlanders, used to the level rice paddies, not mountains. But now they climbed.

Except for eagle flights, they had patrolled at night, but now the hot temperature of the day baked and exhausted them. Pat Graves set the machete down and stared at the blisters forming on his palms. Lieutenant Gomez checked his plastic-covered map, splattering it with drops of sweat. Cool slumped against a tree trunk, digging his heels into the slope, and guzzled half of the Kool-Aid in his canteen. Sergeant Morrison urinated with his pants pulled low, exposing the red splotches of ringworm that covered his buttocks. Doc Tyson handed out malaria pills and salt tablets, while Tiny buried his face into his neck towel.

Mike Brooks wiped the sweat from his brow. This mission, this ordeal had to be part of a trial and error experiment. Even if it were true that Gomez volunteered, why would third platoon have been approved for this mission? It didn't make any sense for a unit used to patrolling in the Mekong Delta to suddenly find itself in triple canopy jungle. There had to be a reason, but he couldn't figure it out.

They had been ordered to avoid contact and find the Communist Central Office and Brooks hoped that could be done without firing a shot. But if that could not be accomplished, he did like one aspect of this assignment---anyone spotted in the jungle would be a combatant, an NVA soldier. This time there would be no questions and no doubt if a firefight erupted. In the Delta, he was never sure and he always felt surrounded by an enemy that was everywhere and nowhere. With no uniforms, they were invisible and no one could feel, see, or touch them until after curfew. Even then, with a body sprawled at their feet, the uncertainty persisted as to whether the corpse was a legal kill. Here, there would be no doubt.

Sergeant Brooks walked to the end of the column and then backtracked uphill to the point, checking the men's condition and reminding them that no one was to smoke during the day on this mission. It was an unneeded reminder for the soldiers. Their nerves and body might crave a cigarette, but all of the men knew this wasn't the time or place. They were all aware that lighting one at night, even under a poncho, made the fabric glow and, if they were smoking, they weren't watching. They all counted on each other and the lack of attention, the smoke, smell, or the glowing embers could be a death warrant for all of them.

In the Delta, they waited until day break or until they returned to Rach Binh to smoke, but no one in third platoon smoked at night. All had heard the story of "the third man on a match". The enemy would see the match light the first cigarette, raise their weapon and aim as the second man's cigarette was lit, and fire at the third man receiving a light. Superstition or not, no one wanted to be the third man and all agreed with a smile that a bullet, even more so than the smoking, could be a real hazard to one's health.

Stopping at the point, Brooks squatted next to Pat Graves. "Seen anything?"

"Nope." Graves slapped a red ant crawling up his shirt sleeve. "It all looks the same after a while."

Brooks listened but saw something up the hill. It was strange, a change of color, maybe a reflection that had grabbed his attention. His face tightened and his body tensed. Squinting his eyes, he leaned forward and tried to figure out what he was seeing.

Graves saw the change in Brooks and his hand tightened on his M-16. "Gooks?"

"Maybe."

Brooks passed the word for the line of men to wait and then he and Graves moved forward fifty meters and stopped near the crest of the hill. They kneeled and crawled to the edge of a smooth dirt road which ran perpendicular to their line of travel. No enemy personnel or vehicles were spotted and the area appeared deserted. But they had been there. The muddy road was covered with tracks from bicycle tires, trucks, and sandals. A glint of light, possibly what Brooks saw, reflected off green metal sheeting that covered a roofed platform and protected numerous gunny sacks on the opposite side of the road. The men waited and listened. It was quiet and the only sign of life was a rusted bicycle, leaning against a tree.

Brooks looked both ways. "Let's check it out."

They ran across the trail, stopped behind the platform, and Brooks tore a small hole along the seam of a bag. Rice dribbled out. "This is not on our ration list."

Graves nodded. "I was afraid of that."

Leaning back, Brooks pointed at a square, ground-level opening. Bamboo formed a perimeter edging, probably used to divert water away from the hole. "Tunnel?"

"I don't know," Graves whispered. In his two months as pointman, he had never seen an entrance like it in the Delta and hoped that the lieutenant would order them to bypass the area.

Within minutes, the column of soldiers trotted across the road with the squads splitting at the rice cache. Lieutenant Gomez acknowledged that the cache wasn't their objective, but the amount of food and possible weapons were definitely worth destroying. The elimination of any supplies would be a setback for the NVA and he figured months or maybe years had been required to bring this rice to the south. Any disruption of the supply lines was a victory.

Gomez estimated their location, marked it on his map, and looked at Brooks. "Pick someone to go in the hole."

"I'll do it," Brooks volunteered rather than sending someone else. He had resigned himself to make the best of the situation and he agreed that any weapons or supplies destroyed in these sanctuaries would help the Americans and South Vietnamese.

Pat Graves looked back at Tiny. His size would be perfect for a tunnel rat, but he also acknowledged that the FNG didn't have any experience. Graves chambered a round in his pistol and switched on a flashlight. "No. I'll go."

Brooks nodded approval and aimed down in the hole as Tiny imitated him. Graves circled the entrance, pointing his .45 and shining the light into the opening. He saw only bamboo mats intricately weaved together and covering the floor and that worried him. The side walls could not be seen, but more importantly, men could be waiting below with their weapons ready to kill him. He thought of Nelson and wondered if he was about to make the same big mistake.

A bamboo ladder lay next to the hole, but Graves had no intention of using it. He could be stepping into a trap, plus he had already ignored two pieces of past advice---never volunteer and toss in a grenade before checking out a tunnel or bunker. He learned that lesson on his first mission when Nelson failed to blow the spider hole and it cost him his life. Now, he had volunteered and he couldn't throw a grenade into the bunker due to the noise. He had no choice but if he was going to die, let it be quick.

Graves jumped into the hole and fell eight feet, splintering the mats and toppling onto his side. He snapped the pistol and flashlight up, spun around, and watched the beam of light dance like a ghost on the sidewalls. He unknowingly chewed on his bottom lip and felt the urge to shoot until he realized what he had hoped---he was alone.

The room was as cool as a crypt and yet his chest burned like the fires of a crematorium and his body anointed itself with sweat. Despite cases of AK-47 ammunition and a single B-40 rocket launcher stacked in a corner, Graves thought this must be a sleeping area…one that would serve to escape the heat and insects and could be easily modified into a fighting position. Crouching next to another tunnel, level with the floor, he ducked his head down and quickly surveyed a passageway which traveled nearly ninety feet and then curved sharply.

Graves guessed that the tunnel was an escape route from fighting or bombing and that it might link up with another bunker. He was deep in thought, concentrating on the tunnel, when those thoughts were shattered by the loud cracking of the bamboo mats behind him. Startled, Graves spun around, pointing the pistol and light, ready to fire.

Brooks swatted the pistol away from his face and yelled as he backed up, realizing he had made a rookie mistake by jumping in the hole and not alerting Graves. "Don't shoot!"

Pat Graves momentarily set down the pistol and then, using his hand and finger, acted like he just shot Brooks. He lowered his head, exhaling loudly and felt his hands shake. "Are you crazy? I almost killed you." He picked up the pistol. "Pull your head out. I'm already jumpy."

Both soldiers inhaled deeply, capturing a breath of air and feeling their edginess ease.

Brooks smiled, lucky to be alive. "You could have spoiled my whole day."

Graves agreed with a half-smile and then removed his helmet and searched the tunnel walls for support beams.

There were none. Only the smell of moisture and tree roots fingered their way into the hole. The passageway was no more than three feet wide and high, but that was enough room. Stretching out his arms, he squeezed in and crawled forward.

His elbows scraped the side walls and, in a matter of feet, they were rubbed raw. Perspiration covered his body and his pistol and flashlight felt slick as the sweat burned the broken blisters on his hands. He didn't like heights, but now he also felt claustrophobic. The walls seemed to close in and the air seemed scarce. Panic built in his chest and he breathed rapidly, picturing himself stuck in the shaft. There was no room to look back and he hoped that the tunnel would lead to a larger room where he could safely emerge.

Sliding forward, clods of dirt tapped his head and he blinked as dust floated into his eyes. At the corner, Graves peeked at what appeared to be another room, lit by a second entrance, and he grinned with satisfaction. He'd soon rejoin the platoon and escape from this hell. He twisted halfway around the corner until a shadow blocked the light. He wondered if another platoon member was checking out the room until he saw an NVA soldier kneeling at the opening and staring at the flashlight. Both men knew trouble was on its way. Shoving the muzzle of his AK into the tunnel, the soldier fired a burst of four shots.

Graves had played it cautious. He had already backed up when he spotted the moving shadows and had just retreated around the corner when the bullets zinged past his head and smashed into the end wall.

"Gooks!" Graves shouted, pushing backwards into the front section of the tunnel and jerking off two random shots into the dark.

Above the ground the shots sounded like distant pops of thunder, but inside the tunnel the discharges boomed. Graves yelled and covered his ears, feeling like his ear drums had ruptured. Scooting backwards, chunks of earth struck his legs.

Brooks looked into the passageway but could do nothing other than watch Graves retreating. He had nearly returned to the safety of the first room when the tunnel's roof collapsed and smashed down on his upper body. Pat Graves tugged and strained, but it was no use. The dirt blocked his ability to push with his arms. The flashlight shined in his face, but he could not move it. His upper body was buried and he had no idea where his pistol was. Clawing and struggling against the dirt and its weight, he was still unable to back up and couldn't see anything other than the light lying against his cheek. His air was nearly gone and, when he tried to breathe, he sucked dirt into his open mouth. Terror struck as he coughed repeatedly, expelling the last air in his lungs and all hope. He was dying in this man-made grave and feelings of helplessness, panic, and doom set in. He was unable to stop it and death was coming. His vision darkened like a black curtain slowly closing and covering his eyes as he lapsed toward unconsciousness.

"Find another entrance!" Brooks shouted to the soldiers above ground and then stretched into the tunnel, grabbing Graves' boots. His fingers tensed, demanding the release. Pulling with all of his might, the body slid into the open room like a baby being forcibly extracted from a mother's womb.

Howard Morrison had recognized the sounds of the AK and had belly-crawled to the second hole. Pulling the pin and releasing the lever of a grenade, he counted until three seconds to detonation and dropped it through the opening. The grenade exploded and white smoke was still rising when he jumped into the opening. The room was clouded with smoke, but Morrison didn't worry about that. He'd stuck his hand out as he landed and a thick wetness now coated it. Jerking away, Morrison saw the man, fired into the NVA's chest, and then realized he'd just shot a dead man.

Pat Graves sat above ground, coughing and wheezing and rubbing his eyes in a futile attempt to soothe the burning. Some relief came when Doc Tyson tilted Graves' head and poured canteen water into his eyes, washing away the dirt. The pointman continued to cough and rub his eyes, then swallowed the water and wiped off his muddy face with his towel. He breathed deeply, sucking in the cool refreshing air, and said a prayer of thanks under his breath.

As his vision cleared, Graves stood and stared at the entrance hole that had become his personal tomb, his premature burial. "Graves in a grave. I don't appreciate the irony and I hope this isn't an omen of the future."

Graves had emerged, dusty and shaken, but unharmed and Lieutenant Gomez was relieved. He needed him as pointman and the lieutenant knew that he had made a mistake by exploring the rice cache and bunker. Hopefully, no one had heard the shots nor would anyone discover the body that would be dragged into the jungle and hidden. He had deviated from the mission and the lieutenant could only hope that there would not be any ramifications.

Chapter 27

Monday, April 27, 1970---9:41 a.m.

None of the third platoon members had ever seen anything like it. And what they observed created immediate tension and fear and they froze, moving only their eyes. They had counted forty-three NVA soldiers walking single file along the road below them and, even though the Americans held the strategic high-ground and could have sprung an efficient ambush, they waited anxiously in hiding as the column passed.

The men had seen only a few NVA in the Delta and most of those had blended in with the Viet Cong. They wore civilian clothes, either black trousers or shorts coupled with a white or black shirt or no shirt at all. These NVA soldiers were dressed differently. They wore complete khaki uniforms, including sandals and pith helmets, and all carried AK-47 rifles. The twenty Americans may have killed all of them if the ambush was sprung properly, but now was not the time. They needed to follow them to their destination, hopefully the Communist Central Office, but not on the road. Walking the trail would be much easier, but they'd be the ones ambushed.

The previous night had been quiet and uneventful as hoped. None had slept well, only dozed, but they felt refreshed and alert and calmer because their worst fears of the night had not been realized. They were calmer but still agitated and worried. Since entering the jungle, none of the men had spoken above a whisper. They continued that mode of operation, using hand signals to communicate, as the platoon moved along the ridge, paralleling the north-south road and following the route of the patrol.

Pat Graves had gained new respect for his fellow pointmen who operated daily in the jungle. He tried to watch his front and the road below, clear a path and be quiet, and see the enemy before they saw him. It was next to impossible. Their faded green fatigues blended well into the jungle, but it was the noise that worried him. A cough, the whistle of the swinging machete, the breaking of brush, or someone spotting their movement would be disastrous. So far they had been lucky. The platoon had been quietly taking a break when they saw the NVA patrol. That alone was a miracle and they could only hope more miracles would follow.

Shoving a branch aside, Graves swore under his breath when the limb recoiled and swatted him on the face. He paused and looked at the blisters and festering scratches of vines and thorns on his hands and then cocked his machete and angrily chopped off the branch that had whipped him. Hacking through the underbrush paralleling the trail was crazy, but following the route of the NVA patrol was fuckin' crazy.

Graves glanced up. The jungle canopy and the overcast sky dimmed the rays and colored the area with shades of green and black. The humidity rose while the clouds hung barely above the jungle, growing thicker and darker. The clouds cooled the temperature but it wasn't enough. Sweat dripped from his face and he could taste the white film sticking to his lips and teeth. He breathed open-mouthed, but the air only seemed to evaporate and vanish as the heat stole it from his lips. This patrol was one of endless steps and numbing fatigue. Not counting his helmet, flak jacket, and M-16, Graves guessed he was humping eighty pounds of ammo, C-rations, grenades, flares, and other equipment in his pack. He tugged on his pack straps to tighten them, hoping to avoid rubbing his shoulders raw. All he wanted was to slouch under the weight and walk, thinking of nothing...but he couldn't do that. In this game, winners won the right to live.

Along the ridge, heat waves bent upwards as the humidity seemed to swell his body, pounding with each heartbeat. It was ironic. His body and shirt were soaked with water but little remained in his canteens. One was empty and he was halfway through his second. He craved the water but knew that he had to wait. There would be no re-supply choppers coming. He had planned for a three day mission in the Delta, not here. Another day and a half of humping the boonies and only half a canteen left and no water source in sight. He didn't know how much longer he could go and wondered whether the temperature or the enemy would strike first.

In less than a mile, Graves received his answer when Tiny passed on the message in a whisper. "Hold up. Someone's down."

In the middle of the column, Cool held his head as if to contain the pounding while rolling over and vomiting. Doc

Tyson shoved Cool's helmet aside and then touched his wrist and checked the pulse.

He counted the beats, glancing up at Mike Brooks and Lieutenant Gomez, and then whistled softly. "One hundred and eighty beats per minute."

"What's normal?" Gomez asked as he stripped off Cool's radio.

"Sixty to eighty beats. His heart's pounding...just like he's running."

Tyson reached into one of his aid bags, pulled out a vial, and shook out four salt tablets while Brooks lifted Cool into a sitting position and tapped his face. Cool rocked dizzily, his eyes opened in a distant gaze, and his lips shivered. Murmuring that he was sorry for holding up the patrol, embarrassed that he was down, Cool took the canteen but lowered it unconsciously. Tyson noticed the disorientation and helped the radioman drink and swallow the tablets.

"How much time do you need?" Gomez asked as he fanned Cool.

Tyson splashed water on the man's head and chest and massaged his arms and legs. "Three hours minimum."

"We can't wait that long and we can't call in a medevac. We'd be pinpointing ourselves." Gomez pulled out his map and pointed to a blue line. "We'll douse him with the water from our canteens and then push to this stream. You have exactly thirty minutes."

Doc Tyson wet his green handkerchief, held it against Cool's forehead, and whispered to Gomez, "You're the boss. But if he travels farther, count on heat stroke."

Within minutes, Tyson's prediction became reality. Clarence Sufficool staggered like a drunkard groping through a maze. His arms swayed, grasping for balance, his legs wobbled, and then he suddenly collapsed, twitching in convulsions. His glazed eyes were unblinking and yet his entire body seemed to vibrate forcing his arms to swing uncontrollably.

Doc Tyson touched Cool's forehead. He was burning up. Unsnapping an aid bag, the medic extracted a bottle of saline solution and then unwound a plastic tube with a cone-shaped plunger on one end and a syringe on the other. He jabbed the plunger into the bottle top and inverted it. His anger bubbled up like the enclosed air and he cursed himself for following Gomez' orders to move and for not starting an IV sooner. As Cool squirmed and the solution ran through the tubing, Tyson hoped it wasn't too late.

Mike Brooks straddled Cool's body, pinning him down and gagging his cries, as Tyson tied surgical tubing around an arm and patted the collapsed veins. He pushed the needle through the skin above the brachial artery, but raised only a hematoma. An ever-enlarging bubble grew under the skin as the blood leaked out. Knowing that the syringe was not properly seated in the artery, Tyson reversed the procedure. He unclamped the tube, leaving the tourniquet in place and adjusted the needle. The blood pressure in the artery, created by the pounding heart and the tourniquet, promptly pushed the blood up the plastic tubing toward the bottle.

"Got it!" Tyson said, unsnapping the tourniquet and allowing the blood to reverse its upward path.

Tyson taped the syringe down and adjusted the saline's drip flow as Cool twisted and curled in total motion. His arm and leg muscles jerked and tightened with spasmodic contractions, his head swung from side to side, and he moaned in varying pitches between his shallow irregular breaths. The fluids within his body had been diminished to critical levels, evaporated by the heat, and he was dying a cruel death.

Doc Tyson touched the dry hot skin of Cool's forehead and hoped that the saline would again create sweat to cool the man. It was evident that the radioman should be airlifted out, but that was impossible. An incoming helicopter would alert the NVA to their exact location and many could die to save one.

The medic stood and whispered to Lieutenant Gomez, not wanting Cool to hear a message that could send him further into shock. "The IV and water will help, but if we don't get him cooled down, he's a dead man."

Chapter 28

Monday, April 27, 1970---2:08 p.m.

The heat and humidity increased the soldiers' sense of urgency and they dropped to their bellies at random potholes, pushed moss and pollywogs aside, and drank the stagnant water. Their canteens were empty, all of the contents splashed on Clarence Sufficool to lower his temperature, and now they were in peril, their bodies crying out for water, any water.

The soldiers' mouths were dry, their tongues seemed to swell, and swallowing became painful. They were not concerned about dysentery or stomach cramps, nor were they concerned with the invisible microorganisms swimming in the brackish "pollywog piss" that they gulped down. In their desperation, they thought of drinking their own urine to prolong life and they accepted the idea as they watched the radioman bounce and convulse on the litter.

Sufficool moaned and squirmed, feeling like his head was exploding, as the litter bearers tried to control their descent and maintain balance. The mud made an orderly evacuation impossible and they slipped and fell and banged his body on the ground. The men strained to control their descent and every few meters the six men stopped, pulled his body back to the center of the portable stretcher, and pushed on.

The men heard the stream's growl about the time the convulsions ceased, but they questioned if it were too late. The weight that the radioman carried exceeded many others and Cool also carried extra munitions, smoke grenades, and hand flares. The heat and the weight had dragged him down, stripping him of his body fluids, and possibly his chance to live. Brooks wondered if there would soon be others. The platoon members, with the exception of Tiny, had sipped from their canteens one last time and then gave up their water to be swallowed by and splashed on Cool. No doubt existed that he would have given up his water for them and, without complaint, they'd do whatever was necessary to save him.

All except one felt that way and Brooks was still angry with Tiny. He begrudgingly relinquished his canteen only after he drank most of the remaining water. Brooks had watched him gulp it down and felt like slapping the canteen from the lips of the spoiled little prick. The FNG had not made any connections with the other soldiers and simply did not care about Cool or anyone else except himself.

Mike Brooks poured the small amount of water into another canteen, combining it for the radioman, and then tossed the empty canteen back into Tiny's chest. Other men had noticed the FNG guzzle down the water and Brooks offered a warning to Tiny, after seeing the men's reaction.

"Count on an ass kicking when we return to the base."

"Yeah," Morrison agreed as several other soldiers nodded. "Count on it."

Blood dripped from Mike Brooks' hand where the litter strap sliced his flesh. Small pebbles and mud clung to the other hand where twice he had shoved it down, fighting to stay upright and holding the stretcher off the ground. His shoulders ached under the weight of his pack and cramps knotted his legs, jabbing him with sharp pains as he struggled to maintain his balance. Little remained of the saline solution splashing in the bottle and there was no time to stop or rest. Brooks hoped for Cool's recovery, but also prayed that the sounds of breaking brush, falls, and swearing in this noisy retreat to the stream would not alert any passing NVA patrols. If they were heard, there'd be hell to pay.

The blue line on Gomez' map represented the stream, but it looked much different than what they expected. Brownish-red colored water, choked with eroded silt and algae, rolled around the granite boulders, roaring and hissing its displeasure at the delay. Only the eddies, hiding behind the smooth rocks, swirled slowly and allowed foam to circle contrary to the main current. The red-tinged water may not have been picturesque, but the color was appropriate and the rushing stream was indeed the lifeblood of the soldiers.

Doc Tyson and Mike Brooks threw down their gear and jumped into the churning water as the other soldiers dragged Cool to the stream's edge and handed him down. His arms were still linked to the IV and floated limply but all were thankful that no other men had fallen to heat stroke.

Lieutenant Gomez directed Pat Graves and half of the platoon to walk a few meters upstream while the other half followed Sergeant Morrison downstream. After the men spread out and the perimeter was established, Gomez pointed to one man from each squad to fill their canteens, drink, and wet their uniforms.

Gomez was the last to partake in the prescribed ritual. He made sure all of the men were watered and rested before he dropped water purification tablets into his own canteen and drank. The lieutenant maintained discipline despite the men's desire for water. Without him, the troops may have randomly jumped in the stream and failed to provide each other with security. The men had waited anxiously for their turn, but they stayed focused and knew that this discipline might keep them alive.

Brooks touched Cool's cheek and felt both a bond of brotherhood but also a feeling of helplessness. It was the same helplessness that he had felt when he and Butterfly had argued two days before. He simply could not do anything to help then or now. Standing in the swirling water, he watched Cool's eyes wander and listened to his incoherent mumbling. For a moment, Brooks' thoughts turned somber as he imagined the growing life of his child and the fading existence of his friend.

"We saddle back up in fifteen minutes," Lieutenant Gomez said, pacing the shore. "We'll have to leave Cool behind."

"The hell we will!" Doc Tyson said, snatching the words from Brooks and jabbing the plunger into another bottle of saline. "I want him stabilized. If you order me to leave him, I will. But if you get hit, don't yell for a medic 'cause I won't hear you. If that happens, you can kiss your ass good-bye."

Doc Tyson was the only man Gomez couldn't replace and the one man whose threats he acknowledged. He had never been wounded, never been hit, not in Korea and not in

Vietnam. He'd always been lucky amid the chaos of exploding mortars and whistling shells, but there was always a first time. Cool would be dead without him and so would many others. Doc might be bluffing, but he wasn't willing to bet his life on it. He nodded his acceptance and then backed off the order to wait.

For a two hour period, Tyson forced Cool to sit in the stream with an IV attached and swallow salt tablets and canteens of water. The effort worked. Cool still felt a little nauseous but appeared almost normal when Mike Brooks knelt on the shore near him.

"Your spa time is about over, sir. But I'll buy you a glass of Kool-Aid at the White Dragon when we get back."

The radioman smiled as Doc Tyson again checked his vital signs. Cool's heart and breathing had slowed, his temperature had dropped, and now beads of sweat dotted his brow. Cool's eyes flashed, awake and alert, and all seemed well until he shivered. The change was not from the cool water but from the movement on the opposite shore. It was surprising that he was the one that noticed, maybe it was the angle of his body or the direction of his sight, but they were there.

Above the water's roar no one had heard the footsteps, laughter, or voices, but seven men carrying rifles and water bags now faced them. Cool lunged onto the bank, reaching for his rifle and radio and yelling, while soldiers on both sides scrambled. Canteens were dropped and C-rations were kicked over as men on both sides of the stream readied their weapons.

The NVA had never encountered Americans this close and they were at a disadvantage. They were outnumbered and outgunned. The Americans sat with their weapons on their laps, had aligned the machine guns, and faced the Vietnamese.

When the NVA dove to the sloped ground, they found themselves in awkward firing positions, their heads on the decline, pointing downward toward the stream. Precious seconds passed as they adjusted, rising to a knee or sitting to fire and both positions exposed them to the incoming fire.

An American machine gun belched out the first shots, but the bullets crashed into the stream, splashing water high into the air. The gunner raised the barrel and fired with a smooth sweeping motion, striking four NVA and rolling their bodies down the hill.

Tiny shut his eyes and plugged his ears in an attempt to escape the noise and ducked behind some rocks as the platoon and the NVA fought. Three NVA returned a hail of bullets toward the machine gunner, hitting the bank harmlessly but blanketing Tiny with whistling chips of granite.

Knowing they were outgunned, the three remaining NVA jumped up and ran, but their journey was cut short when a grenadier exploded an M-79 round and dropped two. The last NVA soldier had run only a few steps further before a curtain of bullets stopped his escape and rolled him near his six comrades.

In less than two minutes, the jungle had changed from peaceful to violent and back. Three minutes before, the Vietnamese men had walked downhill, talking and laughing and enjoying each other's company with no idea of their impending fate or how their casual walk would be turned into a moment of horror and then an eternity of silence. Now, besides the stillness, only the sight and smell of drifting gunsmoke and the sound of the rushing creek remained.

The American soldiers rose cautiously, always expecting more shots. None were fired and Lieutenant Gomez directed them to gather their gear and walk upstream to locate a shallow point to cross.

Slinging his rifle, Brooks stepped knee deep into the swirling water. Howard Morrison grabbed Brooks' wrist, allowing him to side-step farther into the stream. Men added to the chain one-by-one and forded the creek using the line for support.

The soldiers walked back to the bodies and searched them, but opted to leave the NVA's weapons behind. They already carried enough weight and had no desire to add to it. If they returned via this route to their LZ, they would consider grabbing the souvenirs at that time.

Gomez checked his map. Ordinarily he would have taken pride in destroying the enemy and grabbing the spoils of war, but that was not the case now. He figured the men could physically complete the mission. Less than twenty-four hours remained and they had replenished their water, but he questioned how long their luck could last in enemy-held territory. Not long if the gunfire had been heard and if other NVA soldiers were now running to the aid of their comrades. Gomez was still thinking of new strategies to accomplish the mission when his attention was diverted.

Pat Graves rolled one of the NVA onto his back and then jerked back, surprised to see the man's blinking eyes. He tossed the soldier's AK rifle aside and announced, "This one's still alive."

Doc Tyson trotted over and lifted the man's hands and jagged shirt away from his abdomen, exposing his intestines. He was beyond repair. The man's belly had been sliced open by a bullet or shrapnel and a foul odor rose. All watched the NVA wiggling and instinctively pushing at his bowels, vainly holding the rising and shifting intestines like an open container of restless gray and red snakes.

Standing above him, Lieutenant Gomez made a conclusion about the man's injury and fate by tilting his M-16 and firing point-blank into the NVA's head.

Brooks jerked away from the unexpected shot and then reacted to Gomez's action. "Doesn't it bother you?"

"Not the fuckin' least. I'd hope that he'd do the same for me. It's a soldier's code." Gomez looked at the hole drilled above the man's temple and the blood-speckled hair. "Did you want to sell tickets to watch him suffer? He was dying and I just saved him some misery and gave him some dignity…but you wouldn't understand that type of code. If you live long enough, you'll get to the point where it truly 'don't mean nothing'. It goes with the territory and if it eats at you, it will consume you." Gomez shoved in a full magazine. "Enough talk. We have to find the gook headquarters tonight."

Chapter 29

Monday, April 27, 1970---5:13 p.m.

The men had noticed it ever since the column had intersected and paralleled a road running west off the north-south trail. They had not spotted any movement, heard any unusual sounds, nor had any NVA responded to the shots at the stream. It was the smell that alerted them. The column, including Clarence Sufficool, now moved west with only hand signals and with carefully placed steps. No one spoke, not even whispered, and Pat Graves no longer used the machete. He moved slowly, very slowly, weaving through the jungle and they recognized the growing odor as they walked. Their bodies grew more and more tense and their eyes searched. In all directions, they could see only the green vegetation of the jungle, but the smell, strong and pungent, was familiar...a combination of smoke, fish sauce, and burning diesel fuel.

As they drew closer, the sounds of crowing roosters and the drone of motors were added to the wind-blown smells. The soldiers formed a perimeter and concealed themselves in the underbrush of the ridge and nervously waited. They were damn close to the encampment and were willing to bet their mothers' lives on it.

Pfc. Graves low-crawled to the crest of the hill and was followed by Brooks and Gomez. On the ridge, the three men were able to visually follow the route of the steep and curving road. It had been cut by bulldozers years before, incorporated numerous switchbacks, and traversed back and forth across the mountain's face, dropping more than one hundred meters. Hugging the bottom of a cliff and extending into a small, well-concealed valley lay one of the encampments of the Communist Central Office.

The jungle obscured most of their view, but the headquarters was strategically placed. Besides lying in neutral Cambodia, any artillery fired from Vietnam would either fall short into the mountain or fly over the camp. A direct hit could only be delivered from above, but that was improbable. Without precise coordinates, the triple canopy jungle would eliminate any accurate bombing.

The three soldiers could only guess but they estimated that numerous hooches stood below and more were being built. They had heard chickens squawk, the rattling of truck engines, and saw new holes being dug for possible bunkers. Below them and closest to the cliff wall stood a large bamboo hut. Painted green and camouflaged with brush, it was stained a dull gray from a series of generators that smoked and hummed and linked the buildings together with cables. More importantly than what they smelled or saw, Gomez, Brooks, and Graves hoped that they had observed the activities undetected.

"How big do you think the camp is?" Graves asked.

"I don't know," Lieutenant Gomez said as he unfolded his map. "But we're going to find out. What I want are rough dimensions of the camp, more details, and precise locations of the headquarters and jamming areas." He checked his compass and marked the location of the encampment on his map. He had completed his assignment of locating the camp, but he wanted more. "With exact bearings, our bombers could totally destroy them."

"Why don't we just ask the gooks for blueprints?" Brooks asked sarcastically.

"Good idea," Gomez said, returning the sarcasm. "But that would spoil the opportunity for two men to be heroes by sneaking into the base camp and finding out the exact layout." Gomez looked at Brooks. "And I'm ordering you and Morrison to volunteer."

Chapter 30

Monday, April 27, 1970---10:02 p.m.

Low clouds curled through the valleys like silent black snakes spitting venom. The large raindrops rolled off each level of the jungle canopy and then struck the soldiers who huddled under wet poncho liners and sat in an isolated world of darkness.

In the center of the perimeter, Mike Brooks and Howard Morrison smeared mud on their faces to camouflage the slightest reflection and hoped for even more rain to dampen the soil and quiet their footsteps. Still, the storm could work the opposite way. It could allow NVA patrols to move in silence and hamper in-coming helicopters.

Morrison and Brooks squatted next to Lieutenant Gomez. Their faces were muddy and dark and they would have looked laughable under different circumstances. Rain dripped off their helmets, their uniforms were soaked, and a cold chill grasped them.

Both men were ready to proceed when they were surprised by Lieutenant Gomez' words. "Be careful. I want as much information as possible on the camp, but take care." They looked at each other and were further surprised when the officer reached into his pack and handed each a military-issue knife. "Use the blade before your rifle…One shot down there and we're all dead."

The two men said nothing in return and only nodded. They had considered refusing the order and telling Gomez to go to hell, but that decision would create consequences that neither wanted. Mike Brooks understood he'd be court-martialed and lose Butterfly and Howard Morrison knew he'd be given a dishonorable discharge based on his previous jail time.

But more reasons existed. Deep inside, they relished the feeling. Their minds and bodies were challenged and their adrenaline and anxiousness surged. It was a rush of excitement and both knew the ultimate feeling actually occurred before a fight. It was the anticipation of what was about to happen. Brooks figured his father had felt the same rush of feelings so many years ago. He had no idea, but guessed few men had ever sneaked into a VC or NVA stronghold. Their imagination compared it to sticking one's hand through a cage and touching a vicious animal. To be up close and personal facing a challenge that could kill you and yet still survive.

If they succeeded in this mission, they would help other GIs destroy weapons and rice caches and they liked that idea. But there was another reason…Lieutenant Gomez would have his way. He would force two others to go in their place. As platoon sergeant and squad leader, they refused to do that. No one was going except them. They would not shift their burden to their own men.

Both men, like all the others, had removed their packs and had arranged the equipment in front of their fighting positions. But tonight, for the first time, Brooks shared a swig of Morrison's whiskey and coke before they walked away from the safety of their inner circle, moving toward the road and possibly into harm's way. A strong wind and the rain pounding the jungle foliage muted their advance to the dirt road, while their fatigues blended into the green world surrounding them. They squatted and listened, but heard nothing except the rain and the muffled whine of the NVA generators below. They still smelled the jungle rot mixed with smoke and diesel and the triple canopy reflected back a dim light rising from the fires below.

This tinge of light glowed in their faces and hindered their vision, but they pressed on, thinking of Pat Graves' earlier prayer as he climbed and now they were descending into their own valley of death. They walked softly, barely able to see. In a perfect world, shining a red-lens flashlight would have helped maneuver to the top and over the hill. In this world, it meant death. Brooks thought again about his father's night mission, driving through the German lines with no headlights and remembered his words, "Don't worry about the dark, they can't see any better than you."

Brooks prayed that he would see his father, mother, sister, and Butterfly again and guessed Morrison had thought about his wife and daughter. He shook his head, trying to stay focused as they alternately covered each other and crested the hill in minutes. Brooks' chest burned from excitement and fear, remembering Warren Steele being blasted upwards in a cloud of smoke and realizing the only way to locate booby traps in the dark was to trip them.

Walking into the valley and on the road took more balls than brains, but they had no choice. If they headed down slope through the jungle, they would surely slip and a noisy fall would alert someone. Following the road was the only way to quietly advance, but the downgrade surprised both men. The smooth road above was replaced by loose jagged rocks exposed by the bulldozers and they again worried about creating noise that would reveal their position. They did not believe that the NVA, in this neutral zone, would set up trip flares and booby traps across the road each night and chance having their own men killed if the traps were not disarmed daily. Still some security had to exist.

Brooks and Morrison crept along, setting each foot down slowly and quietly. All senses were alive and it seemed that they had not breathed since leaving the perimeter. The raindrops and howling wind helped them move silently, but as they drew closer and closer, they dropped to their hands and knees and crawled. Within the hour, they reached the edge of the camp.

Lying prone together, they waited and watched and were relieved to have reached their destination without detection. Fear gripped them, their breathing seemed non-existent, and their senses were alive as they listened and watched for any clue that their approach had been compromised. Still, they flinched and their adrenaline surged when they heard an unexpected cough. The sound triggered their rapid breathing and they cocked their heads, straining to hear as they shifted their M-16s to "semi". They searched the darkness, waiting and listening and not moving. Laughter occasionally erupted from the encampment, yet the men saw only the silhouettes of bushes and heard the hiss of smoky cooking fires fighting to survive against the rain.

Someone was damn close, but they just couldn't spot him. Raindrops tapped on their helmets and their wait of minutes seemed like hours. Still, they had to move, had to do something. They inched along and heard only their hearts pound until someone coughed again. This time Brooks spotted the man and touched Morrison's arm and pointed. Squatting behind a .51 caliber machine gun, the NVA soldier was not overly alert, only expecting another rainy night in the jungle. Yet his mere presence created more fear. A .51 caliber round could cut a man in half.

They had never seen a live NVA soldier that close without preparing to kill him, but the men backed away and circled the sentry. Crawling forward, their breathing slowed, thankful they were not discovered and thankful the encampment at this point of construction was not surrounded by a fence or wire.

Splitting up, Morrison crept around the perimeter just inside the jungle vegetation while Brooks crawled toward the bamboo huts. After only a few moments, Brooks found his path was blocked by boulders that had been shoved downhill when the road was constructed. In his prone position, he could not see the camp nor could he see a way to move around the rubble. He would have preferred crawling, but that option was closed and he was forced to take a direct path over the boulders. Stepping up, he leaped from one rock to another, almost slipped twice, and then jumped clear, stopping between two huts and behind the whining generators. Chips of broken cement, faint Vietnamese voices, and a humming sound rising from the depths of the bunkers was the only information that he needed. He now counted four bamboo buildings and under each laid the underground headquarters of the communication specialists, experts in both transmitting and interrupting radio messages and directing the infiltration of the south.

As the rain slowed to a light drizzle, high-pitched voices and the sound of laughter yanked Brooks' attention to a cooking fire where NVA soldiers and, much to his surprise, Vietnamese women warmed themselves. The clothing and beauty of one young woman reminded him of Butterfly and he longed to see her and hold her again. He looked further, prodding himself to forget about her or run the risk of being killed.

Brooks figured the encampment could house hundreds of troops as he counted the hooches and surveyed the area. Near the fires, a pole held a red flag with a centered yellow star and represented the PAVN---the People's Army of Vietnam---North Vietnam. The flag flew and snapped in the wind as if whipping the soldiers to quicken their pace. Several trucks and numerous bicycles, modified with poles and saddle bags to carry weapons and rice, were scattered throughout the camp. Scrap metal and unexploded, dud American artillery rounds were piled high, waiting to be transformed into booby traps.

After estimating distances and memorizing details of the camp's layout, Brooks turned to crawl away when he heard the hum of a distant aircraft. The NVA heard the same sound and sprung into action.

At each campfire, an aluminum-type blanket was thrown over the smoldering flames, the whining generators ceased, and the crude electrical lights faded at the bamboo huts. Still the solitary drone was not to be feared. It was the high-flying B-52s that the NVA called "Whispering Death" that they should fear. There was no notice, no preparation, only disintegration and death when the jets released their exploding payloads. This aircraft was not one of them, but it gave Brooks an opportunity to leave.

He checked the time and moved out for his rendezvous with Morrison, reaching the boulders just as the airplane passed. Quickly, the fires were uncovered and the generators puttered back to life. No one seemed alarmed. Brooks hopped onto the boulders, jumped several times, and then slipped onto his back, twisting and banging the stock of his rifle. He twirled around and readied himself for an attack that his clumsiness would surely launch and then realized the noise had not alerted the troops huddling around the campfires. Their conversation, the rain, and the hissing fires had hidden the sound. Still, as he moved, he grumbled at his inability to be silent and yet felt blessed and lucky that no one had heard...But he was wrong.

The NVA sentry jerked at the noise and tried to zero in on it. His comrades would not be among the rocks, but the dilemma existed of whether to leave his post to investigate the sound or simply ignore it. Since it was his duty to protect the camp, the choice was not difficult. A radio was not available to alert the command post, but as he investigated the sound, he had something even better—his rifle.

Brooks laid in the muck, searching for Morrison, and anxiously waited to leave the area. He watched the NVA men and women milling about their fires, but unlike Steele, he had not heard, smelled, or felt the enemy. When he heard the footsteps, he glanced back but his planned retreat with Morrison vanished. His heart seemed to stop and a chill crawled up his spine when he saw the sentry pointing the AK-47 rifle at him.

Brooks expected to be shot immediately, but the man did not fire. The AK was pointed at his back and he shuttered. He'd either be dead in seconds or be a captive wishing he were dead. His only chance was to swing around his M-16 and shoot, but that wouldn't work. Any fast movement would simply trigger his death and his presence, living or dead, would still alert the NVA that other soldiers may be nearby. Swearing, he vowed an oath of silence and hoped the platoon would slip away undetected to complete the mission.

The NVA pushed the rifle's barrel into Brooks' back, poking him repeatedly, and then grabbed and slung the M-16. He motioned for Brooks to stand and he complied, raising his hands. His back slouched under the weight of both his situation and the disbelief that he would soon be dead. He shook his head, glancing back and noting the young sentry's emotions, which mirrored the opposite of what he felt.

A slight smile curved over the man's lips and his heart pounded. He had never expected to capture an American, nor reap the rewards for doing so alone. He would soon display his prisoner amid the cheers of his comrades. His excitement, the nervousness, made his heart swell in pride, but neither would not stop him from shooting. He waved his weapon, pointing it toward a bamboo building, and Brooks stepped forward, lowering his head and feeling the shame and fear of his capture.

Hearing an unusual sound, Brooks turned and saw Howard Morrison closing off the NVA's mouth and nose while smothering the muffled cries of pain. Blood flowed and squirted when Morrison yanked out the knife and thrust it back into the man's chest, just above the heart, and twisted the blade as it sunk. The guard's rifle trembled in his hands and both Americans expected the man's dying reflexes to fire the weapon.

Leaning the man back, Morrison held him against his own body and again plunged the knife into him, whispering into his ear, "Die. Damn it. Drop it and die."

The sentry seemed to follow the request. His fingers tensed and then opened with the fading of life and the relaxation of death. As the rifle fell, Morrison let the dead man crumble into the mud and then, as he looked at Brooks, prayed that retribution would not follow.

Chapter 31

Tuesday, April 28, 1970---12:07 a.m.

The NVA sentry was reported missing at the midnight changing of the guard and his wet and blood-soaked body was discovered after a short search. General Truong, the commander of the camp, immediately tripled the number of guards and placed half of his command on 100% alert. He then ordered four, twenty man patrols to make night-long searches while teams of sappers probed along the jungle trails. He did not believe that the sentry had been killed by another NVA soldier and muddy boot prints near his post verified his belief. If American troops were nearby, he was confident that they would be found and punished for the killing. The death was one issue, but he wanted answers to the unresolved questions in his mind. What would Americans be doing in Cambodia? And if they had a significant force of soldiers, why was only one of his men killed? He hoped to have the information before dawn.

Searching in the dark was difficult, but within twenty minutes of scaling the bluff, one of the sapper units detected the presence of an American patrol. The rain had not fully washed away the tracks of American boots and they found hidden C-ration cans and bent and chopped vegetation paralleling the north-south road. The sappers followed the evidence and, as they sneaked closer, discovered the claymore mines that encircled the platoon.

On guard duty, Pat Graves sat and listened and had heard some movement, but certainly not enough to fire and reveal his position. He had not spotted any enemy soldiers and he figured the rustling could only come from the wind or small nocturnal animals roaming the jungle---no human could be that quiet. He looked through the starlight scope, but with the cloud cover over the triple canopy and raindrops dotting the lenses, it was of little use. He watched and listened, but saw no movement and did not hear any new sounds.

Pat Graves did remember seeing a captured NVA sapper demonstrate his skills of passing through a wire perimeter. Clad only in boxer shorts and using only his hands, no wire cutters, the sapper carefully spread the razor-sharp strands of concertina wire and slipped through. Inch-by-inch, the little man worked so smoothly, so quietly, and never once rattled the empty beer cans hanging like wind chimes from the wire. Twisting, turning, and contorting his body, he slid uncut through twelve rolls of wire and was squatting in front of a bleacher full of new replacements within minutes. He smiled broadly, exhibiting both a gold tooth and his skill, but the recruits knew that this veteran in another time and place would have grinned in a similar fashion after accomplishing his mission of blowing satchel charges or slitting their throats. The demonstration and that devilish smile effectively frightened the FNGs and challenged them to be more alert. Those soldiers could not believe the feat was possible and, even though Graves felt someone was now sneaking up on him, it couldn't be---no one could be that quiet.

The sappers circled the perimeter and one-by-one found the detonator cords. Following the wires, they exposed the hidden claymore mines and marked their locations with strips of illuminate tape, stuck to their side of the nearest tree. Instead of cutting the cords, the scouts reversed the mines, setting them against trees to lessen the back blast, and eagerly anticipated the time when the Americans would explode them on themselves.

After turning all of the mines, the sappers retreated to the road where they contacted the patrol leaders and described the exact bivouac area of the Americans. The NVA leaders relayed the findings back to their camp and then requested an additional forty men to aid in the destruction of, what they correctly believed was, only a twenty man platoon.

Tuesday, April 28, 1970---1:00 a.m.

Tiny's sleep was broken when someone clutched his shoulder. Startled, he groaned and jumped, tossing off his wet poncho liner.

"Relax," Pat Graves whispered as he knelt over him. "It's your guard."

"Sorry. I was dreaming," Tiny apologized and nervously looked around.

"Your dreams may become nightmares...Morrison killed an NVA soldier tonight and Brooks figures that they've already sent out patrols. So we may get hit." Graves pointed toward the road. "I've heard noises. It might have been animals, but maybe not. So stay awake and pass on the information. Remember, radio silence. Any problems wake us up."

As Pat Graves crawled away and lay down, Tiny sat near the radio and felt that his mind was as tangled as the surrounding jungle. Hearing noises was frightening, but hearing the prediction of an attack was terrifying. He hated being the only guard for second squad, especially sitting alone and exposed and having other men rely on him. He was unsure what he would do if he actually saw the enemy, but he looked through the starlight scope and then picked up the claymore detonators, reminding himself about the wire safeties on the clackers. Security and street lights always glowed in the city, but not here. It was black as hell.

This was only his second night in the bush in Vietnam, no Cambodia, he was scared shitless, and he blamed his parents. Two weeks ago, he was home on leave and he had complained that they had not done enough to keep him out of Vietnam. He reminded them that they had purchased their neighbors' home for control because their dogs were a nuisance, barking too much. He yelled, admonishing them for treating him worse than an animal, not helping him control his situation. He pleaded with his father to contact his politician friends and ask for a transfer to the National Guard or talk to the dean of the university and request readmission with a student deferral. His parents explained that it was too late, nothing could be done, and tried to reassure him that he would be okay. But, he wasn't okay...he couldn't stand it.

Tears had welled in his eyes then and the darkness shrouded his vision now. The black night, the rain, the wind, and the jungle could be hiding his killers like an executioner's hood. Blinded by his fears, he imagined being overrun and the first to die in an attack by screaming NVA soldiers. He shivered, chilled by those thoughts and his ever-increasing imagination continued to drive the terror further into his body.

If they were attacked, he hoped that he would react. He had spoken up when Warren Steele was beating the Vietnamese woman, but that wasn't courage. It was an empty threat that worked. Yesterday at the creek, he had only frozen in fear and had not fired a shot. The incident reminded him of the past when a friend was bullied into fighting after school. As his friend swung his fists, two of his opponent's buddies held padlocks in their hands and jumped in, repeatedly hitting his friend in the back of the head with their make-shift brass knuckles. He did not help, did not join in the fray of three against one. His only reaction was to watch in horror as his friend was knocked unconscious.

He now wondered if he would do better. He hoped so. He again checked the claymore detonators. Rain dripped off his helmet and splashed down on his watch. 1:12 a.m. He'd been on guard duty for less than fifteen minutes. He thought about Sergeant Brooks' and Sergeant Morrison's prediction of being beaten for not sharing his water and wished that he had. Maybe the men would forget, but maybe not. He didn't need that kind of trouble. He was already afraid. No, he was terrified.

He cringed each time one of the soldiers turned in their camouflaged blankets, creating the slightest of sounds when they wallowed in the mud. They rested uneasily and it was only through their sheer exhaustion that they slept at all. Men twisted and groaned in low tones and Tiny felt as if he were sitting alone in a graveyard surrounded by corpses awaiting burial. Each time a man would turn, he would jump. The moving bodies startled him and, with each flash of lightning and roll of thunder, his soul followed the stormy night and it grew darker and gloomier.

His hands trembled. His thoughts and fears had taken control of his body and he needed to cope, needed to calm down, and the desire was for immediate relief. Pulling out a vial of heroin from his shirt pocket, he snapped off the top, squeezed off one nostril, and sniffed up half of the white powder. He switched sides and snorted up the remainder. With no idea that the heroin was nearly pure, Tiny opened a second and third vial as the contents of the first rushed into his blood stream and surged his body into a chemical orgasm. Snorting up the powder from both vials, his head felt dizzy and light, almost separate from his body, and his arms and legs tingled and numbed. The sensation was total exhilaration, euphoria of the mind. He opened a fourth vial and inhaled deeply, forgetting his fears of the future and of the night. His mouth dried and he desired water, but a sense of calmness engulfed him, his worries now departed, and he craved sleep.

His brain dulled and blurred under the grasp of the heroin and yet his body was a drowsy turmoil of motion. His torso swayed, his head bobbed, and his eyelids fluttered, increasingly dimming his vision. Leaning back, he mumbled incoherently until his mouth gaped wide and the heroin pushed him quietly and surely into unconsciousness.

Minutes after snorting the first vial, Tiny's breathing slowed to an occasional gasp and his heartbeat became more and more depressed. Rain drops splashed on his face, but he didn't react. His senses were gone and he no longer served as sentry.

As life continued to depart from his body, one hundred and twenty NVA soldiers steadily crawled into an L-shaped ambush, only meters away from the sleeping members of third platoon.

Tuesday, April 28, 1970---2:07 a.m.

Maybe it was his frayed nerves or being in Cambodia or surviving months of war, Brooks did not even consider the reason, but he was wide awake, wet, and chilled by the elevation and the cold. Sleeping…No, trying to sleep in the rain was always difficult. The tapping, the rolling in the mud could only be ignored when sheer exhaustion controlled his body.

With his soaking poncho liner draped over his face like a shroud, Mike Brooks momentarily remained still, thinking of the ghosts of the past, the people killed on both sides, and the stabbed NVA sentry. Maybe he and Morrison should have carried the body back up the hill and hidden it in the jungle further away from the encampment. Maybe that would have given them more time. Neither had been thinking logically at the time, they just wanted out of the camp.

To their surprise, Gomez had reacted calmly to the news of the murdered sentry upon their return. The lieutenant had written notes with a grease pencil on his map, pleased overall with his order and the outcome of his sergeants' observations. The dead soldier did not seem to alarm him. The unexpected happened and the additional information would be vital to both the success of the May 1st Cambodian invasion and the increased odds of his praise. The mission's objectives were now complete, but they couldn't leave. They could not blindly stumble through the jungle at night. As soon as dawn offered enough light to move, the platoon had to leave, had to return to the safety of the original landing zone.

Brooks felt the wet cloth against his face and listened to the raindrops tap. His uniform was soaked and he sat up, sensing that something was very wrong and he was further chilled by that thought. The rain still fell but the wind had shifted, driving the odors of the camp away and blowing in a new weather front. Lightning bolts struck, followed by the rolls of thunder, and heavy rain pelted the soldiers in this first storm of the monsoon. Brooks looked around, checked his watch, and saw that second squad's guard was not sitting near the radio. No one was in position. Pat Graves had the midnight shift and Tiny had the 1 a.m. watch, but Brooks didn't recall who was assigned next. Whoever it was needed their ass chewed out.

Sergeant Brooks crouched over to the radio and jabbed Tiny with his boot, silently swearing at the FNG for being lax. When he did not stir, he kicked him harder and then knelt beside him. He jerked back when lightning flashed and illuminated Tiny's opened eyes, his white flesh, and his mouth hanging open. His hands were tinted blue and his fingers looked like rigid claws. Pulling Tiny to a sitting position, the man's head drooped backwards and his helmet fell off.

Brooks immediately awoke Doc Tyson, saying nothing as he crawled back to the body with the medic following, confused and asking, "What's wrong?"

"He's not breathing," Brooks said.

The corpsman picked up Tiny's wrist but could not feel his pulse. Touching the man's throat, he felt for the carotid arteries and counted as he checked his watch.

"Only eight beats a minute. He's almost gone."

Lying Tiny flat, Tyson checked the airway, hyper-extended the neck, and pinched the nose closed. All thoughts, except to breathe life into this man, had vanished along with the revulsion of touching another man's lips.

Tiny's mouth smelled and tasted of salty vomit as Tyson encircled the opening, blew his air into the unresponsive man, and watched the chest rise. Shoving down with the palms of his hands, the chest cavity sunk under Tyson's weight and then the arms bounced, jiggling when the pressure of the cardiac compression was released.

Tyson motioned to Brooks. "Wake up Morrison. We'll have to work in shifts to save his ass."

Thrusting down on Tiny's chest, Doc Tyson succeeded in breaking the ribs. Doing so would yield a better heart compression, but he wondered what the hell was the use.

Tiny's breathing and heartbeats were so depressed that the brain had already deteriorated, starved for the oxygen that could never be adequately supplied by his shallow puffs of air. Logically, he was trying to revive the dead, offering Tiny a continued existence that called for him to portray a mindless creature confined to a wheelchair. But he couldn't abandon him without casting his own soul into the fires of eternal damnation. As long as a spark of life burned within Tiny, he had to try and rekindle the flame.

There had been no clues as to the source of the illness until Brooks and Morrison returned and scooted over next to the body. Then the answer became evident. Brooks lifted his hand, shaking it. Small slivers of glass and a fine dust covered his palm and a quick search uncovered four empty vials and the shattered remains of the fifth.

Howard Morrison tasted a few flecks of the remaining powder and then spit repeatedly, trying to eliminate the bitterness. "I think it's heroin. Tiny's been in our platoon for four days and in-country for no more than seven and he's already using this shit. It's a fuckin' scourge on all of us." He suddenly dropped the vial and picked up his M-16, twisting toward the road. "Did you hear something?"

Tyson and Brooks did not reply, but an NVA captain had received the message that his men were in attack position. The two Americans listened, responding to Morrison's question, but neither heard any sounds that were reasons for alarm. They were too busy trying to save a man's life, breathing into his mouth and pounding his chest with no visible progress. But their movement and their whispered voices gave the NVA captain a target. Pulling the pin on a captured American grenade, the Vietnamese officer threw the explosive at the Americans.

Brooks, Morrison, and Tyson's eyes widened when it bounced near them and they recognized the shape. It was beyond their reach and still rolling, but in that moment, they did not think of Tiny or attempting to toss it back or throwing themselves on top of the explosive. They only reacted in fear. Scrambling to their feet, they fled, diving away and yelling one word, "Grenade!"

Chapter 32

Tuesday, April 28, 1970---2:47 a.m.

The grenade stopped rolling near Tiny's body, less than nine feet from his head, as the three men dove to the ground and low-crawled away. The seconds passed like an eternity and the time allowed Mike Brooks to curse himself for not trying to throw the explosive back.

Brooks reversed directions just as the grenade exploded. The impact knocked him backwards and catapulted Tiny sideways with his unconscious body absorbing much of the explosion. Shrapnel ripped and tore and disposed of a major portion of his skull. The blast was bright and loud, a horrible wind snuffing out the last flickers of the man's life.

The explosion signaled the NVA infantrymen to fire and a hundred AK-47 rifles did so, propelling lead barely above the ground while a dozen more grenades exploded on the edge of the American perimeter. The men awakened, surprised and panicked, to the terror of explosions and gunfire as the two lines of NVA fire crossed. Green tracers flew by like a swarm of deadly bees. Jagged shrapnel and bullets whistled and cracked the jungle vegetation, raining down broken leaves and twigs. The firefight was an explosion of sights and sounds and of shaking earth. It was a fireworks display gone awry, surrounding the men with tracers of red and green, explosions of yellow and white, and all mixed with equal parts of fear, scrap metal, and death. In a world of flame and smoke, men were blasted upwards and then dropped into a permanent sleep while the deafening bursts smothered the screams of the platoon's wounded and dying. Already the smell of gunpowder, ripped intestine, and blood hung above the men and they pressed against the mud, digging into the bowels of the earth with their fingers to escape the roaring inferno above them.

Mike Brooks lay on the ground stunned and dizzy. His night vision had vanished with the flash of the grenade, but he could hear the bullets and explosions and men yelling. His head ached, his forehead burned, and blood streamed over one eye. Just below the rim of his helmet, a gash had been cut across his temple. But there was something else. He scraped off a gray blob stuck to his cheek and realized that the sticky chunk was part of Tiny's skull and brain.

Flipping it off, his mind teetered on the edge of madness as his vision adjusted and he stared at the world spinning around him. Whispers had changed to yells. Men struggled to be heard in life and death struggles while rifle fire blazed in a deafening tones and American frags and Chi Com grenades exploded.

Chaos was intertwined with order. The total confusion of fear and surprise had grasped the soldiers, but they followed their survival instincts. They stayed low, only slightly raising their heads to fire. Some refused to expose themselves and fired their M-16s above their own heads without looking or aiming. Using trees as protection, first squad crawled forward to face the brunt of the attack. Grenadiers fired low and directly into the line of NVA soldiers, trying to avoid exploding the rounds in the trees and raining shrapnel down on their own men. Belts of M-60 ammunition were fed to the machine gunners, who covered their fields of fire with short bursts. Howard Morrison and Pat Graves sprayed bullets in a semicircle and Doc Tyson tied a tourniquet on a legless soldier.

Lieutenant Gomez yelled into the radio mouthpiece. "Blind Sheep 12, this is Blind Sheep 30. Artillery Fire Mission. Over."

"Go ahead, Blind Sheep 30. Fire Mission. Out."

"Grid 457,823. Desperately need gunships and artillery. NVA headquarters are five hundred meters due north. Approximate grid 452,823. Ambush to north and east of our position. Get us help!"

"Roger. Grid 457,823. Do you ne... HUMMMMM!"

Gomez shook the radio handset, listened again, and figured the NVA were interfering with the transmission. He shoved the receiver-transmitter to Cool. "Check the code book and switch to the alternate net."

"Blow the claymores!" someone yelled. "Blow the fuckin' claymores!"

A grenadier flipped off the wire safety latch on the detonator and squeezed. With no idea that the mines had been reversed, the explosion propelled six hundred ball bearings in his direction and for a frozen moment the soldier convulsed open-mouthed, unaware that he had just executed himself.

The platoon had no idea how many NVA had set the ambush, only that the enemy fire was withering, nor how lucky they were that the two lines of NVA didn't charge.

The platoon only saw the muzzle flashes, blinking brightly like exploding stars and they used the flashes as targets, shooting and throwing their grenades. The Americans held only one slight advantage; they had set up on the ridge in a shallow depression and held the higher ground for the moment.

Morrison lay flat on the ground and awkwardly swatted the cap of a hand flare. The flare ignited and whooshed into the night, but the smoking comet did not shoot up. It was incorrectly angled and flew parallel to the ground and slammed into a tree near the NVA line, where it popped and burned, spinning and shooting out a glowing tail. NVA soldiers were forced to shift positions away from the intense flame and the Americans shot at the first targets they had seen, yelling when three dropped before their destination.

"Cut the claymore det cords and no flares!" Brooks yelled, figuring the claymores had been reversed and the flares would only help the enemy pinpoint their location.

"Smoke out!" Cool yelled just before a 155 mm white phosphorous round exploded, helping them adjust for the actual fire mission. "Fire Direction Center's on this net."

Lieutenant Gomez grabbed the radio receiver-transmitter from Cool's outstretched hand. "The round splashed down," Gomez estimated by the sound and with his experience, "proximity five hundred meters to the north near headquarters. Adjust fire, left two hundred, drop three hundred. Get these gooks off our butts first. Over."

"Roger, left two hun.... HUMMMMM!"

Gomez pressed and released the talk button. "Jammed again!" He tossed the phone to Cool and yelled, "Artillery coming in close!"

Another smoke round whistled over and exploded, lighting the night in a ball of flames. Gomez' again estimated where the artillery rounds would splash down.

Cool raised his head. "Lieutenant. FDC on the first net."

Gomez fired his M-16 again and then took the phone. "Drop seventy-five more and fire."

"That's too close. Danger close," Cool said, hoping the artillery shell would not land short, strike the tree tops, and shower down its deadly rain.

"The gooks are squeezing us by the balls and that's too damn close. If I have to, I'll order the artillery right on top of us."

Lieutenant Gomez doubted that anyone could hear, but he yelled, "Artillery comin' in. Danger close!" He listened to the first artillery shell hit. The blast bellowed and blew and shook the earth, rattling helmets and showering the Americans with mud, leaves, and bits of Vietnamese flesh. Satisfied, he shouted into the radio handset, "Fire for effect!"

The artillery rounds immediately began hammering the ground, while rifle muzzles barked and flashed and bullets popped above Mike Brooks' head. Blood flowed from his forehead, dripping into his eye and blurring his vision. He dabbed mud on his wound and slowed the blood to a trickle, but his head still throbbed, his ears rang, and the battle raged. Soldiers on both sides hoped and prayed while bullets whistled and shells exploded, spewing debris and shaking the ground like man-made earthquakes.

An incoming RPG round exploded and flipped second squad's machine gunner up and onto his weapon, burying the weapon beneath him and burning the man's flesh as he lay on the smoking barrel.

Someone yelled "Medic!" again, but Doc Tyson could not heed another call. Lying near the body of one soldier, he wrapped the leg of another while the infantryman fired his weapon. When Tyson tied off the bandage, he patted the man's back and crawled away dragging his aid bags.

The medic had circled the inside of the perimeter twice, conducting a triage and prioritizing the needs of the wounded soldiers. Where there was no hope or where the wounds were not life threatening, he bypassed them and only offered words of encouragement. In the heat and intensity of the battle, many of the soldiers were unaware that they were bleeding and they simply fought on. Like the rest of the soldiers, Tyson had never been in a firefight of this intensity, never experienced having less firepower than the enemy. Under gunned, the soldiers fired and reloaded quickly, now happy that they had carried more M-60 ammo, loaded additional magazines, and had more grenades to throw. They wanted a field of fire so intense that the NVA would not attempt to penetrate, hoping to keep them at bay and pinned down until helicopters and more artillery fire could arrive.

Reaching the machine gunner, Doc Tyson pulled on him but he did not budge, did not surrender his weapon even in death. The man's hands and cheek oozed a reddish gel, pasting him to the hot steel, and his weight seemed to balance atop the weapon, a weapon that the platoon needed for its firepower. Doc Tyson fired his own weapon and then rose to his knees and yanked the soldier off the machine gun.

As he freed the weapon, two bullets slammed into his chest, instantly crushing the flame of life and propelling Tyson backwards. For a split second, his head drooped sideways and his arms were hurled into the image of a bloody crucifix. But no one noticed.

Lieutenant Gomez' face was dotted with sweat and mud. He yelled into the radio phone, hoping his message would be both heard above the clamor of battle and uninterrupted by NVA jamming stations. He did not expect this, not this. He wanted the glory, but not at this expense and he damn sure didn't want to be remembered for a last stand. Without life, the glory was meaningless.

Gomez' mind reeled as he repeated his plea, "Emergency medevac requested. Six dead. Four wounded: one ambulatory, three litters. Immediate priority. Send all blood types. Half of my men are dead or wounded!"

"Roger, we copy."

"Fuck your copy!" Gomez shouted. "Get the job done...I want air strikes and more artillery!"

Lieutenant Gomez dropped the handset to again face the enemy, shooting and loading swiftly. Maybe Colonel Balfrey's words were right. "Even if you fail…you'll still succeed." Headquarters now had their coordinates of at least one encampment of the Communist Central Office and third platoon had succeeded. With those coordinates, other platoons would find the encampment. But they might find something else…the remains of their bodies. Still, the men struggled to maintain their firepower and he was proud of them. They were a bunch of damn draftees but they were fighting valiantly, holding their position, and keeping the NVA from overrunning them. If they could do that, maybe some would live.

Gomez instinctively looked up and hope surged within him. It was not a dream, only a heavenly sound that raised hope and awakened the men from this nightmare. They cheered the thumping beat of incoming helicopters and prayed that the choppers and the continual pounding of the artillery would be their salvation.

Grabbing the radio receiver, Gomez listened to the gunship pilot's voice vibrating with the rotation of the chopper's blades. "Blind Sheep 30, this is Badger 21. We're here to kick some ass. Please be so kind to pop strobe and we'll take it from here."

"Outstanding! Strobe out," Gomez said, switching on the beam. The light blinked brightly, but was diffused with the flashes of lightning, the artillery, and the NVA flares hanging up in the canopy's branches or drifting down.

"Negative here...We only see a glow through the clouds and jungle. We can't pinpoint you."

The strobe light was not distinct to the pilot, but it was to the NVA and the pulsating light brought more bullets flying by Gomez. Opening his compass, Gomez pointed it toward the sound of the helicopter.

"I'll bring you in by sound. Mark a course bearing 180 degrees."

"You got it, Sheepy Baby. We're slowin' up and comin' down."

The Cobra helicopter's engines howled while Gomez alternately plugged his ears, searching for clues to the chopper's location. As it flew closer, Gomez reported, "You're off course. Our position is approximately one hundred meters to the north. You're passing us...NOW!"

The pilot checked his compass and speed. Banking the helicopter, he estimated the distance and headed in the opposite direction. He noted his bearings to avoid the incoming artillery and then called.

"Throw out the welcome mat 'cause here I come again."

Gomez hoped that the NVA would not jam the radio, would not interfere as he gave his last directions. "Shift fifty meters to the east."

The problem had to be solved. Without exact bearings, the gunship couldn't shoot in this weather and without its firepower, there would be no survival. Gomez' insides burned with both anxiety and hope while he listened to the chopper's approach.

"Stop! You're above us."

"We've got ya, Sheepy. Keep flashin' your strobe 'cause hell is coming."

The young pilot tapped a Playboy bunny painted on his helmet for luck. "I've invited three more Cobras to crash this party and I'll relay your coordinates. Identify the location of friendly forces and target. Over."

"All friendlies are within forty meter radius of my location. NVA troops within ninety to one hundred meters, between due east and two hundred and seventy degrees northwest. Over."

"You lookin' for a rocket up your ass?"

"Shoot the fucking rockets!" Gomez yelled. "Charley's already killing us!"

"Roger that, Sheepy. It's your call…Time to rock and roll," the pilot said as he dove his craft at the target and fired two rockets. "Grab your ass!"

The rockets banged upon ignition and trailed smoke like two comets crashing to earth, exploding on impact into orange fireballs. Circling his craft, the pilot fired his mini-guns. At thousands of rounds per minute, the guns growled like a chainsaw and the tracers seemed to be joined together, forming solid red bolts of lightning.

On his second hot run, the pilot shot again and felt the recoil of the rockets' ignition thrusting the chopper back. He listened to the "crack" as the rockets were fired and the "boom" when they splashed down.

As the pilot adjusted the Cobra's position, the NVA diverted their attention upwards and green tracers and a B-40 rocket screamed past the cockpit. Bullets ricocheted off the craft, plinking and tapping the helicopter's hull. Suddenly, the pilot's hands were thrown off the controls and the craft was propelled upward in a rattling and twisting climb. The rise immediately stopped when the nose dipped and the chopper began spinning uncontrollably without its tail.

Gomez looked up. Something was wrong. He couldn't see the helicopter even though it was directly above him, but the mini-guns had ceased and the familiar thumping had changed.

The pilot re-gripped his controls until his hands and feet were again knocked loose by another RPG round smashing into the belly of the chopper, directly under the seat of the co-pilot. The Warrant Officer's shoulder straps held him in his seat while his stomach felt the sensation of being shoved into his throat and then suddenly yanked out. The pilot tried to regain control of the spinning chopper, but it was impossible.

The helicopter tumbled down. It struck the first level of the triple canopy and exploded into flames, scattering burning limbs and metal debris. A whistling sound caught Lieutenant Gomez' attention and he glanced up in time to see a gleaming portion of the helicopter blade falling toward him. He rolled to the side but the blade dropped like a guillotine and landed on his neck and shoulder, decapitating him with one arm still attached.

Cool trembled wide-eyed and crazed. The blade had barely missed him and yet it reflected the light of the explosions and hid Gomez' head and arm. The body was so close and the wound so severe. He screamed as he stared at Gomez' shivering body and spurting neck. He cried out Gomez' name over and over until Brooks crawled up, shook him and waved the radio handset in front of his eyes.

"You can't help him and we need you. Don't fall apart. Get us more help." He slammed the handset into Cool's palm and waited for the man's eyes to blink and focus. "Are other gunships coming?"

Cool nodded. "Three."

"Tell two of 'em to fire up the north side and the other Cobra to hit the east. They can pound the crap out of those areas until you call. After that, have them cease-fire for five minutes on the eastern flank, so we can get the hell out of here."

Circling the perimeter, Brooks rattled off the plan to Morrison and Graves, dragged the wounded to the southeastern corner, and fired the remaining bullets in the weapons of the dead. He couldn't bear to look at either Gomez or Doc Tyson, but he gathered the lieutenant's map and one of the medic's aid bags.

Unexpectedly, the sound of a whistle and yelling in Vietnamese could be heard. A single voice, shouting instructions, was followed by decreased NVA firing and then a cease-fire. With the NVA firing halted, the jungle seemed almost silent despite the continued firing of the artillery and gunships. The men looked around, seeking an answer, and Brooks hoped that the hush of the moment would last. The NVA could not continue to withstand the artillery and helicopter fire. He faced the perimeter and prayed that the blanketing cannon fire had forced the enemy to retreat. Still, he didn't know what to expect. Breathing deeply, he glanced at Pat Graves and Howard Morrison and felt reassured that he was not alone.

Brooks reloaded as he inched up against a tree, its sap already mending its battle scars. Looking at the scattered, broken bodies of his friends, he was powerless to do more than wish that his buddies had the same ability to heal themselves. There had been so many mistakes: If only Gomez had called in their position and that of the Communist headquarters and then retreated; If they had not been ordered into the encampment; If he had not fallen and alerted the sentry; If Tiny had not overdosed, they may have stopped the ambush. Now, only Brooks, Morrison, Graves, Cool, and four severely wounded soldiers remained. Eight out of twenty men still breathed and hoped, but the moment did not last.

The stillness was broken by loud screams. The yells did not come from the wounded, but from three NVA sappers. Stripped naked except for black shorts, they were running towards them and all carried satchels loaded with explosives.

Chapter 33

Tuesday, April 28, 1970---3:15 a.m.

Mike Brooks aimed at the lead sapper and fired. The bullet spun the NVA soldier around and dropped him onto his exploding charge while the second sapper swung the bag over his head like a Biblical sling and threw it amid the four wounded soldiers.

With one soldier now dead and two others in shock, the rifleman was the only wounded soldier that saw the satchel. He crawled, dragging his mangled foot and leg toward the bag. He wished that he could jump up and either run forward or away, but his wounds stopped him from doing either. It was agony being unable to escape, crawling toward the satchel and knowing that the charges would probably blow up in his face. Stretching for the straps, the soldier never heard the explosion and never realized that he had correctly guessed his fate and that of three others.

The second sapper disappeared into the jungle, but the last sapper weaved and ran toward Howard Morrison. The sergeant shot three times, missed, and then fired again, shattering the man's knee. Toppling forward, the sapper yanked on the lanyard and threw his charges in front of Morrison, who did not budge. He fired a three round burst into the man's chest and then scrambled up. He had taken only two steps when the charge exploded and hurled him forward. The blast blew his helmet off and signaled the NVA to resume firing. Stunned and dazed, he raised up to his knees and two bullets hit him in the back, knocking him onto his face.

Mike Brooks swore loudly as he crawled to his friend and saw the explosion and bullets' devastating effects. It was worse than he expected. Morrison's leg bent sharply away from his knee, hung by only sinews, and blood squirted out with each heartbeat. His hips were twisted away from his lower back like a modified corkscrew and the spinal cord appeared to be slashed. Lifting Morrison's flak jacket, he could see the bubbling bullet holes and hear air hissing out of the pierced lungs.

Brooks' jaw tensed and his throat burned. This was not supposed to happen. Not to this man. Turning him onto his back, Mike Brooks lay next to Morrison and cradled his head against his chest while Cool, Graves, the artillery, and helicopters continued to fire at the NVA forces.

Morrison's eyes opened. He squinted with each explosion and with the rain dripping in his face. He looked at Brooks as if awakening from a trance. But he understood. "I'm full of holes." He coughed, spitting out blood, and then slurred the words, "Why us?"

"I'll get you out," Brooks said, beginning to drag him by the flak jacket, trying to help and in shock seeing his friend in this condition.

Morrison cringed. "NO! No, don't. Won't do no good." He slapped his legs and his chest. His face then saddened. "I'm not goin' anywhere."

Blood oozed from the corner of Morrison's mouth and his mood became somber. He stretched, vainly reaching for his helmet, until Brooks retrieved it for him. Morrison pulled out the red flower from inside the helmet liner and, with shaking hands, squeezed out the picture tucked inside the webbing. Holding the flower against his chest, Morrison touched the photograph of his wife and daughter against his cheek and started to cry. He knew he'd never hold them again, never caress their soft skin, never be a father to his little girl. An emptiness of spirit engulfed him. Death was coming. Sweeping him away before he had really tasted life. He spit blood and he could feel his pain being transformed into a desire for revenge. He remembered Tiny and focused on the moment before the firefight.

He held Brooks' hand and whispered, "Kill the bastard who's pushin' the heroin. He's killed me, he's killed us all. Promise you'll get him."

Mike Brooks figured that his own life would soon be over, but he nodded. "I will."

Morrison moaned loudly when streaks of pain shot through his chest. His nose was bleeding from the concussion and for some reason he watched the blood drip onto his palm and mix with the raindrops. His thoughts spiraled and he was glad that his family would not carry the burden of seeing him like this. He looked at Brooks and spoke one last understandable word, "Why?"

His eyes blinked rapidly and then slowed with heavy lids, his chest heaved unable to secure enough air, and his words became slurred and slow until he was silent. His lips parted, his pain and nausea passed, and he became aware of only Mike Brooks' voice. The screams and the flashes and the explosions had vanished, along with the stench of cordite and burned flesh. The picture of his family was in his mind, but he heard only Brooks' last words, "I don't know why."

The words faded and darkness closed in, smothering Morrison's awareness and his youth. He exhaled long and deep but he did not inhale. His eyes rolled upwards, his life passed, his pain ended, and his arm fell away from Brooks' chest. It seemed to tear out his heart. He would love this man until his own life ended and it was without any shame that he kissed Morrison's cheek and whispered, "Good-bye, my friend."

Brooks lowered the body, placed the flower and picture into his own pocket, and then yelled, "Tell the Cobras we're leaving this hell."

As Cool made the call, Mike Brooks fired, feeling like he was in the center of the netherworld, the place of departed souls, as he glanced at the bodies. Hopefully, all of them would be recovered and sent home, not left on the battlefield to rot.

Cool dropped the radio handset. "Brooks! Graves! We have five minutes. Let's go!"

The three survivors scrambled to the edge of the perimeter, hoping the gunships and artillery had cleared a path for them and hoping to sprint into the darkness. If they could get away to the south, they could hide until dawn and then be airlifted out. The men rose and ran and figured that the jungle would now block the NVA's continuing fire.

Pat Graves took the lead, followed by Brooks and Cool, but the idea was premature. Cool was immediately hit with a single bullet striking him in the throat. Brooks heard him fall, his last gasp of air gurgling through the exit hole, and saw that the man was dead. They had struggled for hours to keep him alive and now Cool was gone in an instant. There was no time to mourn and Brooks pivoted to run when an AK round smashed into his thigh, hitting him with the force of a sledge hammer and dropping him in his tracks. He searched for help, but Graves had run ahead and was not in sight. Brooks grimaced, holding his leg and wondering what to do. Unable to flee, he turned and began crawling back to die with the other men. He didn't want his body discovered away from the platoon. He belonged with them, next to Morrison.

Three minutes remained before the Cobra resumed its firing into the area and Brooks struggled to his feet, feeling dizzy and weak. He had not travelled far enough away from the helicopter's kill zone nor was he close to the platoon. He was in no man's land. His head whirled and his eyes reflected only the turning darkness. When his arm banged into something, it was only then that he realized that he had fallen again.

Reaching out for his rifle, someone grabbed his wrist. He looked up and saw Pat Graves kneeling next to him.

"Where's Cool?" Graves asked and then answered his own question when he spotted the body.

"Dead."

Stripping off his shirt, Graves wrapped it around Brooks' thigh as a compress and then pulled him up. "Can you walk?"

Brooks said nothing, ducking when random bullets flew past them. Pain shot through his leg and his face contorted with the burning flashes, but he had no choice. Using his M-16 rifle as support, he pulled away from Graves, stepped and stumbled. Only seconds remained before the Cobra would strike again and he questioned which direction he wanted to move, to escape or return to the men. "Go ahead. I'll catch up."

"Bullshit," Graves said, lifting him up. He hooked his arm around his waist and made the decision. "I don't want to be out here alone, so we're leaving together."

Trotting and limping southeast, they used their weapons as canes and prayed for more time. How ironic it was that their own gunship might kill them. It was the unplanned consequence of his first official order and nothing could be done to stop the chopper. The radios and medical supplies had been left and they were running short on ammunition. Brooks had Gomez' map shoved into his pants, but he did not think of it. He only pictured a gory image of Lieutenant Gomez laughing his head off at the result of this first and probably last order.

Firing continued on the north side, pounding that area of the "L"-shaped ambush. Once the five minute cease-fire had lapsed, the third Cobra circled, returning to the eastern perimeter as instructed. The initial sortie had opened the door allowing them to escape and the Cobra would now slam the door on any enemy following.

Brooks and Graves heard the helicopter approaching, banking and lining up for its hot runs on the eastern perimeter. The two men swore aloud and then were silent.

Only their breathing, heavy, fast, and open-mouthed, cried out. Each man pushed to the limit and felt their hearts pounding as quickly as the time ticking away.

Running faster, their helmets bounced and dug into the backs of their necks. They threw them aside, hoping that the weight loss would aid in their escape. Brooks' head wound re-opened, slapped by the same vines that clawed Pat Graves' bare chest, and his shirt-bandage dripped with blood running down his leg and soaking his sock and boot. It felt as if he had stepped into a bucket of blood. Both men wanted to stop. Their chests heaved and burned, but they had to push on, running and limping on legs that cramped and ached. There was no other choice.

Brooks and Graves looked back into the darkness and saw nothing, yet they could hear the helicopter pursuing them, hounding them. The two men flinched, startled despite their predictions, and they dove to the ground when the first two rockets exploded near their night-hold position. They lay still, gasping, winded, and exhausted and thanked God that the Cobra was undershooting them, giving them the chance to breathe easy instead of breathing their last.

"That," Graves panted, "was close." He dropped his cheek into the mud as he smiled and looked at Brooks. "Thanks for rubbin' your medal."

Too winded to speak, Brooks inhaled deeply, and then wheezed, "My pleasure." He touched his neck, reaching for Butterfly's good luck gift, but the necklace and charm were gone. Struggling up, Brooks visually searched for the medallion as if it truly held some magical power.

Slinging his rifle, Pat Graves tugged on Brooks urging, "Let's go before the chopper moves closer."

The Cobra gunships continued to pound the north and eastern areas and the pilots hoped that the grunts' plan of escape had worked. The helicopters then moved outward from their original positions, anticipating the NVAs' location and returning fire toward any rising green tracers.

With no radio contact to offer direction or adjustments, the artillery barrage ceased at nearly the same time the three Cobra helicopters had exhausted their ammunition. Turning home, the helicopters left only carnage and a hushed silence hanging in the jungle. The wind and rain dispersed the smoke and diluted the pools of blood and this stillness, along with no return of fire, led the NVA captain to believe the Americans were either dead or conserving their ammunition. He ordered sappers to infiltrate the area again and within twenty minutes they returned and reported that all the Americans were dead.

Thirty-eight wounded and forty-seven dead NVA soldiers were evacuated to the Central Headquarters for surgery and burial. The remaining troops, cursing and swearing revenge, swept through the perimeter and kicked and bayoneted the American corpses. While others stripped the bodies of valuables and claimed M-16s as souvenirs, one trooper lifted Gomez' severed head by its blood-speckled black hair and its dangling one arm and tossed it toward a friend. The man dodged it, unsheathed a machete, and walked away. Moments later, he returned with a pole, sharpened at both ends.

The soldier jabbed the stake into the wet ground and then retrieved the head. With both hands, he plunged it onto the point, driving the sharpened edge upwards into the neck until it struck the bottom of the dry tongue. A dozen NVA soldiers then circled the pole, taunting and shoving pebbles and sticks into Gomez' nostrils, ears, and eyes. Left alone in the center of the perimeter, the head of Gomez stood like a monument to the god of war and, with his protruding tongue, oozing eyes, and an arm rocking with the wind, he seemed to survey the results and beckon others.

At the southern edge of the eastern perimeter, a lone NVA soldier had been assigned to police the ambush area for weapons and search for other bodies. He found two bodies. One was the remains of a comrade, whose split-open chest steamed and smelled. The other was an American, who had been killed in mid-stride by a single bullet passing through his neck. Lowering his rifle, he tried to read the letters on the man's cloth name tag, but stopped abruptly and called for the officer in charge in order to show him two important finds.

First, he showed him a gold chain and medallion, whose fine craftsmanship exhibited a snarling dragon and the Vietnamese words "Good Luck", and secondly he pointed out newly-turned leaves, muddy boot tracks, and a blood trail.

After considering both pieces of evidence, the captain congratulated the observant trooper and then commanded ten of his men to track down the two Americans and destroy them.

Chapter 34

Tuesday, April 28, 1970---6:10 a.m.

Mike Brooks and Pat Graves hobbled to the stream's edge where the rising sun, now unobstructed by the clearing skies, filtered through the trees and shined on their weary faces. Brooks rubbed his beard stubble and bloodshot eyes and watched the water rolling, dipping, and spewing white foam downstream. The water and this jungle world seemed unchanged from the previous day, yet everything had changed for third platoon.

Uncurling his arm from Graves' neck, Brooks hopped forward and awkwardly squatted. He twisted around and stared into a pool of water that was dirty and red and offered no reflection. If the water had mirrored back an image, he would have barely recognized his own battered face. Dried blood and mud, cracked and darkened, caked on his forehead and cheek while the gash remained swollen and jagged. His eyes were sunken and he stared as if in a coma, unblinking and reflecting a deep sadness.

Neither he nor Graves spoke even as their adrenaline slowed. Both were exhausted and empty of spirit. They could not get their minds off the men and all the things that had gone wrong. Neither of them wanted to remember the previous night, but the memories kept running through their minds, haunting their thoughts. Images of Butterfly and the platoon faded in and out, crashing and colliding in vivid contrasts. Brooks pictured Butterfly's skin, an artwork of beauty and bronze, until the thought was replaced by that of torn flesh. He longed to caress her legs, but the vision turned to one of pumping stubs. His thoughts bounced between scenes of life and death, but ultimately returned to the small circle of men, the firefight, and the battle raging within his heart. His death would have been meaningless, but a sense of guilt called from deep inside him and dragged him further into despair. He should have stayed, fought, and died amid the bodies of his family. His escape had only confined him to a prison of shame and a life as an orphan of the war.

Brooks cupped his hands to drink but stopped. His palms were smeared with blood, his blood, Morrison's blood, the blood of his men. He stared at the red stain and then dipped his hands into the water. Choosing not to wash his hands in the stream, he drank the mixture of blood and water and felt a spiritual connection, a communion with his sacrificed brothers. But a feeling of redemption and of forgiveness did not prevail. The tainted water seemed to devour him, poisoning his mind and leaving only a bitterness that fueled his desire for revenge.

All the men were lying where they fell and the image of their crumpled, bloody bodies kept appearing in Brooks' mind. Still it was Morrison's memory that weighed heaviest on him. Morrison had saved his life twice and they had always been together in the most miserable conditions...the mud, rain, and firefights. But they were not together in death and the thought of life without Morrison left a hole in Brooks' heart.

Softly, as if it were an incantation, Brooks recited his vow, "I'll find him and I'll kill him."

Graves too had been deep in thought. "Kill who?"

"Whoever sold Tiny the heroin. Whoever killed our friends."

"Forget it." Graves threw some stones into the water. "It won't bring them back. It's over."

"Not until I keep a promise to Howie." Morrison's name opened the door of sadness again and he touched his shirt pocket where he kept the flower and photo, wondering what life would be like without him.

Brooks slid into the stream. As he waded across, the water cooled and soothed him, baptizing his body but not his mind. That only festered with hate.

The ten NVA soldiers tracked the Americans' blood trail and muddy footprints to the water's edge where they split up and patrolled the bank, watching for a possible ambush or backtracking. They did not find any evidence that the Americans had changed their direction of travel. What they did find further angered them...seven more of their comrades lay dead alongside the river, their bodies and water bags strewn along the bank. The men had been missed, but certainly were not forgotten and the NVA were now further determined to find the Americans.

When the Vietnamese were certain that the Americans had forded the river, they crossed upstream and on the opposite bank divided, searching for signs. Within minutes, one of the five soldiers who had searched to the south discovered the fresh imprints of American boots, tied a red handkerchief to a tree branch, and fired a signal shot.

Brooks reacted to the shot and dove to the ground. He looked up at Pat Graves. "Guess I'm a little jumpy. But that AK couldn't have been more than seven or eight hundred meters behind us."

"Those guys are really starting to piss me off." Graves checked that the barrel of his M-16 wasn't plugged and that a full magazine was inserted. "You think they're after us?"

Mike Brooks reached up to Graves' extended hand. "I don't know. But, let's get the hell out of here."

Chapter 35

Tuesday, April 28, 1970---8:05 a.m.

Hunched over his rifle, Pat Graves crept toward a curve in the trail. They shouldn't be here, not walking the road. They were moving with emotions, not sound judgment, but no better choice existed. Walking through the jungle was safer, but Brooks' mobility had slowed and they followed the fastest route back to the landing zone. Right now, Graves didn't fear any pursuers. They had heard only a single gunshot back at the creek and that shot may not be of any concern. What worried him was what lay ahead around the corner. They could expose themselves to an oncoming patrol and the result would be disastrous.

The road narrowed and the jungle walls inched closer, thrusting him into a run of the gauntlet and reminding him of being trapped in the underground tunnel. He hated the feeling and he listened and watched carefully, but the jungle's gift of concealment forced him to walk into the unknown.

Following the pathway was dangerous but it was the only way to move through the jungle quickly and quietly. Still, the path chewed at his nerves and it was only after he rounded the corner that the pressure eased. Feeling a sense of relief, he jogged back to Brooks to report that the rice cache, not the enemy, lay ahead.

The calm feeling was short-lived and it escaped with the turn of his head and the sudden realization that something else was wrong. Movement jarred his senses and as much as he had wished the hunt was over, his instincts knew better.

Pat Graves dove forward, knocking Brooks to the ground, and then decided to run. Scrambling to their feet, they rounded the corner ahead of their pursuers as the lead NVA soldier shot twice. Brooks hobbled down the trail while Graves jumped back round the bend, shouting and shooting and scattering the NVA. He ran, quickly catching Brooks, whose chest already heaved and his head spun in a dizzy whirl. He was weak from the loss of blood and, even though the bullet had not hit bone, he was unsure how much farther he could travel.

The two men scurried ahead, glancing back every few steps and jerking their rifles toward any sounds. Every moment, every second, they thought of the men behind, hounding them, chasing them. Rounding a second curve, Brooks' leg cramped and he stumbled and fell.

Graves pulled him up. "We damn sure haven't lost them."

"Did they," Brooks gasped, trying to catch his breath, "round the first corner?"

"I don't think so." Graves pointed to the muddy boot tracks. "But they can take their sweet ass time following us."

"That's what we want," Brooks said, limping up the trail. "I'm tired of being pushed."

"Me too, but we don't have a helluva lot of choices. Maybe you'd like to ask them to knock this shit off."

"Let's ask them another way." Brooks looked back. "If you circle back, you could be in a good firing position before they turn the corner. Stay down until I fire, then you open up."

"What the hell," Graves said. "You're tired of being pushed and I'm tired of running."

Down the trail, Brooks saw a dead tree lying alongside the path. He hobbled behind it, gave a wave-salute to Graves, and then watched him running into the obscurity of the jungle. Brooks sat down, wondering whether this plan would work, and yet he felt calm. An unusual serenity embraced him, knowing he was in control of springing the ambush.

He untied his bandolier and counted three full magazines. His shots had to be accurate and he couldn't get into an extended firefight. He didn't have enough ammunition, he could be easily outflanked, and it was obvious that he couldn't outrun them. He bit at his lip and wondered if Graves would be spotted prematurely or if he would be able to help once the firing began.

Brooks slid his rifle between the tangled roots, balancing and aiming, but instinctively ducked when the NVA pointman came into view. His calmness quickly vanished and he could feel his heart beating faster. He took a deep breath and then watched the pointman, followed by four others, moving closer. All sounds of the jungle were lost and he could only hear his heart pound, his quick breathing, and the smacking of the mud clinging to their sandals. It grew louder and nearer with each step, each throb of his head and heart, each beat of an imaginary drum sounding the death march.

Holding the stock of his rifle tightly, Brooks peered above the log and centered the man's chest in his sights. He couldn't wait any longer. He was afraid that they might spot him, afraid they would kill him. Squeezing the trigger, he knocked the pointman back with the first round. Two shots followed without delay, ringing out from Graves, and the last man in the column fell. The three remaining NVA flattened into prone positions and they fired randomly, unsure of the Americans' positions. Brooks aimed again and fired a fraction ahead of Graves, killing the second and fourth men where they lay.

The last man jumped up and sprinted forward. Shooting and weaving, he had spotted Brooks and forced him to duck a hail of bullets, splintering tree roots near his head.

Graves shot at the man, missed, and then ran toward the road, but he couldn't shoot again---the bullets would be in a direct line with Brooks.

The NVA soldier closed in to thirty feet and Brooks heard the sounds of pounding feet and bullets whistling above. Rising up to shoot, the log was again peppered with bullets and fragments of debris smacked into Brooks' face. Twenty feet away. Brooks had to do something. He couldn't let the NVA run up and shoot him behind the log. He had to fight. Fifteen feet. Brooks fired a burst as the man weaved and fired. Both missed with Brooks shooting wide and the NVA's shots going overhead. Brooks was now unsure of how many rounds were left and there was no time to reload.

At less than ten feet away, Brooks pulled the trigger and his last four bullets rattled off. The recoil lifted the muzzle up and he lost sight of the NVA. When the magazine emptied, the rifle barrel lowered and Brooks stood.

On the other side of the log laid the NVA soldier, trembling in the last moments of life. Why in the hell didn't he run into the jungle and attempt to escape? Why did he charge? There was no logic, but Brooks knew the answer and understood the feeling. The death of this man's friends or the loss of the platoon members had taken their toll on both men. Each man stood alone, challenging the other's resolve. It was a test of wills in which neither would bow, yield, or step aside.

Brooks lowered the rifle and stared at the man and recognized the face. The members of the third platoon, along with all of the NVA that had been killed, seemed to capture the same expression. The calm and callous look that always masked the true feelings of pain and fear and of dreams vanished. As this soldier died, his face mirrored the grisly image of a million men in a thousand battles.

Brooks changed magazines and chambered a round as he limped around the log and looked down at the body. In his mind, it was now over and there was no sorrow. Not even a feeling of relief or victory existed in this killing. He felt only that his soul had been diminished to nothing. Even apathy no longer existed. But an odd feeling was growing. A decision that was cold, numbing, and unnerving, crawled into his consciousness and the awareness of that choice made him shiver and accept his change of spirit.

Gomez' ghost haunted him, clawing from deep inside, repeating "It don't mean nothin'" until he surrendered to the command. He hated these men, hated what they had done to his friends, and hated what he had become. He had lost his soul and he could search until the end of his own days, but he would never get it back. He realized it was true and he sealed the pact by squeezing the trigger on full automatic and instantly changing the man's face into a red mask.

Pat Graves walked up to Brooks' side and shook his head in disbelief at what the sergeant had done. The NVA was dead, so why did he mutilate him? It was something that Lieutenant Gomez might have done. Graves looked at Brooks. Behind the muddy, unflinching face and torn forehead, his eyes seemed changed, both older and colder.

There was no explanation and little response when Graves asked, "Why?"

Brooks stared down again, shrugged his shoulders, unable to explain, unable to put the feeling into words.

Graves touched Brooks' shoulder and, with the touch, Brooks turned slowly and the question sunk in as Graves repeated himself, "Why?"

Brooks blinked rapidly and shame entered his mind. He held his hand to his forehead and tears welled in his eyes. "I don't know." Pausing, he repeated the words, "I don't know. I only know that I never wanted this…any of this." He thought of the child he'd killed, Morrison's death, the loss of the platoon, and now this mutilation. Brooks dropped his rifle and sank to his knees as tears rolled down his cheeks. "I just wanted all of us to go home. But not like this."

"I know." Pat Graves picked up the rifle and then helped Brooks to his feet, trying to understand. "We're going home, but guilt and sorrow will be coming with us."

In silence, the two men retraced the platoon's path, glancing at each other and realizing only a short distance of slipping and sliding downhill now separated them from the safety of the landing zone and life.

When they emerged from the jungle's grasp and walked into the meadow, they looked back, thinking of how far they had come and what they had lost and left behind. Only two remained standing. Only two of the twenty gladiators that had stood in the same arena days before and questioned their fate had survived. They were beaten and bloodied and they stood together in silence, holding their feelings and memories inside until they heard the call of their salvation.

The sounds of the distant helicopters lifted Mike Brooks' mood and he managed a half- smile at Pat Graves, who now jumped and danced around him. Surely the helicopters were in route to extract them.

Nothing could stop them now. And yet, at that exact moment, neither would have guessed that the other five NVA soldiers were running up the trail to help their comrades kill the Americans.

Chapter 36

Tuesday, April 28, 1970---9:25 a.m.

Mike Brooks shouted and Pat Graves laughed as they frantically waved at both the descending Huey helicopter and the circling Cobra gunship. The whirling blades and the engines' roar were the sweetest sounds that either had ever heard. They had survived the ordeal, cheated death more than once, and their bodies surged with a joy so complete that all the physical agonies and all the mental strains had momentarily vanished. Neither man would ever forget the past, although they silently hoped it might fade and that time would truly heal. Now, a new notion entered their minds, creeping back from days gone by…they actually believed that they would live.

The second group of five NVA soldiers heard both the Americans yelling and the whine of the helicopters as they stared at the bodies of their friends sprawled out on the trail. Anger grew when they saw the brutality inflicted on one comrade, lying next to the fallen tree. They thought of their friends lost and wounded the previous night, the seven corpses by the stream, and now these five. Pivoting around, they sprinted toward the meadow. They wanted to kill, to expel these invaders from their own country, to return to peace and Vietnam. Still, as they ran, they no longer thought of family or friends or peace. They wanted nothing more than revenge.

The Huey whizzed over Brooks and Graves while one of the door gunners leaned forward and pointed the machine gun at them. When he confirmed them as friendlies over the intercom, the pilot lifted the chopper above the woodline, half-circled, and slowed the horizontal speed, dropping down to the meadow. The helicopter began hovering at ground level just as the five NVA soldiers broke into the clearing.

No one expected this and the presence of the NVA changed the evacuation. Brooks and Graves scrambled up onto the skids as the five NVA soldiers fired. The stationary helicopter became the primary target. It was large and easy to hit, it held even more Americans, and the NVA hammered it. Bullets poked holes into its side and sparks flew when it was hit with glancing blows.

One machine gunner grabbed Graves' hand and the back of Brooks' shirt and pulled until his helmet visor was shattered by a bullet. He fell back and the sudden release of his grip made both men slip and they dangled on the skids as the chopper rose in altitude. The chopper pilot spun the craft in a half-turn, helping protect the two men, while the change of position allowed the other door gunner to fire. Empty shell casings clinked and bounced on the floor while Graves and Brooks struggled into the chopper and the pilot radioed the gunship circling in support.

"Killer Kat 11, we have a hot LZ."

"I read you, Lazy Dog," the Cobra pilot answered. "Killer Kat's a comin'."

The second gunner and the NVA soldiers continued to exchange fire as the Huey pilot dipped the nose of the chopper and picked up speed. Blood circled the helmet of the dead door gunner and pooled on the metal floor, shaking and moving in different directions as the helicopter vibrated and banked.

With Brooks and Graves kneeling helplessly above the dead man, the pilot yelled “goddamnit” over and over, exploding with the shock of losing one man and saving only two, and cursed again when the blood streamed beneath his feet. He continued to swear, but the sound of his voice was lost with the roar and impact of the Cobra’s rockets.

Brooks and Graves were stunned as they sat huddled together on the chopper’s floor watching the lifeless body of the door gunner, hearing the explosions, and feeling the concussion waves shake the helicopter. The blasts seemed to fling the craft upwards like the sudden lift of pallbearers carrying both body and spirit away from an earthly hell and toward an everlasting rest.

Chapter 37

Tuesday, April 28, 1970---4:39 p.m.

Warren Steele threw the mail sack into his truck and crawled up into the cab. He moved as if in a trance, his body stiffened by a venom spreading through his joints and brain. He wasn't the supplier, someone at Tan An was, but five replacement soldiers had overdosed on heroin. All were dead on their third day in-country. Distraught families would demand answers and inquires and searches would result, possibly slowing or eliminating his shipments home. Still, the situation was even worse.

He leaned forward and rested his head on the steering wheel, hanging on to this circle of plastic and metal as if preparing for a self-lynching ceremony with this imaginary noose. Thoughts of suicide as well as the image of his stepfather's mangled head entered his mind. He cursed to himself, a low growl snarling up from inside. He hated the feelings and all of the thoughts frightened and overwhelmed him. There had been no shots, no mortars, none of the fears of a pointman. Only a sinking feeling existed. He was going to be caught, his world of wealth was on the brink of collapse, and he was condemned to dangle under the gallows.

Steele had heard about the mission and now he had heard about the tragedy hitting his former platoon. All of his friends, except two, were reported as killed in action. More importantly, the rumors had been verified as facts when he personally visited the aid station.

Pat Graves had been sitting up in the hospital bed. An IV dripped into his arm for dehydration, but he was in good spirits. The blue Army issue pajamas hid his scratched arms and chest, but those were his only wounds. Eighteen dead, one wounded, and him. He had been the pointman, the first man in the column and the most likely to be killed, and yet he was the only platoon member unscathed. Outwardly, he had walked away with nothing but scratches. In his mind, however, a battle still quietly raged.

Graves had flashed that infectious smile, happy to see Steele's familiar face and willing to share the story with the platoon's former pointman. He broke down, tearfully describing his ordeal in the tunnel, the hellish firefight, and the details of the deaths and of the escape.

In his mixed emotional state, exhilarated at being alive but wondering why he too wasn't dead in the Cambodian jungle, Pat Graves never noticed Warren Steele's face change expression. The outward expression was slight, but inside Steele's heart dropped with the news of Tiny's death and Brooks' promise to Howard Morrison to stop the heroin supplier.

Now, as Steele bent over the steering wheel, he was plagued by the sting of Brooks' vow, demanding revenge and the execution of those who had betrayed a platoon. At first, he wasn't sure what to do or how to get out of the situation. He raised his head slowly as the idea formed, knowing that Brooks would be in the Third Field Hospital. All soldiers in southern Vietnam with head wounds were delivered there.

That would give him time and that's all his plan would need. The verdict was simple and somber, but Tiny's death had sealed the fate of two people. His decision was made amid the salvation of two and the slaughter of many and now he had no choice but to condemn another. He would live and one would die and the results of that plan would guarantee that no one would take away his money and his business.

Steele looked at his hands, now steady and sure, as he flipped the switch on the vehicle and listened to the engine come to life. He touched his shirt pocket as if he were making a cross-the-heart pledge and felt the syringe bubbling with its poison. There was only one other person that knew of the sale of heroin to Tiny, only one other person capable of ruining his plans, and he could not allow the remaining witness to live. Tomorrow morning, he swore, he would kill Butterfly.

Chapter 38

Wednesday, April 29, 1970---6:02 a.m.

"Casualties! More of them!" the orderly yelled as he ran, pushing a soldier on a gurney past the nurses' station and Mike Brooks' hospital room. Sitting up in bed, now clean and shaven, the shouts and screams had startled him while the sight upset him and threw him back to the slaughter of his own men.

The young soldier's right arm seemed to be nothing more than a mass of flesh and blood vessels held together by a tourniquet. His jaw hung open while his tongue continually darted out in an attempt to expel the foamy blood, choking him and his cries. With his uninjured arm, he alternately clenched a silver cross around his neck and then pounded his fist against the stretcher. The pounding increased in speed and intensity and whipped the orderly into a faster pace, rushing frantically through the trail of blood toward the operating room.

Brooks felt sickened, watching the horror until they disappeared. He thought of the men and Morrison and his vow and wondered if he were to blame. If he hadn't fallen, would they be alive? He held his head as if to contain the guilt and felt his eyes being drawn to the words of a plaque hanging in the hallway:

"You've Never Lived
Until You've Almost Died.
Life Has A Flavor
The Protected Will Never Know."

Brooks glanced at his bedside table and stared at Morrison's red poppy and picture, placed there as if it were a shrine. The objects grabbed his attention and he began hitting his fist into his good leg, pounding it harder and harder as if in rhythm with the soldier on the gurney, trying to drive away the thoughts. Soldiers in other beds as well as a nurse noticed the self-inflection of pain, but no one said a word. Without speaking, they all seemed to understand.

Brooks continued the ritual until a young doctor, staring at the blood-splattered floor and feeling fortunate to be a physician and not the patient, walked into the room. The doctor greeted Brooks, gently stopping his pounding fist by touching his wrist and then shaking his hand, apologizing for his haste. The soft words seemed to soothe Brooks' mind, even though the message involved the arrival of new casualties and his limited time to examine the leg and head wounds.

Leaning closer, the doctor touched Brooks' forehead and nodded, approving the look of the wound and the stitches closing it. The leg wound appeared to be draining properly into the compresses and the doctor mentally noted how lucky Brooks had been to have the bullet pass through the leg without hitting bone or major arteries. Neither spoke as the doctor wrote on the patient-chart and Brooks surveyed the other charts, hanging from the end of the other soldiers' beds.

It was amazing how a simple piece of paper---a selective service card, an induction letter, a marriage license, a letter to the family of the deceased, even the medical chart---affected lives.

A high school friend, serving as a gunnery sergeant, had changed his own life by simply writing on his own chart. One night, as the NVA mortared the firebase, he sprinted toward a bunker. He never made it. Running in the darkness, he didn't see the leveled Jeep antenna and he ran directly into the metal rod, piercing his eye and breaking his eye socket. His fellow soldiers found him unconscious after the barrage and he was evacuated to Saigon. After surgery, time in the hospital, and despite severe headaches, the doctors planned to return him to regular duty in Vietnam. That's when the idea formed. Late at night, he wrote "Transfer to Hawaii" on his own medical chart and scribbled a fictitious and illegible doctor's name approving the order. Three words and a signature on a piece of paper and he had altered his fate. One week later, he looked out the aircraft's window at lush vegetation and palm trees as he arrived in Honolulu...far away from the war.

Brooks' attention was brought back to reality when the doctor spoke with both a sad expression and the soft tones of a priest. "Overall, you've been beat up, but you'll be fine. We're conducting an internal triage of all our patients. Your head wound is minor and your leg wound just needs time to heal. So, I'm shipping you back to Rach Binh in about an hour. The corpsmen in the aid station can administer fluids and meds and monitor your leg wound. You're a long way from being healthy but we need the bed." The doctor glanced back to the bloody hallway. "You may have seen one of the presents that we're receiving from the Cambodia invasion."

Chapter 39

Wednesday, April 29, 1970---8:09 a.m.

Warren Steele grabbed the mail bag, stepped up to the front window of the White Dragon and shaded his eyes from the reflection of the glass. He watched Butterfly's body swaying as she leaned over and wiped a table clean. She was beautiful but she was also alone. The bargirls and the other employees lived away from the White Dragon and would not report to work until much later in the morning.

Steele looked around. With the Cambodian invasion, the main street was empty of people and vehicles. Three children played with a dog down the street and his mail truck was parked a block away. Still there seemed to be more activity even here than on the base.

The Rach Binh base was manned only by a skeleton crew. All of the Ninth Infantry Division companies had been transferred to Firebase Jamie to support the First Cavalry and Twenty-fifth Infantry Divisions' push into Cambodia and to prepare for their own June 1st entry.

Although he was sure that he would not need it, Steele brought along the mail bag as a possible alibi, but the deserted streets and bar assured him that he would only need his syringe. He didn't want to harm Butterfly, in fact he had desired her in the past, but there was no other option. Her survival could cost him his fortune, his freedom, and maybe his life. And one more death hardly mattered anymore.

Steele hurried to the back door, twisted the door knob, and found it unlocked. He cracked open the door and peeked through until the sound of footsteps approached from the main room. Butterfly walked down the corridor, humming and swinging a broom, and then entered her bedroom and shut the door.

Stepping into the building, Steele moved carefully and quietly. Each stride was slow and predictable and he imagined himself as pointman again, stalking the prey while listening to her muffled tune. He side-stepped around a creaking section of the floor just as the bedroom door opened. The two suddenly faced each other. Butterfly gasped, startled by his presence, but she reacted. She slammed the door closed, only to have Steele lower his shoulder and smash it open as she fumbled with the lock.

Steele tossed the mail bag aside and then knocked her to the floor. As he locked the door, she grabbed her broom and hit him with it, grunting with each blow until he blocked the handle and yanked it away. Butterfly ran to his side, ducked, and reached for the door. The lock slid halfway up until Steele smashed down on her hand, flattening it against the latch, and then knocked her back. He flipped the door latch and spun around. She clawed at his face. Her finger-nails tore into his cheeks until he jerked her hair back and, with all of his might, threw her against the wall. She hit hard, stunned, and slid to the floor near the window.

He pulled out his syringe, flipped off the needle cover, and then cut off any escape, cornering her. He mocked her, jabbing and swinging the needle as if he were brandishing a sword until he yanked her up and dumped her onto the bed, squeezing between her kicking legs. As she resisted, her movement only excited him and he enjoyed controlling her. He squeezed her neck, making her focus on the syringe, and then held the point next to her jugular.

Lowering his face next to her, his eyes wide in madness, Steele whispered, "Do what I say or you're dead."

He waited, knowing that she would have to die, but he had watched and desired her for months. He would have her, with or without her consent before he silenced her. Her objections to the act did not matter. He had enough rejections in his life, but this would not be one.

Butterfly shivered, feeling the pressure of his body weight, and his sour breath disgusted her. She hated his touch and instinctively curved her spine, trying to flee from the sensation of him rubbing her breasts. She pushed his arm aside, but her struggle only further aroused him. He craved her as a sense of power and control swelled within him and piqued when she began to cry.

Tears flooded Butterfly's eyes, remembering the night by the pond, as she begged, "Don't hurt me."

Steele took the needle away from her neck, pulled her up, and ripped open her blouse. "Strip."

"Me Brook-see girl," she sobbed. "Me have baby."

"And I don't give a shit," Steele said. He touched the tip of her nose with the syringe. "One jab with this and you and your baby are history. Now, do it."

Sobbing, Butterfly slid off her blouse, letting the garment drop to the floor. Steele stripped off her pants and panties and pushed her back on the bed. She laid there in silence and in shock while he stared at her body, never noticing the sound of the incoming Huey.

The helicopter descended slowly toward one of the landing pads at Rach Binh, just outside the front gate. Mike Brooks scooted forward, resting one leg on the skid. He felt tired and alone and the base looked as empty as his heart. Despite his longing for Butterfly, he stepped down from the chopper, leaned against his cane, and paused, searching in a melancholy way for the men who had been left behind. It was not rational but in the back of his mind, he had always held a thin hope, a dream that his friends would be there, waiting for his arrival.

He stood there, a solitary man beneath the vanishing sight and sound of the chopper, and it was only after the crush of loneliness subsided that he hobbled toward the White Dragon alone and unarmed.

Butterfly flinched each time a drop of sweat from either Steele's nose or brow splashed onto her face. She desired only a numbness of the mind and body, a sleepy suspension of any feelings until this man no longer touched her. Still her mind and body could not escape, could not control her loathing of this man. The beads of perspiration, his grunts of passion, and his rough intercourse only snapped Butterfly back to the present and made her skin crawl.

Steele had intended to go slow and extend the pleasure, but his body now pushed and pulled without his control. His body flushed, burning with the heat he wished would never end. He loved conquering her, controlling her, manipulating her. He was in charge and this woman would not reject him. As he closed his eyes, he pictured other women…those that he wanted to hurt. Still he loved touching this woman's soft skin and feeling her wetness. The mental images of his lust propelled him until all control had vanished. Rocking faster and faster, his mind and body exploded in sudden bliss and he moaned deeply.

Outside, the grunting scream of pleasure echoed through the thin walls and had surprised Mike Brooks, who hurried up the back stairs, calling, "Butterfly?"

The recognition of Brooks' voice startled and alarmed Steele and he panicked, cursing the interference. He didn't want it like this, but no alternatives now existed. He would kill Brooks with the needle and then strangle Butterfly. The situation twisted his mind and he reacted like a mad dog penned up in isolation, snapping at all intruders and willing to shed anyone's blood.

Warren Steele pointed the syringe at Butterfly. "Tell him to come in," he whispered. He climbed off the bed and stepped behind the door, buttoning his pants.

Butterfly shook her head, feeling dazed, dirty, and ashamed as she dressed.

Steele stepped toward her. "Call him."

"Brook-see, you come in."

Cocking his arm, Steele unlocked the latch but was immediately knocked against the wall when the door smashed open. Mike Brooks glanced at Butterfly and then charged through the opening, blocking Steele's downward thrust. Brooks shoved him back and slammed the cane against Steele's wrist, knocking the syringe out of his hand.

Like a battering ram, he drove the stick into his stomach and Steele's knees buckled, dropping him to the floor as if he were begging for mercy.

The opposite was true---Steele's face reddened in his rage and desperation, knowing what was at stake. He threw one fist upward, striking Brooks' leg wound and followed the blow with one to the testicles. Brooks fell back, driving splinters into his fingertips and palms, but he noticed only the ache in his groin and the throb of his leg.

Grabbing the cane, Steele whipped Brooks, cracking it into his ribs repeatedly until Butterfly joined the struggle, breaking a bar stool over his back and shattering it into pieces. Spinning round, Steele smacked the cane against Butterfly's cheek and sent her sprawling.

Steele kicked Brooks in the ribs and repeatedly stomped on his bandaged leg. He suddenly stopped and turned. He gasped for air when he felt and saw the sharp point of a shattered bar stool leg, sticking out of his upper back like a harpoon. Yanking it out, he saw Butterfly's surprised expression change to pain when he hit her with the stake, knocking her down into a daze.

Spinning around, Steele picked up the syringe and dove onto Brooks, who was knocked back as he blocked the swing. Steele wrestled forward, centering his weight over his arm, and Brooks knew that he could not stop him. The splinters in his hands were forced farther into his skin as Brooks pushed back with all of his might. His efforts were useless. Whatever was contained in the syringe would soon be in his body.

Steele's weight kept inching the needle's point closer and closer until it was centered above Brooks' right eye. The men's arms trembled and they grimaced under the strain. Steele's hands tensed and the pressure on the plunger created a bubble of strychnine and acid. Hanging from the tip, the drop doubled its size, wobbled, and then fell straight down. Brooks snapped his head to the side, but it was not enough. The rat poison and sulfuric acid splashed down just below the brow and trickled into his eye.

Brooks yelled and shook in horrible pain. His eyeball seemed to explode into red colors, burning and blurring his vision. His eyelid was immediately inflamed, flickered in spasms, and swelled until it was half-closed. He blinked and thrashed his head from side to side, trying to shake out the liquid. He saw double and the pain was nearly unbearable, hot and scorching like a torch being held next to his eye. He felt as if his pupil was melting and oozing down his cheek. When the point moved within an inch of puncturing his eye, Brooks yelled again and pushed with all of his strength.

With the fury of a crazed man, Brooks rotated onto his side and then smashed Steele's hand onto the floor. On the seventh hit, Steele's bloody hand flipped the syringe aside. Besides their hands, it was their only weapon and both had to have it to survive. Steele crawled over, picked up the syringe, and started to stand. Brooks tackled him from behind, driving him against the window and blasting glass and both bodies out of the building and onto to the ground. Reacting immediately, Brooks threw his leg over Steele's back, grabbed his hair and began smashing the man's face into the ground. Steele struggled up, pushing himself up to his knees as he fought to stand, and then collapsed face down.

Brooks again grabbed Steele's hair and repeatedly slammed his face into the ground until he realized the man no longer offered any resistance. Brooks stood, looked back at Butterfly standing behind the broken window, and then turned Steele over. The now-empty syringe stuck out of his neck as the poison pumped into his bloodstream and heart. His skin was pale, his eyes wandered, and his body began convulsing, rolling, and shaking. He chewed on his tongue, dripping blood and a bubbly excretion from the corner of his mouth, while he desperately wheezed for air. Swinging his arm over his chest, it looked like he was displaying the tattooed words "Hell Razor" as the trembling ceased and death captured his soul.

Brooks' vengeance burned as sharply as his eye and he spit on Steele before turning away. This was not the pointman he once knew and he hated the man that tried to kill him and hurt his woman. He glanced back at Butterfly and then limped to her room where they embraced. It felt so good to be in her arms again. Separating and wiping away her tears, Brooks looked at the welt across her cheek, her split lip, and the bump on her forehead.

Butterfly began crying, pressing her cheek against his chest, unconcerned with her face. "Steele make me make love. He tell me he kill."

"Why would he hurt you?"

Butterfly rubbed her eyes and sniffed. "Me see him buy heroin from Major Quan and sell to little soldier."

Brooks gently pushed her back and looked at her face, comprehending what she had just said. Was that the answer? His eye still burned and watered, but his vision appeared to be clearing. Spotting the mail sack in the corner of the room, Brooks limped over to the bag, dumped out the contents, and quickly noticed a package addressed to Steele's wife. He ripped open the box and lifted out a kilo of pure heroin, staring at the white powder and thinking of the misery, the death that the drug had caused.

Unbuttoning his shirt pocket, Brooks lifted out a blood-speckled poppy and handed it to Butterfly, thinking of the poem that he never said aloud to Morrison:

"In Flanders fields the poppies blow
Between the crosses, row on row....
We are the Dead. Short days ago
We lived, felt dawn, saw sunset glow,
Loved and were loved, and now we lie
In Flanders fields...."

Brooks stood there in silence, feeling alone even with Butterfly standing beside him. He and Graves were all that was left of third platoon and they had only lived through the courage of their friends, their platoon brothers. They were still lying alone in the Cambodian jungle and he prayed for them, hoping that they had not died in vain, hoping that their country had not sacrificed them for a lost cause, hoping that they would be remembered and honored. All had only wanted peace, but they had been forced into the dilemma of fighting against ambition, beliefs, and greed…to fight for survival against Gomez, the VC, the NVA, and even Steele. But, for Brooks, the war around him was ending and peace was coming.

He looked at the heroin, cursed the drug, and then stared at Steele's silent body. It represented the fulfillment of his promise to Morrison. The vow had been consummated by the sacrifice of this man, this pointman.

Tears welled in Brooks' eyes as he tried to control his emotions, to keep the nightmares buried deep inside his soul, hidden and unable to escape. His war was over and only time could now heal the wounds. As he remembered Morrison, the men of his platoon, their sacrifice and his redemption, Brooks shredded open the bag, leaned out the broken window, and allowed the wind to scatter the white ashes of heroin across the land.

GLOSSARY

Ao dai —— Vietnamese term for a tightly-fitting silk tunic worn over pantaloons by women. The style was considered decadent in some social circles during the 1960s and 1970s.

AA —— Automatic Ambush; Mechanical booby traps set up by Americans.

Agent Orange —— Code name for one of the herbicides and defoliants used in Vietnam.

AK-47 —— Chinese or Russian made 7.62mm semi or fully automatic assault rifle used by the Viet Cong or North Vietnamese Army.

ALPHA —— The military phonetic for the letter A as in Alpha Company.

AO —— Area of Operations.

ARP —— Aerial Rocket Artillery.

ARVN —— Army of the Republic of Vietnam; Also a South Vietnamese soldier.

AWOL —— Absent Without Leave.

B-40 —— Communist Rocket Propelled Grenade (RPG).

Bac si —— Vietnamese word for "doctor".

Beaucoup——A French word meaning "many". Americans pronounced the word "boo coo".

Bee-bop —— Slang for "walking". See also "ditty-bop".

Bic —— Vietnamese for "understand". "No bic" means "I don't understand".

Binh Xuyen —— An independent military force within the Vietnamese National Army.

Blue —— A river or stream; derived from the blue lines on topographic maps.

Boom-Boom —— Sex with a prostitute.

Boonies —— Anywhere infantrymen patrolled, as in the bush, field, or jungle.

BRAVO-----The military phonetic for the letter B as in Bravo Company.

Bro——Meaning "Brother".

BS-----Bullshit.

Bush——A location to be patrolled; Also a shortened term for "Ambush".

C's——Combat rations; Also C-rats.

C-4-------A white plastic explosive.

CA——Combat Assault.

CHARLIE-----The military phonetic for the letter C as in Charlie Company; Also used as Charley or Chuck to identify the Viet Cong (as in Victor Charles).

Cheap Charley——A soldier who spends very little money on a bargirl.

Cherry——A new soldier.

Chi Com-----Chinese Communist; Typically referred to a hand grenade manufactured in China. Equipped with a wooden handle, it resembled the German "potato masher".

Chieu Hoi——The "Open Arms Amnesty Program"; Enemy soldiers were encouraged to join forces with the South Vietnamese and Americans.

CIB-----The Combat Infantryman Badge was awarded to a soldier, after surviving his first battle.

Clacker——A hand-held firing device for claymore mines.

Claymores——Anti-personnel mines.

Cluster-fuck-----Slang for standing too close to each other and inviting the enemy to fire upon the group.

CO——Commanding Officer.

Cobra——An assault helicopter.

CONEX-----A metal shipping container.

COSVN——(Communist) Central Office for South Vietnam.

CPR-----Cardiac Pulmonary Resuscitation.

Crispy Critters——Burned corpses.

Dee-Dee Mau-----See "Di-Di Mau" below.

DEROS— Date Estimate Return from Overseas. The date a soldier is scheduled to go home.

DI-----Drill instructor.

Di-Di Mau-----From the Vietnamese "di di"---to run. It also meant to "leave quickly" or "get the hell out of here." GIs pronounced the words "dee-dee".

Dinks——A derogatory term referring to the enemy.

Ditty-bop-----Slang for "walking". See also "Bee-bop".

DMZ------Demilitarized Zone between North and South Vietnam.

Dustoff——Medical evacuation by helicopter (Medevac).

ETS——Estimated Termination of Service. The estimated date that a soldier is scheduled to get out of the army.

Eagle flights-----Missions in the Delta whereby infantrymen were inserted via helicopters near marshy wood lines to search for enemy booby traps, bunkers, and personnel; Also Search and Destroy missions.

FDC——Fire Direction Control.

Fire Mission-----A radio request for artillery.

FNG——Fucking New Guy.

Frag——A fragmentation hand grenade.

Fragging-----Using a grenade to kill another soldier, typically an overly aggressive officer.

Freedom Bird——A jet airline that would take a soldier back to the United States.

Free fire zone-----An area whereby anyone, an enemy soldier or civilian, could be shot at any time.

Freq——A frequency on a radio.

GI-----A soldier. In World War II, the term "Government Issue" became synonymous with a member of the armed forces, especially an infantryman.

Gooks——A derogatory term referring to the enemy---both Viet Cong or North Vietnamese; Also used in reference to any Vietnamese.

Grunts——Infantrymen in Vietnam.

Gunship——A heavily armed helicopter, especially the Cobra, which was armed with rockets, cannons, and mini-guns.

HE——High Explosive artillery.

Horn-----The radio.

HQ——Headquarters.

Hooch——A small Vietnamese hut/house; A bamboo and thatched hut.

Huey-----A UH-1 single rotor helicopter, used to transport troops and for medical evacuation.

IV——Intravenous injection. Typically saline solution was used to replace fluid or blood loss.

Jody-----Any young, male civilian, back in the World, trying to take away your girlfriend while you're overseas in Vietnam.

KIA——Killed In Action.

Kilo——A kilogram, which is equal to 2.2 pounds.

Kit Carson scout-----A Vietnamese scout, formerly an NVA or VC, who joined the Americans through the Chieu Hoi amnesty program; See Tiger Scouts.

Klick——A kilometer, which is equal to 1,000 meters or 0.6 miles.

Lifer-----A soldier making a career in the military.

LP------Listening Post.

LZ——Landing Zone.

M-16——American made 5.56mm semi or automatic assault rifle.

M-60——American machine gun; The weapon was belt-fed, air-cooled, and fired on either semi or full automatic.

M-79——American single shot grenade launcher.

MACV——Military Assistance Command—Vietnam.

Mad Minute——A free-fire test of weapons; Used also as a recon by fire.

Medevac-----Medical Evacuation by helicopter (Dustoff).

MOS-----Military Occupation Specialty.

MP——Military Police.

MPC——Military Payment Certificate; Used as money in Vietnam.

Nam——Vietnam.

NCO——Non-Commissioned Officer.

Net——A radio frequency setting.

New Meat——A new soldier.

Numba one——Meaning Number One, mispronounced by the Vietnamese, meaning “the best”.

Numba ten——Meaning Number Ten, mis-pronounced by the Vietnamese, meaning "the worst".

NVA——North Vietnamese Army; Also a North Vietnamese soldier.

P-38——A small can opener.

Pfc.-----Abbreviation for the military rank of private first class.

Piasters-----Vietnamese money.

Piss tube-----A diagonal metal tube partially buried in the ground and used for urination.

Pointman——The first man of a patrol, as in "take the point" and lead.

Poncho liner-----A lightweight, camouflaged blanket.

Pop Smoke-----To ignite a smoke grenade for identification and for wind direction for helicopters. Popping a specific color, like "yellow" or "purple" smoke would further identify the platoon's location.

Punji Pit-----A hole of varying sizes, lined with sharpened bamboo stakes, used as a booby trap.

Purple Heart-----A medal awarded for wounds received in combat.

PX——Post Exchange; A store where various goods could be purchased.

Quad 50's——A grouping of four .50 caliber machine guns.

REMF——Rear Echelon Mother Fucker.

Rock and Roll——Firing on full automatic.

RPG——Rocket Propelled Grenade (B-40 rocket).

R & R-----Rest and Relaxation. A seven day leave, typically to Hawaii for married men and to either Sydney, Australia; Bangkok, Thailand; Hong Kong, China; or Taipei, Taiwan for single GIs.

RTO——Radio-Telephone Operator.

Ruck——A rucksack or backpack.

Sappers——Enemy assault and demolition teams.

Search and Destroy-----Missions whereby infantrymen would seek to locate and destroy the enemy and anything they may consider valuable.

Shake and Bake——A soldier who attended NCO school and earned the rank of sergeant in a relatively short time.

Short——Having one hundred or less days left in-country.

Sit-Rep——A situation report given over a radio.

Slicks——Huey helicopters.

Spec.-----Abbreviation for the military rank as in specialist fourth class (equivalent to a corporal).

Squad-----The smallest group of military personnel. In Vietnam, a squad in the army was typically composed of ten soldiers.

Squelch-----Pressing the transmit button on the radio handset without speaking. "Squelch twice for a negative sit-rep" was a common statement.

Stand down——A short resting period (at a base camp) for infantrymen.

Steel pot——An American helmet.

TB-----Tuberculosis.

Tet-----The Tet Offensive started on January 31, 1968, the first day of the traditional lunar calendar.

Tiger Scout-----A Vietnamese scout, formerly an NVA or VC, who joined the Americans through the Chieu Hoi amnesty program; See Kit Carson scout.

Tunnel rat-----A man assigned to explore VC or NVA tunnels.

VC——Viet Cong; Vietnamese communists.

VD-----Venereal disease.

VFW-----Veterans of Foreign Wars.

Victor Charles——Viet Cong; Also called "Charley".

Vietnamization-----The plan to turn the war over to the South Vietnam military after the Americans returned home.

White Phosphorus-----Also called "WP", "Willie Peter", or "Willy Pete". Used in grenades, artillery, or bombs as weapons, causing serious burns or death. Also used for signaling, smoke, and incendiary purposes.

World——The United States or any place other than Vietnam.

THANK YOU/ACKNOWLEDGEMENTS

To my parents, Frances and Wendell Owens,
who taught me to love, to persevere, and to dream.

and

To my agent, Faye Swetky, who believed in this novel
and made the dream possible.

ABOUT THE AUTHOR

Robert "Bob" Owens graduated from the University of California-Davis prior to entering the U.S. Army. He served in the Mekong Delta and in the Cambodian invasion with the Ninth Infantry Division. Mr. Owens was awarded the Bronze Star, Combat Medical Badge, and Purple Heart medals.

After his tour of duty, the author worked as a teacher, school administrator, and county superintendent of schools.

Mr. Owens lives in California with his wife Kathy and they have two adult children, Alicia and Jeff.